PRAISE FOR J.L. WEIL'S SOUL SYMMETRY

"With more snark than ever, Piper's character development in Black Crow was perfection."

— *-AMAZON REVIEWER* ★★★★★

"I absolutely love this series. The only down side is having to wait for the next one to come out!"

— *-AMAZON REVIEWER* ★★★★★

"As a fan of J.L. Weil books I knew I would love this book. I really enjoyed white Raven so I couldn't wait to read black crow and find out what happens next and black crow was even better than white Raven."

— *-AMAZON REVIEWER* ★★★★★

SOUL SYMMETRY

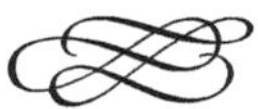

SOUL SYMMETRY

THE RAVEN SERIES, BOOK 3

J. L. WEIL

Published by J. L. Weil

http://www.jlweil.com

First Edition 2016

Edited by Librum Artis Editorial Services
and Alliyson Ma

ALSO BY J. L. WEIL

ELITE OF ELMWOOD ACADEMY

(New Adult Dark High School Romance)

Turmoil

Disorder

Revenge

DIVISA HUNTRESS

(New Adult Paranormal Romance)

Crown of Darkness

Inferno of Darkness

DRAGON DESCENDANTS SERIES

(Upper Teen Reverse Harem Fantasy)

Stealing Tranquility

Absorbing Poison

Taming Fire

Thawing Frost

THE DIVISA SERIES

(Full series completed – Teen Paranormal Romance)

Losing Emma: A Divisa novella

Saving Angel

Hunting Angel

Breaking Emma: A Divisa novella

Chasing Angel

Loving Angel

Redeeming Angel

LUMINESCENCE TRILOGY

(Full series completed – Teen Paranormal Romance)

Luminescence

Amethyst Tears

Moondust

Darkmist – A Luminescence novella

RAVEN SERIES

(Full series completed – Teen Paranormal Romance)

White Raven

Black Crow

Soul Symmetry

BEAUTY NEVER DIES CHRONICLES

(Teen Dystopian Romance)

Slumber

Entangled

Forsaken

NINE TAILS SERIES

(Teen Paranormal Romance)

First Shift

Storm Shift

Flame Shift

Time Shift

Void Shift

Spirit Shift

Tide Shift

Wind Shift

HAVENWOOD FALLS HIGH

(Teen Paranormal Romance)

Falling Deep

Ascending Darkness

SINGLE NOVELS

Starbound

(Teen Paranormal Romance)

Casting Dreams

(New Adult Paranormal Romance)

Ancient Tides

(New Adult Paranormal Romance)

For an updated list of my books, please visit my website:

www.jlweil.com

Join my VIP email list and I'll personally send you an email reminder as soon as my next book is out! Click here to sign up: www.jlweil.com

This book is for you, the reader. Without you, none of this would be possible. Not even this book. I thank you from the bottom of my heart.

PROLOGUE

The boardwalk wasn't a place you'd expect to find a reaper—out in the open, for anyone to see, the slight morning, sea salt breeze blowing over his face. Not a soul had any idea that a harbinger of death was in its midst, and they probably wouldn't have believed it anyway. Humans rarely saw reapers for who they really were; the veil between the living and the dead aiding their true identity. But it was the four frowning hallows beside Heath that were the true concern. The ghosts walked freely among the living, plotting and planning revenge, destruction, and evil, carving a path of devastation.

The five of them were discussing the events from the night before—the coronation. Proceedings hadn't gone according to plan, but lately they hardly ever did. Not since the arrival of Piper Brennan.

There was one thing they all agreed on … She needed to be eliminated.

They slunk under the docks, away from the early stragglers—not that the tourists would have heard them. Heath, the overlord of the Red Hawks, was a phantom reaper whose responsibility was to mark humans for death. His dark suit was newly pressed and stiff, like his personality.

"Your plan failed, overlord," hissed the hallow with shoulder-length blond waves. He stepped forward, letting the reaper know who was in charge.

"Not entirely true," Heath disagreed. "All is not lost. Actually, I don't think things could have gone smoother."

The ghost angled his head in rapid, jerky movements. "How so?"

"Death's heir has fallen." The shock had worn off, and Heath could see the advantage fate had dropped into his palms. He grinned, flashing a row of pearly teeth.

"This aids us how?" asked the smallest of the four hallows, no inflection in his flat voice. Hallows didn't feel emotions other than rage.

A flash of annoyance sparked in Heath's silver eyes. He didn't like being questioned. "The veil has been broken."

The four hallows nodded. "We felt it, but tell us something we don't already know."

"I'm working out the details, but trust me, you'll get what you were promised," Heath said. "We all will."

"Trust?" a hallow echoed, distaste dripping from his tongue.

"You haven't precisely proven to be dependable," another commented, his ghostly outline standing out against the vivid blue ocean.

Water lapped on the shore, leaving behind foam and shells under the dock, but Heath disregarded the rise and fall of the water as easily as he did the four hallows. "I'd wait and hear me out before you pass judgment."

The four hallows exchanged skeptical looks. "We're listening," replied the blond gravely.

"It's about time, because I was beginning to wonder if I'd made a mistake."

A unified hiss erupted. Heath knew working with these chumps had its risks, but the thing about hallows was they were disposable. And there were plenty more where they came from, eager to have a chance at revenge.

As they gathered, a calculating plot began to unfold.

"Your son? Can he be trusted?" asked the ghost of a woman who used to be called Felicity. Her eyes were so pale blue they were almost iridescent. They sharpened.

Heath was steadfast in his conviction. "There is no question where my son's loyalty lies. He will cooperate," *if he knew what was good for him,* Heath added silently. Crash might be unpredictable, disappointing, and often lazy, but he was his blood and his heir. Heath knew the bitter taste of revenge well and knew how it would fuel his son. Estelle's death wouldn't go unpunished. He swore it. And his son *would* do whatever it took, no matter what the costs. He would see to it personally.

Felicity let out a low grumble. "You sound confident. I wish we had the same assurance. He's been seen sniffing around the White Raven since her arrival."

"You dare question me?" Heath's voice was a dangerous whisper, the threat evident. "Remember who brought you here."

The four hallows exchanged silent glares of unease. It was the blond who cleared his throat. "We haven't forgotten. We only want to ensure that there are no bumps in the road. Last night might have ended in our favor, but it could have easily been a disaster."

A blank look remained on Heath's face, and his smooth Celtic accent never wavered. "My scouts will keep us informed. If she so much as sneezes, I'll know about it."

"And when the time comes ..."

A crow squawked somewhere from above the mass of twinkling stars. Even with the roar of the surf, others listened in on the conversation with their keen supernatural abilities. Heath's eyes shifted skyward, and the four vengeful spirits fluttered at the itch of trouble.

A wicked grin spread across Heath's lips. "Oh, you'll know."

"We're counting on you to not screw this up, overlord. The spirit world is flooding with souls ready for their chance to live again."

"I'll do my part." Heath glanced at his watch, impatience leaping into his eyes. "Spread the word, and wait for my command."

"You might have freed us, reaper, but we don't answer to you."

"Just be ready," Heath warned.

The fun and games were over; it was time to get down to business. And Heath had the perfect plan.

CHAPTER 1

I screamed long and loud.

It was more or less my thing—that and collecting souls, a harbinger of death. No prissy, pink bows for this girl. My life was darkness, the afterlife, and souls.

Twelve years ago, on my sixth birthday, I saw my first ghost. To this day, I don't know if it was a spirit or a hallow. There was a big difference. One wanted me dead. And the other wanted to aid or warn me.

Almost a year ago from today, my mom had been taken from me in the most brutal way a daughter could lose her mother—murder.

I came to Raven Hollow because of her death to spend a summer with my Grandma Rose—a woman I didn't have the pleasure of knowing until it was too late. Now, she was one of those spirits who abetted me.

It was strange how a journey could change you. That's what coming to this island had been—a journey of self-discovery. The things I had learned about myself couldn't be taught in school. It was one of those life lessons you had to experience, and experience I did. I learned the truth about who I was and what I was capable of. Those two things were life altering.

My abilities were amplified since Zander had died and I'd taken his soul—a formidable task that hadn't been my choice. I had tried to save him, but no matter how powerful I was, some things were still out of my control.

It didn't really matter now. He was gone. The boy who was supposed to be my husband was dead.

A fire began to kindle inside me, a satisfying burn and purpose I'd never felt before. Losing Zander had snapped something inside me. Never again would I sit back in silence and do nothing. The hallows weren't just dead, they were a threat to us all. And now I was personally invested, and I had the power to stop them. Being a banshee no longer seemed like a hindrance. The hallows might have found a way to lift the veil between realms, but they hadn't done so on their own. It wasn't possible, not without help.

Time to weed out the traitors and clean house; if you weren't on the side of the living, then you were dead. No more sweet, nice Piper — not that I was ever actually sweet. Despite all the unknowns, I was stronger and more focused than I'd ever been. For the first time, I didn't doubt myself. I was going to kick some serious hallow ass.

The most immediate problem was how I was going to put the veil back in place. I had no clue, but hallows were sucking reaper souls, lapping them up like they were the last banana split on Earth. Someone had to stop them. I always got the short end of the stick, but lucky for me, I had one kickass, very hot, and dangerous boyfriend.

Speaking of Zane …

Holy Scooby snacks.

He was standing on the open balcony, the wind whipping through his dark locks, carrying in the night and the sea. His face was angled, a five o'clock shadow lining his jaw. I blinked. Seeing him, I felt like a different girl than the one who had stepped foot on the island just weeks ago, angry at the world. Zane had played a big part in my transformation—him and the intense feelings he aroused inside me.

Then I remembered. The scream. Crash. It all came tumbling back in waves of fear, pain, and uncertainty. After what had been a train wreck of a night, Crash had snuck into my room, much like a stalker.

He'd made it clear his sister's death would not be forgotten, and the person responsible—in this case me—would pay. The whole conversation left me shaken and confused. Was he warning me or threatening me? No doubt Crash was long gone after his dramatic exit and threats, but he'd left me trembling in his wake.

Zane was a force to be reckoned with, and those who knew him well knew it. By the expression on his face, he was very much not okay. I wasn't even going to ask. Pain and hurt refracted in his stormy blue eyes, yet he'd still come to my rescue. A little late, but who could blame him? He wasn't in top form. I was honestly surprised he was here at all.

"You came," I whispered, placing a hand on the wall to steady my racing heart. Between Crash's unexpected visit and Zane's presence, my heart was overtaxed.

His voice was gruff when he replied. "I will always come."

It meant a thousand times more to me, hearing him say it. Zane was bound by an ancient oath to protect me. "I-I just thought with everything that happened—" My voice caught as tears began to swell in my eyes, closing off my throat. The sight of him broke down my walls. I didn't have to be strong or tough.

He stepped inside, closing the double glass doors behind him. "I'm not taking any chances with you. What happened?"

I swallowed, forcing the tears to remain at bay. "Crash. That's what happened," I said and waited for him to turn green and go Hulk. I wasn't disappointed, minus the green skin.

His eyes went dark, veins exploding down his face. "He was here?" he rumbled from deep in his chest. "He dared to show his face?"

I picked the half-peeled black cherry nail polish from my fingertips. "He came to give me a warning … I think." I was honestly left a little perplexed by Crash and his actions.

Zane clearly didn't trust him. "I'm going to kill him. His soul is mine."

This was pretty much the reaction I'd expected. I circled around the bed to the center of the room, where he stood rigid and unyielding. Tonight of all nights was not the best time to piss Zane off. Crash must have had a death wish, because I wasn't certain I'd be able to stop Zane from sending him to an early grave. Against the reaper rules or not, Zane was angry enough to act now and screw the consequences. Luckily for him, I was the White Raven. "Normally, I would argue with you, but maybe you're right."

His lustrous eyes glowed eerily in the dark. If I hadn't know him, I would have been frightened. "I'm always right, Princess."

And just like that, his arrogance became part of his armor. Zane was a complex guy, and under the hard shell and temper, he was hurting. And that brought on the guilt. "I shouldn't have sent the distress signal. You should be at home with your family, not here. Crash didn't hurt me. I'm not in danger at the present moment." Other than my shaken nerves and the uncontrollable need to feel safe, I was fine. Although I wasn't sure I'd ever truly be safe again.

His icy eyes thawed. It was possible he'd caught a flicker of my unease, but it was misplaced. It was *him* I was worried about. As if my skin was made of porcelain, he lightly ran a finger along my jaw. "I should have come sooner."

"He didn't hurt me," I reiterated before Zane got any ideas about going commando on Crash. I shouldn't have felt the need to object. Yet, regardless of what had transpired, I understood Crash's actions. I would have done anything to make the people responsible for my mother's death pay, suffer, even.

Maybe that was what he was doing. Taunting me, before he made his final move to strike me dead.

I knew now that muggers hadn't killed my mom, but instead reapers, probably Red Hawks. Knowing the truth didn't diminish the anger or desire for revenge. It had once blazed inside me, spreading until I thought of nothing else, and in my rage, I'd made some pretty stupid mistakes I could never take back.

Zane shook his head, wisps of his windblown hair partially obscuring his eyes. "That's not the point, Piper. He could have hurt you ... or worse. Apparently, it doesn't matter how much security we assign. Unless someone is stationed by your side twenty-four seven, you're exposed."

A deep ache filled my chest. Looking at Zane, I was glad I hadn't screamed sooner. He would have killed Crash. The glare in his eyes was murderous. There had been enough death in the last twenty-four hours, and I didn't want more blood on my hands, not until I was certain where Crash's loyalties laid. The odds were stacked against him, but I couldn't afford to jump to conclusions and risk making monumental mistakes. We needed all the facts before condemning someone to death. There'd already been too much bloodshed.

Zane … not so much.

But I'd always known who Zane was, what he was, and none of it changed my feelings for him. He might be a ruthless reaper with a rap sheet longer than even the most prolific serial killers, but when I saw him, I didn't see a destroyer of souls. I saw the guy I was hopelessly in love with.

And feeling his fractured pain, I wanted to wrap my arms around him and absorb his agony. The only thing worse than death was being the person left behind to deal with the loss and the anguish. It was times like this that made our linked souls overwhelming—when emotions were tremendous. His feelings hurtled into me, and my blood pressure escalated. "And that someone is going to be you?" I assumed.

"For tonight," he responded in a strangled voice.

I reached out, grabbing his forearm before he could turn away from me. "I appreciate the offer, but I'm okay. Really. I don't need a babysitter."

He wasn't convinced, maybe because I was gnawing on my lip to keep it from trembling. "I'm not leaving." And to prove his point, he kicked off his shoes.

We could go back and forth all night, but someone was going to have to cave. And he'd already been through too much for me to be a thorn in his backside. "Zane, what about your family …?"

"They'll understand. Trust me. I need to be here tonight, with you."

I think my heart stopped. "Okay," I agreed, pressing my forehead to his chest.

His arms immediately encircled me, enveloping me in his cool, midnight scent. It felt like I'd waited forever to be able to be with Zane and have him return my affections without pushing me away. I was afraid it wasn't real, that in the morning, I would wake up and nothing would have changed.

"Thank you," I whispered against his shirt, my hands flattened on his chest.

"For what, Princess?" The deep timbre of his voice vibrated against my face.

I lifted my head and gazed into his startling eyes. The dark reaper veins had faded. "Coming back." I wasn't talking about tonight, but coming home and back to me.

His fingers weaved through my slightly damp waves. "I never should have left."

We stared at each other. The cuts and bruises from our fight just hours before were gone from his face. A wealth of emotion transpired between us. Neither of us knew what to do or say next. I could have offered him one of the spare rooms to sleep in, but we both knew he wasn't going to let me out of his sight.

Time elapsed; neither of us budged. It was that kind of night. Emotions ran high, and my mind and body were not in sync. I imagined he felt the same.

"Come on," he urged. "You should try and get some sleep."

I stepped back, but his hands remained at my hips. "What about you?"

"I don't think I could if I tried." His jaw flexed. "I'll keep watch. Make sure you don't have any other unexpected intruders."

Always the tough guy, but he didn't need to be with me. "Or I could slip you a bottle of sleeping pills," I mumbled.

He sauntered across the room. "It wouldn't do anything."

"Because human drugs have no effect on us?" I guessed.

Bending down, he tugged back the covers. "None."

Well, that explained a lot. I slipped the robe off and threw it on the chair. "Fine. Will you at least hold me?" I asked, padding across the room.

He was silent for a blink. "It depends."

"On what?"

"Is that what you're wearing to bed?" he asked with a trace of his Celtic accent.

I arched a brow. "Do you have a problem with my nightshirt?"

"Not the shirt, just how short it is ..." His eyes roamed down my legs. "... and the fact that I'm not certain you have on anything else."

"Perfect. I was going for distraction." I climbed to the edge of the bed, snugging my feet under the covers, making sure to leave plenty of room in hopes I'd persuaded him to join me. I looked up, his entire face shrouded in darkness. "Don't steal the covers."

The bed dipped with his weight, and a second later I felt him give a yank on the blanket. He was really something else. Without thinking, I grabbed the ends and pulled them up to my chin, and maybe I took more than my share. He was too big or the bed was too small. Opening his arm, I settled in alongside him, my head nestled on his shoulder.

His body was firm as he held me. I hadn't been able to save his brother, but maybe I could, for a night, calm his troubled soul and take some of the pain. Whether he was willing to admit it or not, he needed the rest as much as I did.

Cool lips pressed against my neck, a brief, light touch. "Get some sleep," he murmured.

The only one sleeping was going to be him. I closed my eyes and drew my power around me, letting the tendrils trickle into Zane. I didn't need pills. Our bond provided an IV straight to his bloodstream.

In moments, his body relaxed, and the even rhythm of his breathing filled the quietness. The hurt of losing Zander was still fresh and raw. He was drained physically and emotionally. I was able to quiet his soul so he could fall into a sleep he desperately needed. I kept watch, unable to follow him into the unknowing bliss of slumber. Too well I knew the scars left behind from losing someone and how they didn't ever quite heal.

Dawn was only right around the corner. A few hours would do him good. What I hadn't expected was what it would do for me.

Regardless of the traumatic evening, being in Zane's arms was nothing short of miraculous. A part of me had truly thought we'd never be able to be together. But I hadn't given up hope, and although we hadn't had a chance to discuss our relationship, he was here. And that was all that mattered in the world.

There was no denying the peace, tranquility, and harmony of lying beside him. Not to mention safety. It wasn't only my soul that sighed; it was my heart as well. For the first time, the two were joined in mutual contentment, and a ribbon of happiness I hadn't felt since before my mom died twirled inside me.

I wanted to hold onto it, bottle it for a bad day, but it was hard to appreciate the glow inside me after the events of the past twelve hours. My guilt was overwhelming. How could I possibly feel a shred of happiness when Zander was gone? But the small fragments of happiness couldn't completely mask the agony and anger that lived inside me. I wouldn't forget what had happened or who was responsible. I wouldn't forget my role in his death. I vowed to myself, to Zane, and to Zander, his death wouldn't be in vain. It was a promise I meant to keep at whatever cost.

The world sort of depended on it.

CHAPTER 2

I don't know what woke me. It could have been the sunlight streaming in through the sheer curtains or the squawking of a hawk. My room was otherwise peacefully quiet. But as I rolled to my side, I got an eerie sensation I wasn't alone.

And then I remembered. I wasn't alone. Zane had stayed the night … or morning, depending how you looked at it.

I opened my eyes and blinked, expecting to see his dark blue eyes rimmed with silver spurts of light. My gaze roamed to the spot beside me. It was empty. Go figure.

But I wasn't alone.

Eyes the color of dew-covered grass stared into mine from across the room. My first instinct was to scream and give him a sonic blast strong enough to knock him into next week, but I blinked again.

"Oliver?" I croaked.

Oliver was a Blue Sparrow and one of my security details who normally patrolled the manor and maintained the entrance. He hadn't exactly done a bang-up job, considering Crash had managed to weasel his way into my room not once, but twice. He was lounging against the wall, cleaning his nails with a pocketknife and looking very bored.

Clutching the end of the blanket to my chest, I sat up and cleared my throat. "Uh, what are you doing here? And by here, I mean in my bedroom."

"I've been ordered to keep eyes on you at all times, Princess," he replied in an almost robotic tone without any inflection.

"Don't call me that," I snapped. He didn't so much as flinch. "Ordered by who?" I asked, though I already knew the answer. This had Zane written all over it.

He showed the slightest emotion—amusement. "The Death Scythe."

I rolled my eyes. "Where is he?"

Oliver lowered his gaze, dark lashes fanning over angular cheeks. He was tall and built like Zane, but that was where the comparison ended. "He had to leave. I believe his family is paying their respects."

I wanted to be there for Zane and his family, but it wasn't my place to show up at something so personal. A deep pang radiated inside me, and I slumped back against the white, pin cushion headboard. "Oh," I responded. I lost my grip on the blanket as it slipped down.

Oliver flipped closed his knife. "He also said you were not to go anywhere until he got back."

Over the past year, I'd grown used to doing things my way, going and coming as I pleased and answering to no one. Losing my privacy didn't bode well for me. There was also the little fact I hadn't had my coffee yet. "Who died and made him king?"

Oliver wore an unapologetic grin.

I pulled my knees up, contemplating how I was going to get out of bed without Oliver seeing more of me than I was comfortable with. "I'm guessing it wouldn't do any good if I told you to leave?" I asked.

He crossed his arms and frowned. "None."

"Wonderful," I grumbled. "So Oliver, any chance part of your job description is to fetch me coffee?"

"I liked it better when you were sleeping. Less questions."

Yeah, he seemed like a guy who was more action and less talk. "I just bet. So I take it that's a no on the coffee?"

He snorted. "Affirmative, Princess."

Couldn't he just say no? Fine. I could stay in bed, but now that I was thinking about coffee, I really wanted a cup. Or an entire pot. Yawning, I considered rolling over and pulling the covers past my head, or I could wrap the sheet around myself and truck it down to the kitchen. I nibbled on my lip, contemplating. I loved sleep, but I think I loved coffee more. Gathering the sheets around me, I scooted to the edge of the bed when Oliver stiffened.

Veins the color of sapphire pooled down over his cheeks. "Someone's coming."

My fingers dug into the bed, and ten seconds later, Parker popped his head into the room. Sandy hair messy from sleep, he stood in the doorway in rumpled flannel pajama bottoms and, of course, a manga shirt. Parker was so predictable in his wardrobe ... and generally in life. It was what I loved about him. Dependable Parker.

I let out a whoosh of air. Thank God it wasn't a hallow or something worse—ten hallows.

Parker's gaze slipped from me to Oliver and back to me. "Uh, I didn't realize you had company."

"*Oliver* is not company," I informed him, unclenching my hands. "Apparently, he's been assigned to stick to me like white on rice."

Oliver returned to leaning one shoulder against the wall. He was strategically placed in the room so he could see all the exits.

"Oh." Parker sauntered over to the bed and handed me a cup of coffee.

I could have kissed him. "You're a godsend," I replied, sipping from the mug and letting the steam warm my face.

His amber eyes sparkled behind his glasses. "You mean Gracie is. She made it. I just poured and delivered."

I closed my eyes a moment and savored the sweet and bitter brew. "Remind me to tell her I love her."

He sat on the edge of the bed. "If I had known this was a slumber party, I would have brought the whole pot and my sleeping bag."

"Trust me, it wasn't my idea, and Tonto over there won't listen." Between Oliver and me, we both knew I had the power to make him leave. I just didn't have the strength or heart. This was important to

Zane. I was important to him, and at least for today while his family grieved, I would behave.

"Well, that might be a good thing, considering the world is about to go to shit," he said.

I glared. I didn't see the upside to having someone shadow me every second of every day. Gah, was he even going to watch me pee? But after last night, everyone was still shaken up, so whether I agreed with the extra precautions or not, I did understand them. "You okay?" I asked.

He stared down at his cup. "Define okay. I don't think I will ever be okay again. My best friend is a banshee, the universe is out of whack, and I didn't sleep at all last night."

"Me neither," I replied. "This whole thing is so messed up. How the heck am I supposed to fix it? I don't even know how to put the veil back in place. I can barely think straight."

I hadn't really expected Parker to give me an answer, but he did. "You don't need to decide right this minute. Breathe while you can. Anyway, I don't pretend to understand how, but you seem to always know what to do at the critical moment."

Maybe I had today, a week, or a month, but regardless how much time I had before things got past the point of redemption, I wasn't willing to bet the lives of those I cared about on my instincts. "God, I wish I knew when they will strike again," I said, frustrated. "I'm afraid the next time we won't be able to defeat them. Or someone else will die." We had reached the point where Parker needed to leave Raven Hollow. Yesterday had been another demonstration of how unsafe it was for him to be here. Hell, I wasn't sure anyone was safe anywhere.

Parker shoved a hand into his hair. "Wow, this is some heavy stuff for …" he glanced at the nightstand "… eleven-thirty in the morning."

I sighed. "Sorry. Reaper time. It won't be long before I'm completely nocturnal." My gaze shifted to the ceiling as my thoughts wandered. "I can't believe Zander is gone."

He set aside his coffee and scooted up on the bed, putting his arm around me. "Your fiancé. I never got the chance to get to know him. Tell me about him."

Parker's feelings about Zane were crystal clear, but Zander … I think they would have gotten along. I laid my head on his shoulder and sighed. "You would have liked him. Everyone liked him."

"So he wasn't a colossal asshat like his brother?" Parker asked.

I snorted. "No, he wasn't an ass-anything. He was far more than I deserved, considering the way I treated him."

He shifted on the bed, trying to find a comfortable spot. "Some things are out of our control."

"I hate not being in control."

He gave my shoulder a squeeze. "I know."

I sighed, watching Parker fidget on the bed for the second time. "What's up with you?" It wasn't like him to be so antsy. Something was on his mind.

"So I've been thinking," he started.

"Does this require more coffee?" I asked, staring at my nearly empty mug.

Oliver's lips twitched as he stood in the corner. I was tempted to ask if his legs ever got tired. Mine would be jelly in an hour.

"It might require something stronger," Parker advised.

"Now you've got me worried."

"My mom called."

"Is everything all right?" My mind ran in a million directions. With the veil down, no one was safe. Had something happened?

"Yeah, she's good. But she wanted to know when we would be coming back. School starts in three weeks, and you know how she gets."

I exhaled. Summer was almost over, meaning we were about to embark on our senior year. Believe it or not, reapers went to high school. We were homeschooled, I had learned. I doubted very much the education I was going to get was anything like my school back in Chicago.

But I hadn't told Parker of my plans. I had kind of assumed he understood I wouldn't be leaving Raven Hollow. This was my home. "I'm not going back, Parks."

He took a deep breath. "I knew you were going to say that."

"I'm sorry. I know we had this plan."

A sad, almost wistful half-smile touched his lips. "Right, the one where we skip our graduation ceremony and go grab breakfast at Over Easy Café so we can talk shit about all the lame-os we never have to see again."

"And then we were going to spend the summer road tripping across the States before enrolling in the Art Institute. I haven't forgotten, but I don't think college is in the cards for me anymore. You're going to have to go without me."

His eyes sobered. "That's the thing though. I don't want to."

"Parker, you can't give up on your dreams. I know how much you want to create. That you have a passion for manga most people don't understand. There have been too many dreams crushed, too many lives destroyed. I need you to live, for both of us. Do all the things we promised ourselves we would do."

He was stubborn. "Everything's changed. What if the things I used to want are no longer important?"

"It's true; everything is different now, but that doesn't mean you still can't have a future. Get married. Have 2.5 kids, a dog, and a house with a white picket fence. If that's what you want, you can have it all."

"You make it sound so easy. How can you expect me to forget there are ghosts with anger issues running around killing people? To forget about you?" There was anger behind his words.

I swallowed. "I don't want you to forget or forget me. I want you to be safe. And very, very happy."

He glanced up. His expression tugged at my heart. "Life without my best friend doesn't sound happy. I'm not delusional enough to think that once I leave this island we'll ever see each other again."

I fumbled with one of the rings on my finger. "You can't be sure of that. Neither of us knows what the future might hold."

I had no idea what was going to happen from here on out. Even thinking about the possibilities scared the ever-loving crap out of me. Parker didn't deal well with surprises, and I was starting to dislike them, especially since all my *surprises* ended up with me fighting for my life. Tomorrow wasn't guaranteed, especially in my line of work.

CHAPTER 3

"Did you know that you snore … if you could call the cute kitten noises you make snoring? It's more like a purr."

With my head laying on my hands, I opened one eye. "I do not," I groggily mumbled.

His head was on the pillow beside me, our faces close enough that I could almost taste his breath. In typical Zane fashion, he raised a brow at me, calling me out.

Okay, so maybe I snored, a little. "Yeah, well, you drool." I'd grown restless cooped up inside, waiting for Zane, and apparently had dozed off.

He pressed a kiss to the tip of my nose. "You might sleep like a kitten, but you wake with a roar."

I stretched, drinking in the sight of him. The anxiousness I'd been feeling all day evaporated at his touch. "What time is it?"

The changing of the guards had happened while I'd taken a little catnap. Declan stood silently in the room. "Declan, I can take it from here," Zane said, without moving his eyes off mine, and relieved Declan of his babysitting duties.

Declan gave Zane a nod before he morphed into a hawk and took flight.

I rubbed my eyes. I still hadn't gotten used to watching someone turn into an animal in nothing more than a quick blink.

Cool fingers brushed my cheek. "Everything quiet?"

"Believe it or not, the world didn't crumble around me and no one tried to kill me today. Overall, I'd say it was a pretty normal day." My eyes ran over his face, trying to judge his mood. "How about you? You okay?"

"Better now."

I dropped my gaze. The heightened sense of his emotions was a bit of a struggle for me. I noticed since the night I'd renounced my engagement to Zander, the link between Zane and me was sharper. "You didn't have to come back, you know. Your hounds are doing a superb job of following me."

"Good. But I wanted to see you." He twined our fingers, bringing our joined hands to his chest. "Being here with you is the only time the pain is bearable."

My heart wobbled. Hearing him admit how much he needed to see me did funny things to my innards. I pressed a soft kiss to his sad, soft lips. "I wish I could have done more."

His hand squeezed mine, and for a moment, neither of us moved. It had been a casual gesture, just a kiss meant to comfort, but static crackled in the air between us. Unable to pull my gaze from his, I felt myself drowning in his darkness. He was a temptation, and even in that moment, I deconstructed the way he made me feel: the way his body leaned into mine, making my skin shudder, his wild scent teasing my senses, and my heart thudding in my chest.

His mouth hit mine again in a cool wave of twilight. And this time, it was a very different kind of kiss. It was three months worth of kissing. My lips came alive under his, tasting his desire mixed with mine. My mind shut off—precisely what I wanted: to feel and not think. For once, there was nothing standing in our way.

And I was free.

I opened my eyes, pressing my lips together to savor the tingling feel. He had ended the kiss far too soon for me.

This was the second time I'd waken up with Zane in my bed and nothing had happened.

He must have read my thoughts. "The next time I get you in bed, I promise we won't be sleeping."

Familiar tingles skated down my neck, and my blood began to sing. "That is a promise I am going to hold you to, Zaney."

"I know what you did last night," he murmured.

My fingers ran through his hair, linking around his neck. "What do you mean?" I replied, my mind still floating on his kiss.

"No one's ever manipulated my emotions before." He brushed a strand of hair behind my ear. "And truth be told, I haven't been in control of them since you stepped foot on this island."

I swallowed hard. Right. That. "I only wanted to help."

"I know." He tucked his arm behind his head and smiled. "It's going to take some adjustment, letting you in."

I didn't want to assume anything about our relationship and get all goofy. I wouldn't press him yet, but we were going to have to talk. There was no doubt in my mind what I wanted or the lengths I would go to love him, but I could still feel his reservations. Even now, he was holding back.

"Try having someone shadow your every move. Not something I want to get used to," I mumbled.

"It's only until we figure out how to restore the veil," he reasoned.

I sighed. "That could be never."

He rotated his head, staring up at the ceiling. "Don't say that. We'll find a way to stop them. It's what we do."

It was what *he* did. Zane was a death reaper. He destroyed souls and absorbed them. If he killed you, there was no coming back, no afterlife. You were pretty much nonexistent at that point. Not all reapers were the same. There were others who harvested a soul and brought them to the other side and those who marked humans for death.

We all had our part to play in keeping the balance of life, except someone had gone and screwed it all up. I chewed on the inside of my lip. "How much time do you think we have until things go haywire?"

His jaw worked from side to side, and his entire face darkened. "I don't know, but when they do, they'll come with everything they've got, and we're going to annihilate them all."

I wished I had his confidence. It wasn't only the hallows I was worried about, but also the reaper or reapers who were assisting them. "When do we start? Where do we start?"

He rolled over, snaking an arm over my waist. "Tomorrow. Crash is first on the list."

I rolled my eyes. "Zaaaane."

"Piper Longstocking," he replied, tugging at the ends of my braids. "I don't trust him. He's threatened you. That alone in my book makes him a dead man."

"He and his family have reasons to hate me." I had killed Crash's sister, even though it had been self-defense. Dead was dead. "But we don't know that Crash is the one who released the hallows," I argued. "He's had plenty of opportunities to hurt me, yet he never has." I just wasn't ready to write Crash off as the traitor.

Zane growled. "Maybe, but I'm not taking the chance. He's never played by the rules and has been more of an interference than an asset. I can't ignore the fact that he wasn't at the ceremony. We don't know where he was or what he was doing."

"I saw Heath slinking off just as shit went sideways. It could easily have been him."

"Even more reason to suspect Crash. He's probably conspiring with his father."

"What could they gain by dropping the veil?"

"Your death," he stated flatly.

I picked at a loose string on the bed. "Nowadays, it feels like more people want me dead than alive."

Zane played with my hair, twisting strands around his finger as we talked. "Not true. I definitely don't want you dead."

I shoved him on the shoulder. "You might be the exception. What do we do now that everyone knows our secret?"

"First, we're done hiding. Second, we use it. Together we're more powerful. We might not have the element of surprise, but they don't know what we can do."

And that posed a question. "Do you know what we can do?"

His lips twitched. "Not fully. I know we have the ability to share our powers and our souls naturally align when we're near each other, which has some interesting benefits."

My eyes narrowed. I knew about the weird emotion-altering thing. "Interesting how?"

"That's what we're going to find out."

"When? Now?" I asked, unable to keep the enthusiasm from my voice.

"Uh, I was thinking of some place more structured to handle explosions, unless you want to destroy another room in this historic joint."

Oh crap. I'd completely forgotten about the mess left behind from my train wreck coronation. "That reminds me. I need to do something about the cathedral room. I'll be screwed if it decides to rain. That hole in the ceiling is like an open window."

"We'll get the guys from the club to come down and help."

It felt good making plans to restore what the hallows had destroyed. "So, back to our soul symmetry. Are you scared what we might discover?"

He frowned and somehow managed to look ridiculously sexy doing so. "No. Neither should you. If you haven't figured it out yet, there's nothing you can't handle, Princess."

I wasn't afraid of the link between us, but I wanted him to talk to me, tell me what was going on in that head of his. "You're not afraid of anything."

He ran a hand through his disheveled hair. "Not true."

"What could *you* be afraid of?"

"There's only one thing that petrifies me." His blue eyes hit mine. "Losing you."

My heart toppled over and then squeezed as his face became pained with real fear. Zane knew better than anyone what we were up against, and after just losing his brother, it was a fear we both felt. "That's not going to happen."

"Swear you won't do anything reckless. *And* you won't make Oliver and Declan's job difficult. I don't know what I would do if—"

I affixed my lips to his. "I promise," I said. "I don't want to die. I want to get rid of those who would upset the balance. I understand what my purpose is. I'm not going to run."

Judging by the fading of the harsh lines around his eyes, he believed me. "Good, because I would only come after you."

His cool breath washed over my face, making my pulse flutter as emotions swirled between us. "I've had plenty of practice being invisible."

"I think we've established you can't hide from me," he murmured—all seriousness as one hand gently framed my cheek.

I leaned into his touch, and—

"Piper!" My name bellowed from outside my bedroom door, echoing over the expansive house.

Zane's eyes collided with mine. "Expecting company?"

It sounded again. "Piper!"

This time I recognized the voice and jumped up. "TJ," I muttered.

The dark lines around Zane's eyes softened as I withdrew myself from his arms and clumsily jumped out of bed. And by jump, I mean I rolled off the side and landed on my butt. Scrambling to my feet, I reached the hallway in seconds, racing toward the stairs. "TJ," I blurted out.

He rounded the top step, and I flung my arms around his neck. "You're okay." I exhaled.

He glanced down at me like I'd grown devil horns. "Of course, I'm okay. What is Parker doing in my room?"

"What are *you* doing here?" I countered, dodging the question. The sanctity of his room was the least of my concerns.

"Don't be mad. I know you don't want me here—"

"TJ, that's not true," I interjected. "I was so worried about you. I must have called you a gazillion times."

"Chill. My phone broke."

If I hadn't been so happy to see him, I would have punched him for making me worry sick about him. It wasn't a good feeling. "You didn't think to borrow a phone?"

He rubbed the back of his neck. "I don't know your number," he admitted sheepishly. "And I didn't know what else to do, so I came back. You're not mad?"

A million and one questions raced through my mind. Where did he get the money to make the trip? Please tell me he hadn't hitchhiked. Did he know Dad was dead? My face paled. "No, I'm not mad. I never should have made you leave to begin with." Hindsight was twenty-twenty. It was clear the safest place for TJ was with me, where Zane and I could protect him. And seeing him in the flesh, it hit me. TJ was all the family I had left.

"What is Parker doing here?"

"Um, he showed up the same day you left."

"That's bullshit."

Judging by his usual teenage angst, I was going to assume he didn't know about Dad. "Language," I scolded.

He looked frazzled and tired. "I've had a helluva week. Dad took off on one of his disappearing acts and basically fell off the Earth."

I choked.

He crossed his lanky arms. "Parker's got ten minutes to gather his shit and find himself a new place to crash."

"It might be fun to have a roommate," I suggested, thinking the two of them could keep an eye on one another.

"What are we, ten? There are four other unused bedrooms," he so obviously pointed out.

"Fine," I agreed. It wasn't worth fighting over. We did have ample space for all of us and then some.

Satisfied, he hiked his bag over his shoulder and turned to leave, but something else was on his mind. "Hey, Piper?"

"Yeah," I answered.

He shuffled his feet, glancing at the ground. "Something weird is going on."

My hand tightened on the banister. "What do you mean?"

He gave kind of a half shrug, unsure of himself. "I don't know. You're going to laugh at me."

I wanted to snort. "If anyone understands weird, it's me. I promise

I won't laugh."

"I've been seeing things," he announced.

"What kind of things?" I asked, but I was pretty sure I already knew the answer.

There was a long pause as if he was deciding if I could be trusted. "I don't know ... ghosts, I guess," he said, his voice wavering.

I closed my eyes. *Damn.* I was going to have to tell TJ the truth ... soon. Before he saw me in all my banshee glory. Something must have triggered the ability for him to see the dead, maybe the death of our father.

"I told you it was crazy." There was a pinch of fear in his gaze.

Our eyes met. "It's not crazy. I believe you, TJ."

I watched as the strain he'd been holding left his shoulders. "You do?"

I smiled. "Yeah. I'm your sister. I know when you're lying."

TJ ran his palms over his thighs. When he was troubled, he got fidgety. "The things I've been seeing, if I didn't know better, I'd think I was on drugs. It doesn't make sense."

I ruffled his hair, a habit that annoyed the crapola out of him. "It's going to be okay. You're home now. Get some sleep, and tell Parker to pick a room, any room. We'll talk in the morning."

"Sure, as long as it's not about me going back to Chicago."

"Pinky swear." I held out my little finger.

His lips twitched as he looped his pinky around mine. "You're still lame."

Some things never changed.

Zane choose that moment to lean against the open doorway. He did one of those guy nods of hello to TJ, who reciprocated.

TJ shook his head, snickering. "Now I know why it took you so long to come out of your room. I'm giving Parker ten minutes to get all his crap out. I just want to crash and forget the last ten hours," he said as he and his duffle bag trotted down the hall.

I could relate. I suddenly wasn't feeling too spiffy.

"That was unexpected," Zane said.

My back was pressed into the wall. "You're telling me."

CHAPTER 4

I let myself into the Black Crow's "secret" room with Declan on my heels and found Aspyn beating the pulp out of a dummy. Apparently, I wasn't the only one with issues to work out. Three days had come and gone and nothing had happened. Nada. Zilch. Diddly-squat. But each day I grew more fretful not only because there hadn't been any hallow attacks, but also because I needed to have a discussion with my little brother I had never thought I would have to have. And no, it wasn't the sex talk. Unfortunately I wished it were as basic as the birds and the bees.

Things were awkward between TJ and me. He knew I was hiding something—that I knew more about the ghosts he'd been seeing than I was revealing. Procrastination was one of my biggest flaws. Along with about twenty other things I could think of off the top of my head.

Perfect? ... Not even close.

But when I was stressed to the max, I tended to be more introverted, at least until I worked through the problem. Without a single hallow or spirit sighting, I started to doubt the veil had been fractured. If it was really gone, why weren't we being overrun by hallows?

Why weren't they exacting their vengeance? It didn't make any sense. I wasn't the only one who was concerned, either.

The entire island was on red alert.

Then there was Zane. Every day we'd practice aligning our souls, stretching our abilities. We could do some really amazing things together, but I didn't know how any of it was going to help us.

Aspyn spun around as the door to the training room swung shut with a clack. I tackled the stairs, aware that her eyes followed me. She wiped the sweat from her brow with the back of her arm as I approached. "I see you got a new accessory." Her eyes lifted to a frowning Declan behind me.

Tension flittered through the air. I got the vibe there was some history between them, and it hadn't ended well. *Awkward*. "A gift from Zane."

"Aspyn," Declan said flatly, his arms crossed, sunglasses shielding his eyes.

She was wearing a crop top and boy shorts, owning it. "Declan, glad to see your sparkling personality hasn't dulled."

My lips cracked. In the short time I'd spent with Declan, there hadn't been a whole lot of banter. He was a pretty closed-lipped kind of dude and took his job seriously, unlike Oliver, who had more of a sense of humor.

Declan stood in his bodyguard stance, peering down at Aspyn behind his shades. "Just don't cause any trouble."

"I wouldn't dream of it," she cooed.

I rolled my eyes. Seriously, how much trouble could two girls cause in a secured training room? "I'll be fine, Declan. You want to take advantage of the gym and work on beefing up those pythons you call arms?"

I swear his mouth twitched. It was hard to tell. "No funny business."

"Cross my heart and hope to—"

"Don't say it, Princess," Declan warned.

Aspyn laughed. "Epic."

Declan walked over to the weights, shaking his head.

Gathering my hair on top of my head, I secured it into a messy bun. "Mind if I take the dummy for a few spins?"

Even with her skin glistening with perspiration, Aspyn was beautiful. If she worked out like this daily, no wonder she had a banging body. "He's all yours. Actually, I'm surprised to see you here."

I stepped up to the armless and legless dummy. "I needed to get out of the manor. I hate being boxed in. What about you?" I extended my leg and gave the poor guy a kick to the gut.

"That restlessness you feel, it's a reaper thing." The earlier mischief in her eyes wasn't present. "I've got some baggage I'm trying to unleash."

"Don't we all," I mumbled.

A strand of hair clung to her damp, pale cheek. "I still can't believe he's gone."

Word of Zander's death had spread over the island like wildfire. Everyone had a million questions, including my merger with the Crows and who would be Death's heir. I was supposed to unite the White Raven lineage with the Black Crows'. It was my duty to make sure that I had a successor. The sudden pressure to marry and have a child was prickling at my neck. I was only eighteen, yet I felt like I was thirty. I pressed my back to the dummy, facing Aspyn. "Neither can I. Every morning I wake up and, for a few seconds, I've forgotten—blissfully unaware. Then I remember what happened," *and the agony plunges inside me, so forcefully it robs me of air,* I added silently.

"It sucks." She swiped the corner of her eyes. "There's a pit in my stomach, and no matter how hard I punch that dummy, it doesn't dull the ache."

I glanced over my shoulder at Bob, the punching dummy. "So you're telling me this isn't going to help?"

"Nope," she confirmed. "I know the circumstances surrounding your relationship with Zander were less than ideal, but I also know you grew to care about him."

"I did." There was a strange shift between us—a comprehension stemming from the depth of Aspyn's pain. I felt it. Her heart was weeping. Since absorbing Zander's powers, I had noticed enhances in my own. Nothing major, but small things, like being able to sense Aspyn's emotions on a different level. My connection to other reapers appeared to be heightened.

The bigger question was how had I not known Aspyn had a thing for Zander. It was a blow. The more I thought I knew about Aspyn, the more secrets she seemed to have. My mouth dropped. "Oh wow," I whispered. "I didn't know."

Her eyes glassed over for a second. "It was before your engagement, but he was more than just some guy, ya know? I know I have a reputation for going through guys like hotcakes, but I'm not heartless. He made me feel ... special."

I did know. All too well. I only wished one of them had told me. I had always thought of Aspyn as just a flirt. "I'm sorry. I never meant to—"

She waved a hand in the air. "Don't apologize. He ended things the moment his father told him about you. Zander was an honorable guy."

I nodded. "He was. And a good friend. I only wish I could have saved him."

There was no blame or judgment in her gray eyes. "No matter how hard you try, Piper, you can't save everyone. And trust me, I know you want to, but this life, it's encompassed in death."

Aspyn had grown up as a reaper, and death was a part of her everyday life. She had saved me once as a child. I didn't remember it, but she was right. I couldn't save everyone. I knew that, as hard as it was to swallow. "I'm coming to terms with it," I replied.

"How's Zane?"

I shrugged. "On the outside he's a tough guy, but inside, his heart is splintered."

"Zane's made from a different kind of reaper cloth. And I don't care what those elder bozos say. Pureblood or not, Zane is more reaper than half the ones I know."

She wasn't going to get an argument from me. It didn't matter if Zane was half demon or part gargoyle, in my heart we were destined to be together. Fate had linked us for a reason, and I wasn't about to spit on fate. We needed to embrace the power between us, not hide it. "You should tell that to Zane."

"Don't tell me; the Death Scythe is still resisting you."

"No, not exactly." But he still put up walls. It could be an old habit, or it could be he was holding back.

A ghost of a smile splayed on her lips. "So," she said, a twinkle in her silver eyes, "are you and Zane really together? Is it true you finally grew some balls?"

There was always something about Aspyn and her choice of words that lightened my mood. She was good for my soul. A smile tugged at my lips. "What exactly do you mean by 'together'?" I asked, knowing how Aspyn's mind worked.

She flipped the tail end of her ponytail off her shoulder. "Do you need me to spell it out for you? S-E-X."

"Aspyn!" I shrieked, stealing a glance at Declan. He was lifting the barbell over his head with at least a hundred pounds on either side. Show off. But he appeared too involved in his workout to have overheard, or he was doing a fantastic job pretending otherwise.

"Okay, by your virtuous blush and your unease at the word *sex*," she whispered over the last bit, "I'm going to assume you and Zane have not done the freaky-deaky. So I ask, what are you waiting for?"

Good question. There was no doubt in my mind that I wanted to be with Zane. "Timing," I replied, shrugging.

She wrapped a white sweat towel around her neck, holding onto the ends with either hand. "Let me tell you, timing is not everything. Trust me. If you wait for the perfect moment, you might never get the chance. I think we've proven life is precious and unexpected. None of us know how long it's going to last. Even as *the* banshee, sometimes opportunity slips through your fingers."

I pushed off the dummy. "You're absolutely right."

She came up beside me and karate chopped the dummy in the chest, making him wobble back and forth. "Go get him, girl."

I wrinkled my nose. "Now?"

"No time like the present."

I faced the dummy and gave him a solid whack with my fist. "I'm gross and sweaty."

"Trust me, guys like it dirty."

The smile spreading across my lips couldn't be helped. "We've waited three months … I think a few more hours aren't going to hurt."

"Suit yourself."

"Glad we cleared that up," I muttered, turning my attention back to beating the piss out of Bob. My feet danced over the mat as I swung.

Aspyn held on to the back of the dummy, keeping his wonky form still while I took turns alternating between kicks and punches. "I'm happy for you, for both of you. I've known Zane my whole life, and if anyone deserves a chance at love, it's him. But boy, you guys have some obstacles to overcome, don't you? I bet the overlords are shitting a brick."

"That's one way to put it," I panted.

"They're going to want to make a match for your husband. We both know Zane is not a candidate. They will choose one of the overlord's heirs."

My fist slipped, completely missing my mark, but my body followed through with the motion. I caught my balance, planting both feet on the mat. "So again I'm not free to choose?"

"You're free to choose one of the four. That will be the only freedoms the divine will allow," she said, leaning a hip on Bob.

I shook my head. "No. I won't do it." Injustice tore through me, and an absurd idea popped into my head. "Is that why you think Zane and I should, uh, seal the deal? Would it make a difference?"

She grinned at my awkwardness. "If you're talking about your virtue, then no, it won't matter to them. But if you were carrying his child …"

Sweet baby Jesus. She wasn't suggesting … She couldn't be implying … Dear God, she was. Me? Pregnant? "You're joking."

Her expression didn't waver.

"Oh my God, you're not joking. Is that the only way?" This conversation had taken a bizarre twist.

"There are no guarantees in life. But it doesn't hurt to swing the odds in your direction. If you had his baby, you could prove to the stuck-in-their-way fuddy-duddys that your daughter can rule. That she will be a full-fledged banshee."

"But what if she isn't? What if they're right? Then what?"

"I don't know, Piper. All I know is, the little girl I spared so many years ago, *she* was destined for greatness. I felt it then. And I feel it now. If anyone can break the norm, it's you and Zane. There is a reason why your souls resonate. And I don't think you should ignore it."

Once the shock wore off, the idea was ... enchanting. I could see her. A little girl with raven hair and emerald eyes, with the ability to cloak herself in shadows, just like her daddy. Our daughter. She was adorable, and I fell instantly in love with the little girl in the vision.

Everything Aspyn said were thoughts I'd already had, and it only strengthened my resolve. "Thank you," I replied drolly.

Her lips split into a grin. "What are friends for?"

"Now all I have to do is convince Zane. I don't know which is going to be the bigger challenge: standing up to the divine or telling Zane I want to have his baby."

She winked. "Who says you have to tell him?"

I shouldn't have been shocked by her implied deception, but I was. "I couldn't do that. Not to Zane."

"And this is exactly why you're the White Raven and I'm not."

Another burden to shoulder. Zane didn't have my love-conquers-all belief. It had nothing to do with his feelings for me, because he loved me. He was hung up by century-old rules and that his reaper blood wasn't pure.

"So, I have a *thing* tonight," Aspyn said, lifting her brows. I interpreted the *thing* she was referring to as she had a soul to devour. "Why don't you come with me? Get some hands-on experience? You can even bring tight-ass over there."

Declan had finished his workout and was pulling on a shirt. He frowned.

I chewed on my lower lip. Zane wouldn't like it, which, not going to lie, kind of made me want to do it even more. Everyone had their part in keeping the balance between life and death. I was the banshee, the siren of death. Reaping souls wasn't my specialty, but if I wanted to be a kickass White Raven, I needed to know the ins and outs of all aspects of reaping. It was past time I went on a reap, and my curiosity was piqued. "What time should I be ready?" I said, jumping at the chance to get off the island, even for a night.

"Midnight, of course."

CHAPTER 5

I stood on the balcony for several moments, listening to the roaring of the surf and the whistling of the wind, letting it take my thoughts to dark places. Midnight was drawing near, and all I could think about was the difficult journey I had set out in front of me. Not the reaping I would be doing with Aspyn tonight, but the choices I had to make about my future.

It wasn't only about me. The decisions I made would affect everyone. There was so much to accomplish in such a short time. I still had to talk to TJ and Zane, and the sheer silence of the island was getting to me.

If there was nothing happening here, maybe there was activity on the mainland. It was risky leaving Hallow Island, but if I was going to figure out a way to restore the seal, I needed to know what we were up against.

Who the heck knew? Maybe we were all wrong and the barrier wasn't gone. Maybe we were all stressing for nothing.

The fleeting thought might have come too soon, as the newscaster's voice flowed through the TV, urgent and grave.

Tonight, roughly ten accounts of ghost sightings have been reported in and around the New Orleans area. But the numbers are multiplying as details of the encounters are reported: tales of ghastly figures attacking the public, causing harm, destruction, and even death. The city is in chaos. People are locking themselves up in their homes. Descriptions of the sightings are disturbing: muted skin, soulless eyes, even floating in the air. The reporter's voice showed some stress. *The flood of emergency calls to local stations are overwhelming law enforcement.*

Most alarming are the bodies that are piling up along the French Quarter. Just what is going on in the city? Some have suggested this is the result of chemical or water pollution. One thing is certain, New Orleans has never witnessed such horror and, at this moment, seems to have no ability to stop it.

My balance wavered as the room started to spin. I reached for the edge of the dresser, steadying myself, absorbing the shock of what had been reported. *Dammit,* the world was already starting to crack. The end was not far behind.

"We're going to be busy tonight."

Startled, I jumped at the sound of Aspyn's voice. "Did you see this?" I asked, pointing to the images flashing across the screen.

She nodded. "We've got work to do, girl. Ready to rock?" Aspyn was dressed in head-to-toe black leather. Her pants were sucking the life out of her thighs. At her hip, a silver blade sparkled in the moonlight. She looked like she was about to go postal on some vampires.

I wrinkled my nose. "As long as you don't expect me to dress like that."

She puckered her lips. "You could totally pull it off, you know, but your jeans and T-shirt will do," she huffed, as if my fashion offended her Catwoman persona.

Woo-hoo. "Fantastic, because there's no way I'm showing that much cleavage."

She put her hands on her hips, smiling. "You don't know what you're missing out on. It's liberating. I mean, what's the point in having them, if you can't flaunt them?"

"I guess that's one way of looking at it."

She gave a slight nod. "Come on. We need to get started. Where's the entourage?"

My eyes drifted to the corner of the room where, just beside the

TV, sat a German Shepherd with soft, fluffy fur. "Uh, we both needed a little space, so he went into stealth mode."

A wily smile quirked her lips. "Ahh, isn't he just a cute little pooch," she cooed, strutting across the room.

Declan growled, baring his sharp canines.

Aspyn's grin only widened as she patted the top of his head. "Down boy."

He snapped at her hand.

Note to self: don't pet the dog. "So how do we do this?" I intervened before blood was shed. My bedroom floors had seen enough.

Aspyn shot Declan a smug glare before she spun around to address my question. "I'll show you. Ever been to New Orleans?"

I secured my hair into a tight ponytail, preparing for business. "Nope."

She grabbed ahold of my hand, her ruby red lips curving. "This is going to be fun. I hope you like things spicy."

I glanced up, meeting her eyes as a tingle of power radiated down my forearm, and I took a deep breath. Maybe I should have been nervous, but I was excited.

Nothing prepared me for moving through time and space as a reaper. It was like what I imagined having an out-of-body experience would feel like. Each cell in my body seemed to come apart—minuscule molecules that floated in the air. And when I was put back together, Aspyn, Declan, and I were no longer in my room. Declan was no longer a German Shepherd. Aspyn was still beautiful. And I was sick off my ass.

Doubling over, I turned around, giving Aspyn and Declan my back as I littered the ground with the cheeseburger, fries, and chocolate shake I'd had for dinner. Disgusting. After I finished hurling my guts all over Bourbon Street, I wiped the back of my hand over my mouth and stood up. I hated puking. It always burned the back of my throat and left a rotten taste in my mouth.

"You okay?" Declan asked. He lightly rested a hand on my shoulder.

I nodded, feeling my pale green skin start to tinge pink in mortification. "What was that?" I asked.

Her pretty painted mouth thinned into a straight line. "Don't worry. It is perfectly normal to feel out of sorts after a jump."

"You should have warned her," Declan scolded.

If they kept bickering all night, I was going to get a migraine along with the upset stomach, but at the moment, I was more concerned with my body. My hands raced over my arms and chest, verifying I was fully intact and that I wasn't missing a finger or toe or tit. I exhaled, positive I was in one piece and my gut was going to stay where it was. "Anyone have gum?"

Aspyn chuckled. "Here you go." She pulled a slim pack of Trident from her back pocket.

I withdrew a piece and popped it into my mouth. My first reap wasn't going so hot. *Can't wait to see what happens next.* I had so many questions, but only one that mattered at the moment. "How did you do that?"

"All reapers are capable of jumping—the ability to move from one place to another no matter space or distance."

"You still haven't explained how you did it," I pointed out.

"Well ..." she drawled out. "It's not exactly easy to put into words. We're naturally pulled toward death. The simplest jump is when a human has been marked. All it takes is their name; your body and energy do the rest."

"If you say so." There was no need for me to pretend I understood. She made it sound simple, but there was nothing simple about the way I felt afterwards.

I took in my surroundings. Streetlamps hung from poles lining both sides of the road, lighting up the heart of the French Quarter. Tourism usually made the streets full of life, but tonight it was comatose. Not a sign of life was detected, but in the dark alleys and concealed crevices hid more than thugs and the homeless. Ghostly predators. The air smelled of death ... and my regurgitated dinner—not pleasant scents.

The three of us weren't worried about the few lingering humans who were oblivious to the danger they were in. They couldn't see us, except for maybe the frail, white-haired old man whose scruffy and unkempt silver beard gleamed under the moonlight. "Don't hurt me. I'm not ready to die," he rambled as we walked by.

"We need to move," Declan instructed, coming to my side. There was a calm lethality to his watchful eyes.

I rubbed my hands up and down my arms, but nothing I did would chase the chill that had settled in my blood. "I can feel them."

Aspyn nodded. "They're ready to move on, find peace. Their souls call to you."

The first body we stumbled upon was a woman in her twenties. She was dressed in a killer little black dress with stellar heels on feet angled oddly. Her legs were bent in almost the shape of a W. I cringed, knowing her death hadn't been painless or easy. The contours of her face were twisted in a cry of agony.

Declan placed his hand to her heart, and the red veins trailing down his hand trickled into the body, releasing her soul.

His glamour hummed in the air, and I felt the first real emotion from Declan. Remorse. He was exceptionably good at being stoic. At times, I had wondered if he was capable of anything other than stoic expressions. It was nice to know he wasn't a machine.

"Glad to see you still got the touch and bodyguarding hasn't made you a complete tool," Aspyn chimed in a flat voice.

Declan extended his legs, giving Aspyn a look of half annoyance. "You do your job; I'll do mine."

Here we go again. It was like a ride along with Princess Leia and Han Solo. The tension was electric. They needed to kiss and just get it over with, but I wasn't going to be the one making the suggestion.

Aspyn stepped over the woman's body. "Whatever you say, boss."

We ventured deeper into the French Quarter, moving steadily toward our goal—the souls of the dead. But as we rounded a corner, I got a weird prickly sensation. My eyes scanned the area around me, but there was nothing.

Aspyn came to a dead stop, her arm extending out in front of me. "No sudden movements," she whispered. "We're not alone." She had that right. At the mouth of the narrow alley, a dark shadow slowly came into focus.

Declan stiffened just as I did. His bulky form was suddenly in front of me. I stood on my toes, glancing over his shoulder, trying to get a glimpse at what was coming at us. Logic said it was probably a hallow … or fifty. But there was something familiar about the tingles radiating inside me. They escalated as whatever was in the shadows grew closer.

I should have been afraid or nervous, but oddly I was neither, and that only meant one thing.

Zane.

My whole body sighed.

He stepped out from the shadows, the streetlamp casting a beam of light over his dark cheekbones. His eyes bypassed over me and landed straight on Declan and Aspyn. The expression on his face wasn't outright hostile, but that didn't say much. Zane could be a ticking time bomb. You never knew when he might go off.

I decided to defuse the torpedo before we all went boom. "Goddammit, you scared the crap out of me." My fingers gripped the front of his shirt and tightened.

Zane ignored me. "What the hell is she doing here?" he hissed over my head at Declan.

I almost felt sorry for my bodyguard. "Keep your boxers on, Zaney," I replied in Declan's defense. "He is only doing his job … Plus, I didn't give him a choice."

Serious anger clung to his features as his eyes shifted downward. "And you thought this was a good idea?"

"I—"

"Actually, it was my idea," Aspyn said, stepping forward.

"Oh, I'll deal with you later." A chill passed through the air, but he kept his artic gaze on me. He rubbed his palms roughly over his face. "Do you have any idea what is happening?"

"Of course I do," I said, unclutching my hand from his shirt. "And nothing you can say or do is going to make me leave."

"Then I don't think I need to tell you how stupid it was to step foot off the island tonight of all nights."

"Here's the deal. When I decided to go, I didn't know there was going to be a massacre tonight. Regardless, what are *you* doing here? Spying on me?"

He snorted. "I don't need to spy on you to know you're always getting yourself in trouble. And no. The city is swarming with hallows. Death summoned all Crows to defend the city while the others release the souls already gone."

"These deaths weren't supposed to happen." The balance of the world was already being tipped to the wrong side—the dead. "Were they?"

Zane shook his head. "No. This is only the beginning. More people will die if we don't stop them. And for the safety of mankind, you shouldn't be here. If something happens to you, there will be no way to restore the balance. Don't you see how important you are?" His hands were on either side of my arms.

"I can't hide away forever. This is my fight too." Not to mention, what about him? It was okay for Zane to put himself in danger? He wasn't the only one who worried.

We stood staring at each other with the wind howling in the distance. His eyes showed how much he wanted to argue with me, but that was because he was thinking with his emotions. It was second nature for Zane to protect me, given the oath he'd taken and how he felt about me, but in that moment, he realized it was my duty to be here. I needed to show the sectors that I cared, that I was invested, and I meant business.

Aspyn cleared her throat. "Guys, we can stand here and argue about Piper breaking out of jail, or we can release the souls and destroy as many of these dead assholes as we can find."

Finally, something we could all agree on.

Zane relented, but he let us all know he wasn't happy about it. "If anything happens, it is on you," he snarled at Aspyn.

She gave a humorless giggle and angled her head. "I thought one of you was bad. Now we get the douche-tastic duo. Which one of you—"

A crash sounded not too far in the distance, and Zane went rigid in front of me, eyes darkening to midnight glass. Black veins spidered over the sharp angles of his face, trailing down his neck and over his shoulders. That was as far as I could see, but I knew his entire body was pumping with Crow blood.

Shit was about to go sideways.

Eyes shining in the darkness, Zane, in one fluid motion, eased me behind him. "Princess, stay close."

That's the goal.

I was going to be stuck to him like Krazy Glue. My heart rate jacked up as I pulled forth my core power as a precaution. If whatever was coming at us wasn't alive, I would be ready. Fear was a natural instinct at the onset of danger, but I refused to let my fear rule me.

My body went into an automatic protective mode, clearing my mind as I concentrated on the sights and sounds of my surroundings. No matter how many hallows I came in contact with, it still came as a surprise. A pale figure tore out from around the corner of the brick building. His clothes might have been nice and neat at one time, like when he was alive.

For a moment, no one moved.

I lunged forward.

"Piper!" Zane called.

CHAPTER 6

My hand flung out, and a powerful hit sent the hallow flying. He was hurled into a bunch of trash cans, knocking them down as he fell on top of them. Hitting them wouldn't feel good, but a couple of metal cans weren't going to stop a vengeful spirit.

I swore silently.

The hallow regained his composure and pounced on Zane. If his plan was to take out the best first, then Zane had been the perfect choice. The problem was, though, Zane was remarkably fast. He dodged the blow and struck low, aiming for the hallow's legs, which happened to be floating a few inches off the ground. The blow had him staggering, giving Zane time to summon his shadows.

I'd been so centered on Zane I had forgotten about Aspyn and Declan. The two of them were engaged in their own battles. Declan's lip was bleeding, but he continued, fighting with determination. A flash of silver appeared in Aspyn's hand, and she managed to swipe it through the air, nicking the hallow across the cheek. The ghost hissed. It wasn't a lethal cut, but it still hurt like a bitch.

The shaggy hallow snarled, teeth gleaming in the dark right before he backhanded Aspyn. I winced as the sound cracked down the damp and musky alley, the force of the blow sending her stumbling backwards and straight into me. Unlike the other, seasoned reapers who had real fighting skills, I wasn't as quick on my feet.

Aspyn barreled into me. She grabbed onto my arms and barely managed to stay on her feet. It was her quick thinking and incredible ability to shift her balance that kept us from kissing the ground. "Thanks for the cushy landing." She grinned for a second before she spun around and leapt up at the hallow.

Like a spider monkey, Aspyn attached herself on to the back of her attacker. He bellowed, revolving in circles, and somehow managed to weasel his hand into her hair and yank. Aspyn shrieked. Her silver eyes teared with pain. Before I thought about what I was doing, I intervened. "Hey, asshole," I yelled.

His head angled in jerky movements toward me, eyes rimmed in thick black gloom. He shouted something incomprehensible at me that didn't sound friendly. Good thing I wasn't in the mood to chitchat, though I did understand one word. *Die*. How accurate he was. One of us was going to be executed. And it wasn't my time.

I threw my arms out, my veins glowing silver under the moonlight. Duel blades of white light burned in both of my hands. Zane's voice sounded in my head, reminding me I had a small window of opportunity to destroy him. I needed to take it. The longer you fought with a hallow, the greater your chances of a mishap. They didn't tire, not like beings with a beating heart.

Yet, as my arm was arched to deliver a blow to exterminate him, I saw a chance for information I couldn't pass up. It was my responsibility to restore the veil. To do that, I needed to grill someone from the other side. This guy just won the interrogation lotto.

At the last second, I dropped my arm and shifted my body weight and landed a swift kick into his stomach. I needed to incapacitate him, keep him from blasting me with a bolt of dark light. True to the speed of a hallow, he recovered before I took my next breath, coming back at me, but all I needed was that split second to spring. I heaved myself up, using my body's weight to keep him off balance.

"I got you, girl!" Aspyn shouted over my right shoulder.

No questions asked, Aspyn was at my side. Between the two of us, we managed to wrestle him against a building. It hadn't been a cinch, but Aspyn grabbed his hands as he thrashed. Limbs twisting sporadically, dark beams of light shot everywhere. I was beginning to think this had been a dumb plan. If we didn't get the upper hand … if he managed to get away …

Another set of hands joined us, reinforcing the hold we had and giving Aspyn the opportunity to secure his wrists. Declan was a welcome sight. His lip was still bleeding, but otherwise he was just peachy.

I moved forward, letting the tip of my blade press firmly into the center of his chest. It would only take the slightest pressure and poof—bye-bye. "No funny business," I seethed, putting a bit of pressure on my blade to get my point across.

"What's the plan here?" Aspyn asked. "I assume you have one, since you didn't take the kill."

"We're going to get this poltergeist douche to talk," I replied, out of breath.

The laugh that pulled from his pale lips was haunting and nightmarish. "What makes you think I will tell you anything, *banssshee*?" He made a gurgling sound in the back of his throat over the last word.

I gave him a smile full of malice, leaning forward. "Oh, I'm thinking the blade to your heart might be motivation enough. I may be fairly new to the inner workings of life and death, but I do know if you want any chance at getting your soul, you don't want me staking you. Because, you see, this blade won't send you back to the other side … It will incinerate you. Now talk."

A dark shadow fell over me.

"Death Scythe," the hallow hissed, his eyes centered over my head.

"In the flesh." Zane's voice was disquieting.

My heart sighed in relief. Hearing his voice, however ominous, meant he was okay, and it gave me a burst of renewed energy.

"I'm not looking to play games," the hallow rasped.

After everything I'd been through, something inside me had hardened. I took my blade and swiped it across his shoulder, an action that a few months ago would have made me squirm. The hallow cried out, but his pain was just a means to an end. "Too bad. I like games, and we're going to keep playing my kind of games until the sun comes up or you talk, whichever comes first."

"Well, since you asked so nicely, what do you want to know, *Princesssss?*"

Zane let out a dark sound from the back of his throat.

"What do you know about restoring the veil between our realm and yours?" I demanded.

"Why would you want to?"

I sunk the blade farther into his chest, feeling the first inklings of his abolishment. I tried not to think about the smell of rot that accosted my nostrils. His head fell back, and he screamed in pain. Those soulless pits shined with pure evil and malice when they met mine again. "Just a friendly reminder who is asking the questions. Do you need another?"

His dry blue lips spread into a tight-lipped grin. "Are you going to let me go if I tell you what I know?"

"I don't negotiate."

"Then neither of us will get what we want," he snarled.

"Look, bucko," I said, my teeth clenched, "I don't have your soul."

"You can find the reaper that doesss."

"I could … but I probably won't. Now let's start again. I want to restore order. Tell me what you know." I angled my head condescendingly. "Or are you not privy to such important information?" When in doubt, shame them.

He laughed a twisted, demented cackle. "You might want to look closer to home for answers."

Okay, so that plan backfired. He wasn't giving me any information I didn't already know. "You got any names?"

He tested his restraints, but Declan slammed him back against the wall. "Stay put," Declan warned.

"Maybe you should give him another reminder," Aspyn said beside me.

I agreed. Torture wasn't really my style, but with Earth's future at stake, I found myself willing to do things I'd never considered. Taking the blade still shining in my hand, I stuck it into the cut I'd made earlier on his shoulder and dug in, widening the gash. His cries pierced the silent night.

"This guy is useless," Zane said. "Let me kill him."

I was thinking about it. "You've got two minutes before I give you to him," I informed the hallow.

His shifty eyes swung between Zane and me. "Give me your word you will release me."

This could go on all night, and we didn't have that kind of time. There were still souls who'd been taken before their time because of asshats like him. "Depends on how vital your information is." I wasn't a fool. I couldn't trust a ghost. I prodded him with the knife, prepared to cut him a hundred times if necessary. And I might have, if an unwelcome visitor hadn't interrupted me.

"What's this? A hostage party?" An arrogant voice I knew well broadcasted from around the corner of the building.

Zane and Declan both stiffened.

I tilted my head slightly, keeping an eye on the hallow. A small circular glow of amber burned in the nightfall, followed by the scent of smoke. Those two things were only present in one person dumb enough to intrude, and even without those clues, I would have known who it was. My reaper detection was on point and getting sharper.

Crash.

He had balls; I'd give him that.

Blowing a puff of smoke above his head, Crash walked under the lamppost, an egotistical curve to his lips. "And you started without me." He made a tsking sound with his tongue. "Crows have all the fun."

Three things happened at once.

Zane wrapped Crash up in a shadow burrito.

The hallow took advantage of our momentary surprise, squirming like a damn fish.

And Aspyn lost her grip on his hands as he managed to break one free.

Son of a bitch.

A plasma charge hit me in the gut, sending me sailing backwards. I hit the pavement on my side with such jarring force that it knocked the stupor out of me. Things were quickly unraveling. I staggered to my feet and twisted at the waist, but another blast whizzed past me, sending me to my knees. It hit the brick building behind me before fizzing out.

Pushing the hair out of my face, I lifted my head just as the opalescent bastard swatted Aspyn aside. Her shriek exploded over Declan's enraged shout. He maintained a hold on the hallow, but I could see from his eyes he wasn't going to be able to hold him for long. I jumped to my feet.

Shit. Shit. Shit.

This had been my call: interrogating him instead of running my blade through his heart. I couldn't live with myself if anyone else got hurt. Time seemed to slow to a crawl. Zane had Crash pinned to a building. The hallow threw his head back and laughed. It was a skin-crawling sound.

My gaze dipped to check on Aspyn. She was shaking the gravel out of her hair as she pushed to her feet. Then Zane was screaming my name. At first I didn't know what was wrong, but it didn't take long before I realized I was in trouble. One minute I was staring at Zane, fear radiating in his eyes, and the next, I was falling backwards, staring at the sky.

The guileful bastard had escaped and grabbed hold of my feet, pulling the ground out from underneath me. Of course it didn't end there. He took off, dragging me across the ground. My head thumped along the grass. I cried out in pain as my head hit a rock and black dots swarmed behind my eyes.

Yet, through the torment of being pulled around like a sack of potatoes, a tingle divulged at my raven mark, and it was followed by a burst of power. Zane's power. His dark shadows merged within me as our souls fused. Amazing things happened when our souls synchronized.

Without a thought to what I was doing or how I was doing it, I channeled all that energy building up inside me and let it loose. Not in a scream as I normally would, but into the environment around me. My heels and nails dug into the dirt, stopping our forward motion. The hallow snapped back in an unexpected jerk.

Take that, doofus-bord! I'll be super pissed if I die in this craphole a virgin.

Steadier in both mind and body, I stood up, letting the crackle of power feed into the Earth. The ground under me quaked, and I was ready to kick his ass every which way from Sunday. I slammed my foot down, and a violent shockwave rippled the pavement, knocking him flat on his back. Squatting down, I extended the blade of light I summoned in my hand. My body might be suffering from the worst road rash ever, but I ignored all the searing burns and aches. In a life and death situation, adrenaline kicked in, foregoing any thoughts of anything other than surviving. I would heal in time. I couldn't say the same for him. All deals were off. "Wrong move, jerk," I said.

The cheeky prick spat in my face. It wasn't like humans' saliva. Hallows didn't have bodily functions or secretions. The air from his lungs came out in a dark mist that iced over my face.

There was scuffling behind me followed by grunts and groans. I thought Zane was going to run him through right then and there, but it was Crash who sunk a knife into the hallow's heart.

Wow. Didn't see that coming.

The hallow burst into a thousand little pieces.

I closed my eyes a moment to steady my thumping heart, until a familiar chill skittered over the nape of my neck and down my spine.

"You okay?" Zane whispered. His arms were around me, lifting me to my feet.

I nodded, leaning against him.

"Good, because I need to take care of something."

I went to put my arm on his, but he was already gone, and I didn't have the strength to stop him. Spinning on my heels, Aspyn and Declan moved to stand on either side of me. I wasn't quite sure if it was for my protection or to keep me from interfering.

An artic gust trembled through the air as Zane cloaked himself in darkness, his eyes on his target. "Crash," he growled. He made his name sound dirty, like a cuss word.

For the love of reapers. Crash's timing sucked. Not only had he singlehandedly botched my interrogation, but Zane had been itching to confront Crash, and it wasn't going to be a civil conversation.

"Why the hell are you here?" Zane demanded, blue eyes luminous in the shadows.

Crash dug in his pocket, pulling out a lighter and a pack of smokes. "It's nice to see you too, Death Scythe."

Zane was having none of it. He was neither amused nor happy. "Care to explain why you executed our hostage?"

Crash put the slim stick in between his lips and flicked the end of the lighter. The flame burned brightly in the dark. "Does it matter? I came to save your ass."

I blinked, and in that second, Zane had Crash wrapped in head-to-toe darkness, his fist curled on the front of his shirt. "When have I ever needed your help? I think you were spying on us, you little traitor."

I couldn't believe this was happening. Were we always doomed to fight among ourselves? I was going to have to intervene. Again. Aspyn and Declan were clearly not going to get involved. The two of them were standing on either side of me, seemingly enjoying the show.

Crash blew a puff of smoke in Zane's face. "Whatever makes you sleep better. Or I heard the world was on the brink of an apocalypse and thought I would lend a hand."

Zane snorted. "As if a good deed has ever crossed your mind. You've spent your entire life abusing your position."

Crash stuck his cigarette in his mouth and swept his arm down over the hold Zane had on his shirt. "Hands off the merchandise, unless you want to lose the hand."

Zane stepped forward, muscles bunched, and I made my move. "Guys!" I yelled, weaseling my way in the middle. "Can we not do this now?"

Crash held up his hands, backing off, and Zane glanced down at my face, seeing the exhaustion and pain. Even if I were a skilled enough actress to hide the suffering I was feeling, Zane would have still known. He would always know. The tie between our souls made sure of it.

Crash leaned up on the brick building. "Truce, for the night. We can go back to hating one another when the sun comes up."

"Fine," Zane reluctantly agreed, mostly for my benefit.

"Thank you," I whispered.

"You sure you're okay, doll?" Crash asked, dropping the half-smoked cigarette on the ground and crushing it under his foot. "You look like death."

"Good thing I'm not trying to win a beauty pageant," I replied sharply.

Aspyn chuckled softly.

Crash was right though. I was beat and on the verge of collapsing, but the night was still young. The stench of death was everywhere. Wordlessly, I took a moment to look at my surroundings. The hallow had dragged me into the open street. There were bodies littered along the road—souls waiting to be released.

Seeing all the bodies churned my stomach. It seemed unnecessary that so many innocent souls were taken tonight. I shuffled around a corpse of a ten-year-old boy whose clothes were ripped, and his skin was an unsightly gray. I glanced up and knew Zane and I were both thinking about our brothers. Mine was still alive, but Zander, he was gone.

"Let's finish what we came to do," I said, letting my outrage fuel my body with the energy I would need to get me through this night.

CHAPTER 7

The sun was rising, casting beams of soft orange and yellow over the horizon as I stood on the balcony. I held my breath, still braced for a fight, even though I was home. After several tense moments, I relaxed. Zane had put his hand on the side of my waist, bringing me back from the gruesome images haunting my memory.

I don't know how they did what we had just done, night after night. It tripped me up and had me second-guessing whether I was the right person for the job. A Raven was supposed to be a leader: strong, with a stomach of steel.

"Hey, Princess," Zane said, his voice slightly hoarse.

The cloudiness lifted from my eyes, and a strangled laugh bubbled out. "That wasn't a dream?"

He placed the tip of his fingers under my chin, examining my face. "Afraid not."

I exhaled and closed my eyes. Everyone had bad days. Today was mine. Luckily, tomorrow was a new day and just around the corner. I'd pick myself back up and remember what I had to do. And after seeing firsthand what the hallows were capable of and getting a glimpse at what the world might look like if I didn't restore the veil, my resolve was even stronger. "I'm running out of time," I stated. "I can feel it. Tonight was only the tip of the freaking iceberg."

Zane gave me a piercing look. "What's the plan?"

"That was plan A," I replied, walking through the double doors and kicking off my shoes.

"Plan A never works," he told me.

I rubbed the sore muscles at my neck. "Obviously. You got any suggestions?"

"I have plenty." He leaned a jean-clad hip on the doorway as his eyes roamed over my body. "But none of them have anything to do with restoring order and everything to do with getting you out of those grimy clothes."

Holy hot reaper babies. Zane had made plenty of advances at me, but not when we were free to actually act upon them. We'd grown accustomed to one of us always putting on the brakes, but not tonight. He wasn't going to get an argument. Not from moi. Actually, I was going to knock his socks off, because I was damn tired of fighting the attraction between us.

I'd had a hellish night, and all I wanted at this moment, besides a hot shower, was all six-foot plus inches of Zane. Heck, I was going to have both—Zane and the shower—together. Once the idea took root, it was all I could think about.

Before I lost my nerve, I grabbed the ends of my shirt. I locked eyes with his, and my blood roared. "I can help you with that." I tugged the tattered cotton over my head and let it slip to the floor. This wasn't the first time I had stood in front of Zane in only a black lacy bra, but this time my cheeks didn't flame from embarrassment. Instead, it was a different kind of fever.

Keeping my eyes on his, I was encouraged by the dark gleam that followed. The entire room seemed to spark. I walked forward, invading his personal space so our bodies brushed. Anticipation heightening, I ran my hands over his shoulders and down his chest. "You're wearing too many clothes. Lose the shirt."

He arched his brows. "Piper, what are you doing?"

I slipped both my hands under the cotton material, and his

stomach jumped under my touch. "The fact that you have to ask makes me think I'm doing something wrong."

The hue of his eyes burned extraordinarily bright. "No, you're definitely doing it right. And that's the problem."

I lifted up on my toes, aligning our mouths. "The only problem is you're not kissing me."

His gaze moved to my lips. "That can be fixed." Slowly, as if he had all the time in the world, his head dipped.

Unfortunately, I wasn't a very patient person. My fingers sunk behind his head and closed the distance between us, sealing our lips in a kiss that started soft and tender but quickly turned into something neither of us could contain. A blazing fire. He was kissing me as if it was his dying wish.

In an effortless turn, he pressed my back against the wall, lips trailing the side of my jaw and then tasting the sensitive spot on my neck. My body reacted. I pulled him closer, chest-to-chest, flesh-to-flesh, causing us both to shiver.

Running my fingers down his stomach and along the angles of his hip, I wound my fingers with his. "Speaking of dirty … I stink." I rubbed the tip of my nose along his cheek. "And so do you," I whispered.

"Let me guess, you have a solution," he murmured.

"I really, really want to get this funk off me," I said, nipping at his bottom lip. I took a step back but kept my hand in his, not letting him get away. I wasn't ready to stop touching him. Walking backwards, my eyes imprisoned his as I guided the two of us into the adjoining bathroom. Scents of candy and apples, much like my soap and shampoo, perfumed the room.

He raised my hand to his lips, pressing a kiss at the center of my palm. "I can't stop thinking about you," he whispered.

"Don't stop, okay? I don't want you to ever stop thinking about me." *Or touching me.*

He moved into the shower, turning the handle to hot. The hiss of the water brought a smile to my face, and steam slowly began to fill the room. I hooked my finger behind my back, unsnapping my bra before wiggling out of the rest of my clothes.

I felt him stop breathing for a moment, and the look he gave me had my blood humming. His form blurred, darkening at the edges. For a second, I thought we might end up on the bathroom floor. "You first," he stated and pressed a kiss to my nose before closing the curtain.

I waited, assuming he was undressing to join me. I stood dunking my head under the spray. The steady stream of water plastered over my face and cascaded over my body, soothing the cuts, burns, and tender muscles that were already beginning to heal.

Where was he? I was feeling a bit lonely ... Pulling back a corner of the shower curtain, I stared at an empty bathroom. Zane was nowhere to be found. Dumbfounded, I realized he wasn't joining me. I was torn between stomping out of the shower soaking wet to give him a piece of my mind or just enjoying the rest of my shower.

The nearly scalding water did the trick, washing away the dirt and blood stuck to my skin. My annoyance and disappointment soon gave way to bliss. He didn't know what he was missing. Bubbles from all the fragrant shampoo and soap pooled around my feet, and I tried not to think about why the water was tinged pink.

The shower was nearly cold by the time I was finished. Shrugging into a robe, I ran a brush through my hair and attended to my teeth before stepping out of the foggy room.

Shirtless, Zane was lounging in my room, his hair slightly damp. Our eyes locked. "You showered," I blurted.

"I did. You smell amazing," he said.

I wrinkled my nose. "You mean I don't smell like dirt, sweat, and death."

"Precisely, Princess." His accent thickened, and the veins spidering down over his eyes shone in a wealth of emotion.

I padded over to the bed and climbed in. "That was a dirty trick," I pouted.

He rolled over on his side, propping up on his elbow. "I could say the same. You don't play fair."

"Tell me again why we need to?" I should have taken a cold shower. Seeing him half-naked wasn't helping to control this overwhelming urge to do more than kiss.

His smile was secretive. "Some things shouldn't be rushed."

My thumb swept over his bottom lip, and his dark eyes drifted shut. "Let's not sleep, just yet," I whispered.

Zane and I had unfinished business, and it seemed like the kind of night to clear the air. I wanted a resolution, and I wanted it now. As I stared into his face, Aspyn's suggestion played in my mind. *Zane and I having a baby?* The idea was preposterous. I mean, we were supposed to be married before we thought about having a kid.

But perhaps it was the solution. Nothing about my life was normal or traditional. So why should my relationship with Zane be any different? Regardless, I didn't want our first time to be about anything other than us. It was a big deal, and not only because I was still holding the V card.

The edges of his form were outlined in shadows, and there was a ghost of a smile on his lips. "What did you have in mind?"

Gazing into Zane's eyes, I lifted my face to kiss him. "I'm more of a show than tell kind of girl." His hot mouth met mine, and there was no turning back. The moment our lips connected, all self-control went flying out the open window. Sparks ignited. Feelings intensified. I had never felt more excited or more ready for anything in my life. He had a taste that was deliciously cool and intoxicating. I reached up, placing a less than steady hand on his cheek.

Darkness as snappy as winter blanketed around us. But in the moment, with Zane kissing my brains out, I didn't give it a second thought. His frosty shadows glided us from the center of the room to the bed. Zane pulled me onto his lap all while kissing me until I was breathless. He paused only to brush the robe off my shoulders.

My hands roamed, moving from over the cords of his neck and shoulders to his chest and stomach. His breath quickened as my fingers slipped lower over the planes of his belly. I fumbled with the button on his jeans, looping it through the hoop. I pressed against him, and a fresh bout of unbridled power trembled in the air. He gazed at me in a way that touched my soul.

I had no idea what to do, but it seemed my body knew. Each touch, each kiss, made me feel closer to Zane than I'd ever been with anyone. Words couldn't express what was going on inside me—not just my body, but also my soul. This was nothing like the making out we'd done before. This was so much more. More feelings. More intense. More serious. The veins inside me glowed brighter everywhere his hands lingered. And they were everywhere. Not in a rush. He took his time, as if he was searing every moment to memory.

I trusted him explicitly. But I'd never done this before with anyone. It was only natural that my nerves kicked in as clothes began to shed and ended up scattered on the floor. As we lay next to each other, no barriers, his mouth found that spot just under my ear that sent my senses spiraling and drove me crazy. I brought his mouth down to mine again. Deepening the kiss, our tongues danced, charging the electricity between us.

Our bodies weren't the only things that merged together—so did our souls. I remembered everything I'd ever heard about a girl's first time—the uncomfortable pain, the blood. In the moment, I couldn't fathom either. Nothing about how Zane was making me feel was scary or alarming. Just the opposite. I was drowning in pleasure. Every pore in my body was alive.

Yet, right before the moment, I stiffened, braced for the unknown.

He pressed a kiss on either side of my mouth. "If you want me to stop, you only have to say the word." His voice was dark and rough as his breath washed over my face.

I looked into his eyes. "Don't stop."

His five o'clock shadow brushed against my cheek. "Do you trust me?"

The feeling of a bit of roughness against my smooth skin made me shiver. I bit my lip and nodded. There was no one I trusted more.

"Relax, Princess," he whispered.

When his lips met mine, all trepidation fled. A fire ignited inside me and spread like wildfire. I swear I would have burst into flames if it weren't for his cool body covering the length of mine.

Being with him so intimately had been like merging our souls, only a thousand times more potent. It had been absolutely perfect. Yeah, there was a pinch of pain, but Zane had vowed to always protect me. And he did. Because of our bond, he was able to make me forget the discomfort before I really realized it was there.

Afterward, sunlight bathed the room. The warm breeze streamed through the open windows, setting the sheer curtains in a twirl, and while the rest of the world was waking up to start their day, we were just lying down. I shouldn't have been so relaxed or happy, not after all the death I'd seen.

Feeling utterly languid, like a kitty cat licking the last drop of milk, I rolled onto my side and tucked my hands under my pillow. I tilted up my face toward his, content to stay wrapped up in him for all eternity.

Zane trailed a finger over my arm. "You're glowing," he whispered in awe. "It's beautiful. I've never seen anything as beautiful as you."

I rubbed my cheek on the pillow, amazed by the tingles budding over my skin. "I love you," I murmured, my heart soaring and my bones feeling like mush. I was ridiculously happy.

His eyes searched mine. "Not nearly as much as I love you." Only Zane and I could compete over who loved whom more.

I thought I saw a flicker of sadness, but it was gone before I could be sure. My chest squeezed. *I'm no longer a virgin.*

Zane's mouth traced over the curve where my shoulder met my neck, sending tingles down my spine. "So was it everything you thought it would be?"

A smile teased my lips. "Are you fishing for a compliment?"

"Maybe."

"You were amazing."

He grinned like a wolf after the hunt. "Like fifty shades of amazing?"

"Better," I whispered before closing my eyes, and in what felt like only minutes, I was fast asleep, only awake in my dreams.

It was another day. Nothing special. TJ was sitting on the couch, yelling at the TV, a remote control in his hand. His fingers punched the little keys, frustration lining his face.

I stared down at the sketch in my lap. "Why do you play those stupid games if they make you so mad?" It was a question I'd asked countless times.

"Mind your own business," TJ snapped, eyes in a trance, mesmerized by the movement on the screen.

"I was just saying," I barked. To me it seemed obvious. If something pissed me off enough that I had to throw a controller across the room, then maybe I shouldn't play anymore. I glanced up in time to see the guy's brains on the screen spatter everywhere. Disgusting.

"Dammit, Piper," TJ swore, giving me the death stare. "You got me killed."

"Tragic." Parker's voice came through the TV, not sounding remorseful in the least.

TJ stretched out his legs so they were covering the coffee table and in the process knocked my pencils on the floor. "Why don't you dabble somewhere else, somewhere far from me?" he suggested in a not-so-nice way.

Ugh. I'd forgotten what a pain in the ass TJ could be. "Why don't you go jump off a cliff?"

TJ scrunched up his face at me, only to return to his video game.

Yep. It was a typical Friday night in the Brennan household—TJ and I bickering, while Dad was closed off in his room waiting for inspiration to strike. Mom was … I wasn't sure.

I looked over my shoulder. We were in Chicago, at our old apartment, and regardless of TJ being a total butt plug, I was happy. Settling back into the worn couch, I turned my attention to my drawing—the girl with the whip. My hand carved out the scar just below the girl's face on my sketchpad. It was in the shape of a star. She had big sultry eyes and long, dark red hair. To offset the hard lines of the whip she held, I added a flower to the side of her hair.

While TJ was absorbed in his video game, I was engrossed in creating, and neither of us noticed the temperature change in the room. The windows frosted, and the cold sucked the color right out of the room. It was what finally alerted me that there was something wrong.

My pencil hovered just over the page. I blinked. And blinked again. "What the—" All the bright colors on my drawing seeped off the paper.

Ooo-kay. My dreams had always been messed up and bizarre. I never gave them a second thought. Why would I? But now, I was scared they meant something more. And that thought proved to be frightening.

I set the pad aside and moved to the edge of the couch. The air in my lungs went stale. I wasn't sure where they came from, and it didn't really matter. What did was they were in my home. I recognized the white figures floating from the dark corners of the room weren't from this realm. They didn't belong here.

My two worlds slammed together. The girl I used to be and the banshee I was now.

I knew what they were, and the knowledge was like ice in my veins. *Hallows.*

This is only a dream, I told myself, but no matter how many times I recited the phrase, the ghosts swarming the room made me question my reality.

"TJ," I murmured, careful not to make any sudden movements.

"Not now," he responded, clueless.

I wanted to rip the controller out of his hands and tell him to open his eyes. "I'm serious. We need to get out of here."

He finally tore his gaze from the TV to glare at me, but his expression went through an array of emotions, starting from annoyance, turning to shock, and ending in confusion with a touch of apprehension. "Piper?"

"There's no escaping." The entire gang of hallows spoke. Their mouths never moved, but their eerie voices chorused in unison.

"You can't hurt us here," I responded.

"Are you so sure? Dreams are just another realm. We've already breached the veil between the living and the dead, why not the dream world as well?"

They had a point, unfortunately. But I wasn't willing to risk my life or TJ's to test the theory. I closed my eyes, clenching my fists and willing myself to wake up.

The laugh of a thousand hallows erupted.

Shit on a sandwich. My eyes popped open, wide with dread. I reached for TJ's hand and tugged him to his feet, squaring off. I didn't really have a plan, not a solid one. It was pretty simple —don't die.

I summoned my core power, prepared to fry these imbeciles, except nothing happened. Zippo. No glowing veins. No radiant swords. Nada. I stared down at my hands, horrified. "Just great." My only weapon was my mouth and my wits. We were so screwed.

"What were you expecting?" TJ asked, giving me a funny look. "You're not one of those kickass girls you're always drawing."

"That's what you think," I mumbled.

The dream was so vivid, as was my fear. I backed us up to the edge of the couch, but that was as far as I got. The hallows closed in, in ranks, stalking toward us as their outlines flickered like a faulty lightbulb. "We're coming for him," they all echoed at the same time.

"No!" I yelled. "Don't hurt him."

"You're not safe. Not anywhere. Not anyone," they warned.

No shit, Einstein.

I was just about to tell TJ to make a run for it when they decided to attack, all at once, in a unified assault. There was only a nanosecond to make a decision, so I shoved TJ to the side, taking the full brunt of the hit. *Thwack.* I landed on the coffee table with a crash. My head hit the wood, splintering and causing me to bite my lip. My mouth filled with the metallic taste of my own blood.

Groaning like an eighty-year-old woman, I stared up. The ceiling was littered with the ghosts of the dead. *Ugh, that went well.* As I stared into their see-through pale faces and hollow black eyes, there was no way I was getting out of here. Fear ricocheted inside me.

I quickly lifted my head, searching the floor for TJ to make sure he was okay and order him to get out. Horror hit me in the gut.

My head shook back and forth. "No, no, no," I kept repeating over and over again. I refused to believe what I was seeing, and I'd completely forgotten this was supposed to be a dream. It was hard to remember what was real and what wasn't, especially at the sight before me.

Much like the video games he loved, his blood splattered over the couch, spraying the legs of the coffee table and soaking into the carpet fibers. I hadn't even heard him make a peep. My brother lay motionless on the floor, eyes open but lifeless, and his mouth agape in a silent cry. He was dead. I knew death. And my baby brother was no longer a part of the living.

"A warning," the hallows chorused.

"TJ!" I screamed.

The entire room burst into a blinding white light.

CHAPTER 8

I woke sitting straight up, covered in a cold sweat, and bellowing. The sound stretched, moving over the island, traveling with the wind. I didn't know the extent of my voice, how far it journeyed, how it moved, only that it held power. I could do things with my voice, unimaginable things. So when I woke up screaming, the entire reaper race knew something was wrong.

Zane was beside me, his hands framing my face, until my eyes finally focused on him. My gaze moved around the room as I slowly put together where I was and what happened. The dream? TJ? Alarm raced through me, my eyes going wild. I wanted to jump out of the bed and run down the hall to his room, but then I remembered I was naked.

"Piper?" Zane spoke my name gently. "Is everything okay?"

I blinked. It was midday. The sun was beaming through the windows, and there was a relaxing breeze bringing in the scent of flowers and sea. "I-I'm not sure." My hand went to my scratchy throat. It was raw and hoarse after the screaming. "I had a dream."

Worry leapt into his dark eyes. "You're bleeding," he stated, swiping a finger across my lip.

I licked the edge of my mouth. Pain seared at the open wound. "I'm fine." Or so I hoped. I didn't need him to tell me it wasn't normal for a dream to draw blood. I could still taste it. The horror. The blood. The sheer fear. "God, what was that?"

His brows furrowed. "I was going to ask you the same thing. Tell me."

I relayed the events of the dream, from being back in my old apartment to being surrounded by hallows, and I got choked up when I told him what happened to TJ.

"Your banshee abilities are coming in hot," he said when I finished. "It won't be long until they're at full force."

"Joy. Don't tell me my dreams might actually mean something. Am I suddenly going to levitate and be able to spin my head around like an owl?"

His lips curved. "Not entirely. It could be the dream was nothing more than a caution. Or it could be someone was sending you a warning."

"Are you sure?" I asked, feeling anything but confident.

He shrugged. "At this point I am only sure of one thing."

"And what might that be?" I prompted.

"How I feel about you," he murmured, pressing his lips softly to mine.

I sighed. Zane wasn't a hearts and flowers guy, so when something sweet left his lips, it meant that much more.

His fingers pulled slightly at the ends of my hair. "Your abilities are ingrained inside of you, even in your dreams. They're tied to your soul. It doesn't matter what realm you find yourself in."

"And therefore tied to you," I added, and he nodded. "But that doesn't explain why I couldn't use my powers then."

"It could have been fear," he suggested.

I pinched him under the arm. "That wasn't it. I could feel my powers, but nothing happened. It was like I was shooting blanks."

The corners of his mouth twitched. "Even when you're alone, you're not. If you had called for me, even in your dream, I would have been able to help. You're a banshee. The laws of nature don't apply to you. Don't be skeptical of your own abilities."

Wrapping a sheet around my body, I scooted out of bed. It was silly. Zane had already seen me naked, but I couldn't repress the modesty. Things between us were still so new and fresh. "I need to see him."

"Who?" Zane asked.

I rolled my eyes. He needed to keep up. "TJ," I replied. "If my dreams are as prophetic as you imply, I need to make sure he's okay—that he's safe. I need to tell him the truth about me."

He tossed me a shirt. "Put this on first. I don't want your brother hurting himself by trying to give me a black eye."

He was right—not about the black eye, that was laughable; I couldn't go traipsing through the house in nothing but a flimsy sheet. Slipping his oversized T-shirt down over my head, I was swathed in his scent. I tugged on a pair of cotton shorts I found tossed over the desk lamp and combed my fingers through my tousled hair.

Shirtless, Zane stood in a pair of dark denim jeans. "You ready for this?"

"To tell my brother I'm a banshee? I don't think I'll ever be prepared, but I need to tell him. Keeping him in the dark could put him in more danger. As much as I'm dreading this conversation, everything inside me is pushing me to do it. Immediately."

Zane followed me into the hall as I went to find my brother. It wasn't a difficult task. Just follow the sounds of whooping and hollering and the smell of week-old food. TJ whipped open the door a moment after I knocked, a cookie dangling between his teeth. His light brown hair was too long, but to my surprise, it looked clean. "Did you just wake up?" he asked, cookie bits crumbling to the floor as he bit down.

I was so relieved and happy to see him looking unharmed that my worry turned to irritation. "You know, you're going to get ants." I plucked the other half of his uneaten cookie and plopped it into my mouth.

He frowned. "Did you come to eat all my snacks or yell at me?"

Zane leaned in the doorway behind me, snickering.

I put an elbow into his gut, only making his smirk stretch.

Someone was feeling pretty damn pleased with himself. "Neither," I replied, moving past TJ into his room. Parker was there, sitting on one of the beanbag-like chairs, a game controller in his hand.

Parker pushed up his glasses. "Hey, Pipes."

"Hey," I automatically responded and then turned around to face TJ.

He had his arms crossed. "Come right in," he mumbled. TJ glanced between Zane and me and back to me. "Is he just going to stand there and keep guard?" he asked, being a smartass.

"Yep."

"Did you two ..." He made an obscene gesture with his finger and hand.

Parker cleared his throat, turning an adorable shade of crimson.

I hadn't come here to talk about my sex life. "That's none of your business, and not what I wanted to talk to you about."

He let out a whoosh of air. "Thank God, because I never want to think about you doing the nasty with anyone. Ever."

"Glad we got that cleared up." I wrung my hands together and began pacing the room. This was a lot harder in person than it had been in my head. I opened my mouth and then quickly snapped it shut.

"Oh, boy. Here comes the lecture," TJ said flatly.

"Yep," Parker agreed. "She's definitely got something on her mind."

I paused in my aimless circles. "Will the two of you stop talking about me as if I'm not in the room? This is kind of important, and I need to find the right words to tell you."

"Does this have anything to do with what I told you? About what I saw?" His voice got quieter.

"Yes," I exhaled.

Now it was his turn to fidget uncomfortably. "Are you sure we should be talking about this with an audience?"

"It's fine. Parker and Zane already know."

"You told them?" he blurted out, looking like a wounded puppy. His brown eyes were big and filled with accusation, as if I'd broken a sacred sisterly vow.

The expression on my face softened. "It's not that I told them. Both Parker and Zane have seen them, too." I didn't want him to think he was alone in any of this craziness.

His eyes narrowed in skepticism. But he had no reason to believe I was lying. If there was one thing TJ knew, it was that I wasn't a liar. "Are you going to tell me what the hell is going on now?"

I crossed my arms. "That's the plan."

"Good, because I'm tired of everyone acting so weird. What was it?"

"A hallow," Zane supplied, shifting so he was no longer at an angle but was facing us, his back pressed into the wall.

Parker perked up, understanding dawning in his amber eyes. He set aside his controller and spun around in the chair, giving me a nod of support. He would back me up.

"And that means what?" TJ asked.

Having Parker's approval gave me a boost of confidence. I had people who cared and supported me. "It's essentially a restless spirit who has unfinished business here on Earth."

"A ghost," he deduced. "So I was right?"

"There's a first for everything," I mumbled, falling back into old habits.

"I'm going to ignore your snide comments, only because I want to know more about the ghosts. How can we see them?"

His enthusiasm worried me. "Normally, we can't, but because our lives have been touched by death, it weakens the glamour that hides them from human eyes."

"Mom," he mouthed.

He was taking this far too well, but I guess deep down he'd had his suspicions, and I was confirming he wasn't going crazy. I knew the feeling. "It's complex. She wasn't killed by gang members; that's for sure."

Tossing the controller aside on the bed, he said, "Piper, this is seriously messed up. Okay. I don't understand. Why would a ghost kill Mom?"

"It's complex."

"Is this why you wouldn't let me stay in Raven Hollow?"

The questions kept coming. TJ had a young, curious mind. "I had to. Things weren't safe for you here and only got worse when Rose died."

His eyes darted around the room. "How do you guys know so much about this stuff, anyway?"

I tugged at the hem of Zane's shirt, and my gaze habitually moved to Zane. He gave me a wink that said, *You can do this, Piper.* My gaze returned to TJ, who was anxiously waiting for an answer. "This isn't easy for me to tell you," I started. "I've been trying to figure out the right words, but there aren't any."

TJ's eyes narrowed. He could see how jittery I was. "You've never had a problem speaking your mind before."

"There's more. Ghosts aren't the only thing in our world. There are reapers who are essential for death to occur, and they hunt the hallows." I tried to put it in simple terms without going into too much detail.

"Reapers," he echoed. "Let me guess, your boyfriend is one of these so called reapers." He was being sarcastic, but he was dead on.

"A death reaper to be exact," Zane interjected.

TJ threw his hands in the air. "I'm glad you guys think this is a joke."

Parker leaned his elbows on his knees, giving TJ a straightforward look. "It's true, man. Zane is a reaper. I've seen what he can do."

Zane drew to his full height. "Do you require proof?"

TJ turned to Zane, his brows drawn. "What could you possibly do to make me think you're anything beyond the guy macking on my sister?"

Zane stepped into the room and did his thing. First, the dark veins webbed around his eyes, spreading down his jaw before covering his chest and disappearing beneath his jeans. Then the shadows gathered. From the dark corners of the room, from underneath the bed, and beneath the doorways, darkness responded to Zane, congregating at his feet. He held out his hand, and on call, the shadows morphed into a weapon—a scythe. As always, I was fascinated by him; my soul called to him.

"Holy shit," TJ gasped, bug-eyed.

Zane twirled the scythe in a complete circle. "And so we're clear, I'm not macking on your sister. I love her."

My heart skipped. Hearing Zane express his feelings never got old. Actually, he didn't say it enough. I wanted to hear him say those three little words hourly. I'd settle for daily.

"Wow." TJ shoved a hand through his hair. "I'm not sure you being a *reaper* makes dating my sister any better." He eyed Zane leeringly. "How did you do that?"

Zane's face twisted into a serious scowl. "You're still not entirely convinced I'm a harbinger of death." He wasn't used to not being taken seriously.

"It's a lot to process. Ghosts. Reapers," TJ reasoned.

"It is," I agreed. "Trust me, I get it, but I need you to take this seriously. Things are about to get … hairy."

Hairy, Zane mouthed.

I shrugged. It was all that I could come up with in the spur of the moment. It wasn't like I had a speech rehearsed.

TJ was watching me curiously. "Piper, you're glowing. Like glow-worm glowing."

I tucked my hair behind my ear, gazing at the ground. "Um, about that. There's something else I need to tell you." I choked up a moment before finding the courage to look at him. "I'm a reaper, a banshee."

"You're a banshee?" he echoed. Then he did the most annoying brotherly thing. He burst out laughing. "Yeah, right. And I'm Superman."

"TJ, this isn't a laughing matter, you little twerp." I flicked him in the ear. "I'm trying to be open and honest with you. You're in danger. We're all in very real danger."

Since no one else in the room saw any humor in the situation, TJ's condescending smirk vanished. The silence made him rethink the possibilities. "What kind of danger?"

"The kind that will put you six feet under and me in the very crushing position of having to release your soul. You're the only family I have left, TJ. I'm telling you all of this because I can't lose you." The lines on his face changed. It was the same expression I'd seen when he'd been younger and there'd been a thunderstorm. Fear. "I'm not trying to scare you, but caution you. I came to the conclusion that your ignorance was no longer bliss, but a hindrance, a crutch. If we are going to survive this apocalypse, you need to take your blinders off and see the real world."

"Uh, so if you're a reaper, does that mean ..." I knew where this was going. "Am I one too?"

Now that I had this burden off my chest, I took a seat on the edge of the bed beside him. "Here's the deal; it's a female thing. The banshee gene is passed to the firstborn who indefinitely happens to be a girl."

"But Zane is a—"

"Death reaper," I finished. "And not of our bloodline."

"The banshee, or White Raven, is an elite reaper," Zane said. "She's responsible for keeping the balance between the living and the dead."

"That's such a crock of shit," TJ swore at the injustice.

"Tell me about it," Parker grumbled. One of fifty manga T-shirts in his closet stretched across his lanky shoulders.

I angled my head and shot him a you're-not-helping look. "Being a reaper isn't a walk in the park. And I'm not exactly doing a bang-up job of keeping the equilibrium between realms," I reminded Parker. "People are dying because the veil that protects them from the dead is gone, and I'm entirely responsible."

Zane locked eyes with me. The dark veins had receded, and his shadows dissipated back into the hidden crevices in the room. "You're being a little hard on yourself, Princess. This battle started long before you became the White Raven. You just happened to take the reins in the middle of the stampede."

For a moment, I'd forgotten that he was shirtless and barefoot. I repressed the urge to stare. "Nice analogy, Aristotle. Still doesn't change the fact that all the sectors will hold me responsible. I ultimately have one job, and I managed to screw it up minutes after being inducted as the White Raven. Guinness world record."

"But you have a plan, right?" TJ asked, suddenly onboard, ready for action, and looking to me for all the answers.

That was my role. His big sister who fixed everything, not just the scraped knees or the spilled milk. I couldn't disappoint him or let him see how scared I really was. "I'm working on it. *But* I don't want you doing anything heroic or rash. I didn't tell you this to put you in the middle, but to protect you. Make no mistake, if you get any half-baked ideas, you'll be confined to these four walls."

No doubt about it. TJ wasn't pleased, and knowing my little brother, he was going to be a nuisance. It was a good thing Parker was here. He'd just been assigned babysitting duties. And they were both getting security detail.

"Hey, Pipes, can we talk later?" Parker asked as I got up to leave.

I glanced over my shoulder. "Sure thing. Should I be worried?"

He shook his head. "Nah. I just want to run something by you."

I nodded.

CHAPTER 9

Zane wrapped an arm around my waist, pulling me beside him as we walked down the hall. "Do you feel better?"

I laid my head on his shoulder. "You know I do." Our soul connection tied our emotions.

"You're right. I do, but I wanted to hear you say that you did the right thing by telling him. Of course, you broke another sacred reaper rule by doing so. And that is the reason why you're going to make an exceptional Raven." He ran his lips over the top of my head.

We'd reached my door. I turned to face him and stood on my tippy-toes to press a kiss on his lips. Seeing me with TJ had dredged up the fresh wounds of losing Zander. I wanted to erase the heavy pain of loss. "I'd been thinking about doing that for the last half hour."

"Your self-control is admirable." His hand moved to my hips as he backed me into the door. His eyes moved into the room and settled on the bed. I didn't like the look that melded on his face—seriousness with a touch of sadness. "You know, this shouldn't have happened."

He didn't need to explain. We were talking about the most intimate and memorable moment of my life. "Are you saying it was a mistake?" There was a possibility I might put my fist into his gut, depending on his response.

Zane reacted before I barely finished the question. He boxed me in. "Never. Not in a million years." His eyes were bright as he spoke. "But the elders are going to do everything in their power to make sure you align your blood with a reaper heir."

The back of my head pressed into the wall. "I won't let that happen."

"I know. After what transpired between us last night, I would eliminate anyone who tried to take you from me. I just want you to be prepared for what we have to go up against."

I frowned. "What do you mean 'eliminate'?"

He waggled his brows. "Do you want details?"

I yawned right in his face. Talk about romantic, but then again, waking up screaming wasn't the lovey-dovey morning after I'd envisioned. I ducked underneath his arm and strolled into my bedroom. "Zane, you can't go killing each reaper the elders try to force me to marry."

He was on my heels. "Watch me." He put a hand on my shoulder, turning me to face him. "I'm not going to lose you, and I won't share you. You're mine. You've been mine from the moment you stepped foot on the island. Probably before."

My breath caught. "No regrets."

The pad of his thumb outlined my jaw. "My only regret is that it didn't happen sooner."

I smiled. "Me too." Other couples have weird after morning moments. Zane and me, our whole existence was made up of awkwardness.

Concern colored his blue eyes. "You okay? I mean, after last night?"

I nuzzled my head into the spot between his shoulder and chest that was perfectly made for me. "I've never felt better. Can we do it again?"

He laughed, the deep sound rumbling under my ear. "Most definitely. I tend to have that effect. Once is never enough."

I cut him a bland look. "You might be magical in bed, but I'm not a two-bit floozy."

"I guess this means you're a—"

"If you say I'm a woman now, I will projectile vomit on you."

His lips twitched. "I could do this for the rest of my life."

I angled my head to the side. "What?"

"This. The sweet and sarcasm. The back and forth. I'll never get tired of you, Princess, or what we have."

"Good," I replied, for once without a witty comeback. "Because you're stuck with me." In this life and the next.

With all this talk about us being together and the challenges we were up against with the elders, now might have been the opportune moment to tell him about Aspyn's suggestion. However, when I glanced up into his face, I couldn't bring myself to do it. My hands flattened on his bare chest, his heart beating under my palm. I bit my lip. There was no way I could deceive Zane into getting me pregnant. Our relationship couldn't be built on lies. He, of course, had been responsible. Sorry to say, Aspyn would not be happy to learn there was no chance I was pregnant. The idea gave me mixed feelings. I picked at his shirt, contemplating.

He tilted his head down, a worry line spreading over his forehead. "Do you have something on your mind?"

I chickened out. "Only how adorable you are."

"Touché." His head dipped.

I pressed a finger to his descending, edible lips. "Hold that thought. I've got to pee," I announced and padded to the bathroom.

Zane chuckled.

DAYS CAME AND WENT. The last week seemed to fit together like a stained glass window—a hundred different little pieces of colored glass much like my mood. All the ups and downs, the highs and the lows, but when you combined all those emotions, it created a picture. My crazy life.

I had no appetite.

Forget sleeping at night.

And my anxiety was through the roof.

Every time I closed my eyes, I saw death. The world was overrun by hallows to the point where there were more ghosts occupying Earth than the living. The dreams came every night, haunting me with the death of someone I loved. Parker, Aspyn, Zoe, TJ, but the worst were the dreams of Zane. His death would not only crush my heart but would shatter my soul into a million broken pieces. No one needed to tell me that if anything happened to Zane, my body, mind, and spirit would never be the same. I often wondered if I would be able to survive without him. My soul was intertwined with his in a bond that made us both stronger and weaker. And now that we'd gone public with our soul symmetry, my enemies knew where to hit me the hardest.

I couldn't shake the feeling that these nightly nightmares were visions of what could be if I didn't figure out a way to restore the veil. And pronto. The clock was ticking. Yet I was no closer to figuring out the puzzle, and knowing that Zane was out there evening after evening, fighting hallows, made my blood run cold.

I needed to do something. I needed answers. Before it was too late.

I swept a coat of mascara over my lashes. Makeup was a minimal thing for me. I dabbed on some shiny lip gloss and smacked my lips. The simple action got me thinking about kissing Zane, and so much more. Not even my wildest dreams came close to the feeling of being treasured by him.

It was then, while I was doing the trivial human action, that the idea came to me. Zane would absolutely despise the idea, and that was precisely why I wasn't going to tell him. He would undoubtedly try to stop me or change my mind. Neither was possible. Once I set my brainpower to a task, I could be as relentless as he was.

There had been another attack tonight. Las Vegas this time, and after each one, my guilt mounted. I hated sitting here, unable to do anything to stop it and feeling useless. And that ended today.

I pressed my lips together, staring at myself in the mirror. Time to put my plan in motion, and the first order of business was finding an outfit. Swinging around on the stool, I padded over to the dresser to rummage through the drawers, looking for the perfect disguise for a spy. I was going undercover.

Just as I pulled on a little black dress, a knock sounded on the door. My eyes darted around the room as if I had just been caught red-handed robbing Starbucks for the last cup of coffee. A moment or two of silence went by before Parker called my name.

"Pipes?"

Exhaling, I jogged to the door. Oliver, my detail for the night, was outside in the hallway, and Parker was standing on the other side of the door, his hands shoved into his pockets. A sandy lock fell over the left side of his face, partially covering his eyes. His gaze lifted from the floor to meet mine. "Hey, you got a minute?"

I glanced at the clock on the bedside table. Almost ten o'clock at night, prime reaper time, but Parker and I hadn't seen much of each other lately. I couldn't brush him off. "Sure," I said, swinging the door all the way open.

"Going out?" he asked, eyeing my unusual getup.

"Uh, yeah, reaper stuff," I replied, trying to make it sound boring and unimportant. It wasn't a lie, but it wasn't entirely the truth—something I'd always given Parker. *It's for his protection,* I reasoned.

He didn't ask the usual where, when, and why questions and seemed on edge, more so than was typical. Fiddling with his glasses, he said, "I want to ask you something. And before you get your panties in a wad, hear me out. That's all I ask."

Great. Now he had *me* on edge. I sat on the end of the bed, tucking my feet underneath me. "Ooo-kay, what's up?"

"I've put a lot of thought into this, and it's not just a whim." He stuffed his hands back into his pockets as if he didn't know what to do with them.

"Good. I'm glad to hear you say that, I think. I wouldn't want you making any rash decisions, but what are we talking about here?"

"I'm not going back to Chicago," he blurted out.

"You're not?" It wasn't the worst thing he could have said. For a second, I thought he was going to tell me something crazy. Like he wanted to be a reaper.

"No," he insisted, letting out a ragged breath and puffing out his chest.

My brows pushed together in worry. "Why not? I don't get it. Don't you want to graduate high school?"

"How can I possibly worry about a diploma when we don't even know if Earth will still be standing?" he argued.

That was a bit melodramatic and presumptuous. "Wow, Parks. Where's your sense of faith in me? Are you telling me you don't think I'll be able to reestablish the barrier?" Truthfully, I didn't blame him. Right now, my self-confidence had reached a new low, and just when I was starting to think I was tough shit.

"No, of course I believe in you," he retorted. "I'm just saying I can't go on pretending the world isn't plummeting down the crapper. I know you will find a way to fix it, but school just doesn't seem as important as being here with you and doing anything I can to help."

I wanted to ask him just how he thought he could help me, but I curbed my wicked tongue before it got the best of me and hurt Parker's feelings in the process. He had only good intentions. "What are you suggesting then?" We needed to quit beating around the bush and get to the point.

His foot scuffed over the hardwood floors, his eyes avoiding mine. "Oh man, this is a lot harder than I imagined."

"Why do I get the feeling I'm not going to like where this is going?"

He ran a hand through his hair. "Because you know me too well."

I held up a finger and said, "Give me a minute to prepare myself." Then I wiggled on the bed until I found a comfortable spot and crossed my legs. Oliver was in the hall shaking his head, trying to keep a straight face. "Okay, I'm ready. Lay it on me."

"No sharp objects?" Parker asked with a nervous laugh.

I pinned him with the evil eyes.

He exhaled and wiped his sweaty palms on his flannel pants. "Here goes nothing. I want you to turn me," he bluntly stated.

I stared at him, dumbfounded. "Turn you into what?"

He lifted both his brows. "I think it should be obvious. I want to be like you—a reaper."

Oh hell no! "What the shit? Are you certifiably crazy?" At this point, I had jumped off the bed. "I'm not turning my best friend into a harbinger of death. How can you ask that of me?"

"I'm not crazy. I'm being realistic. How long do you think I have before another hallow or a rogue reaper tries to gut me again? Being human makes me weak, and I don't want to be weak, Piper. I want to help you."

"Does this have anything to do with Zoe? If it does, you do know you don't have to become a reaper to date her."

He shook his head. "No. I mean, it would help, but no. She isn't the primary reason. You are."

"Me? Parker, this isn't a life I would choose for myself. You have a choice. You can live a normal life."

"Come on. Let's be real. I've never been normal. I can't explain it, but I feel like this *is* what I'm supposed to do."

"What about your mom?" I reminded him. "She is alone in the city. You're just going to leave her behind? She'll be so disappointed and hurt if you don't go back." Like me, Parker didn't have a lot of family. His dad was out of the picture. Other than an aunt he never saw, it was only his mom and him. My family had always been his as well.

"S-she'll be okay," he stammered, convincing himself more than me. "My mom is a tough cookie, and it's not like I'll never see her again, which might be the case if you don't turn me."

I understood his need to survive and not always relying on someone else to protect you. I understood the need to do something and make a difference. I'd felt all of those things. But the difference was, I wasn't human. And he was my best friend. He didn't comprehend all the sacrifices, all the death. "I'm sorry. I can't do it. I won't do it."

"You're being ridiculous. And selfish!" he said, raising his voice.

"Me? I'm being ridiculous? That's rich," I snapped back. Parker had come up with some harebrained ideas in his days, but this took the cake. *Parker ... a reaper?* The last thing I wanted to do was fight with him.

"Whatever." The crestfallen look that sprang onto his face made my heart sink. "You're making a mistake."

My mouth dried. "Let's hope not." I glanced out the window. Night had fully descended. "I've got to go." And before Parker could say another word, I grabbed my bag and was out the door. TJ was coming up the stairs. I brushed past him, our shoulders bumping.

"What's going on?" he asked, hearing all the commotion.

"Nothing," I replied, not stopping.

"Where are you going?" he asked as I rushed down the stairs.

"Out!" I barked.

CHAPTER 10

The night was cool. I could already taste the end of summer. Soon the trees would turn from green and lush to vibrant colors. But for now, the garden at the manor was still in full bloom, perfuming the air. Sticking to the shadows, which were a comfort more than a distress, I snuck off the grounds.

I turned down the nearly empty street, a shortcut to Atmosfear. Heath, Crash's father, owned the seedy club. He was on my hit list tonight.

If anything shady was going on and Heath or Crash was involved, Atmosfear would be the place to find answers.

There was a slow roll of fog tumbling in over the island from shallow shores. With the brisk evening wind sneaking up under my hoodie, I heard the soft sound of footsteps. They paused briefly as I did, then picked up again when I creeped along the side of a building. The prickles of being followed radiated from the nape of my neck.

Well, I had news for him; he wasn't going to get the drop on me.

As an afterthought, it probably would have been a smart idea to have enlisted Oliver or Declan for my little plan. No doubt I was going to pay for it later, once Oliver realized I was no longer anywhere in the manor. I would have to make it up to him … bring him a peace offering, maybe coffee or candy.

I resisted the urge to look over my shoulder and raise the suspicion of my stalker. I might be small and wearing three-inch wedges, but I'd learned I could handle myself against even the toughest of opponents. After walking around the island the last few months, I knew most of its twists and turns, hopefully allowing me to use an element of surprise. I was kind of counting on it.

I stepped quietly out of my clunky black shoes—great for clobbering someone over the head. I wasn't above using whatever means necessary. The pavement was cold under my bare feet. It had rained earlier, leaving the ground damp, and small pools of water gathered due to the changes in elevation. My discomfort was currently ranked below my need to survive. It was sort of sad, but I wasn't nearly as freaked out or scared as I should have been. Actually, if someone didn't try to kill me at least once a week, I wondered what was wrong. How pathetic.

Ducking behind the building, I waited until a shadow appeared on the ground, cast from a nearby street lamp. My fingers wrapped around one of my heels as I brought it up over my head. If I could get one clean thwack …

The footsteps came to a stop, and I held my breath, waiting and poised for damage. Reapers were trained to be stealthy; this predator was sloppy and careless. I shouldn't have been able to pick up on him following me so easily. And if it was a reaper, I should have been able to sense them. My sonar abilities were stronger.

Of course, it could be a hallow, but the lack of temperature change in the air confused me. If it wasn't a reaper or a hallow, then just who or what was tailing me? I was about to find out.

I made my move, leaping around the corner, my fingers tightening on my makeshift weapon, and I froze. The shoe halted inches before knocking its intended target into next week.

What the frick?

My pursuer most definitely wasn't a hallow or a reaper. It was TJ.

"What are you doing here?" I demanded, slapping him on the back of the head with my palm. "I almost bashed you with my shoe."

He scowled, eyes moving from the weapon clutched in my hand back to my face. "Following you."

I lowered the shoe. "I figured that part out, deputy dipshit. But why?"

"Because you've been acting weirder than usual. And that's saying something."

I whacked him again.

He rubbed at the back of his head. "Will you stop that?"

"I will if you stop acting like a moron," I replied, slipping my wedges back on my cold and damp feet. "Do you know how dangerous it is out here? I thought I explained this to you the other day. The world is going to hell in a handbasket."

"If that is true, what are you doing sneaking around in the dark? Isn't it just as unsafe for you?" he questioned.

It was, but I wasn't going to admit it. "You're forgetting one important fact. I can take care of myself."

He rolled his eyes. "Oh, I saw. With a shoe, right? I didn't realize that was what banshees used to defend themselves."

"Hey, you've got to work with what you have."

"Don't you have like super powers?"

I lowered my voice. "I can't go around blasting everyone I come into contact with. If I did, you'd be twenty feet away lying flat on your back."

He scrunched his face. "Vain much?"

Miffed, I started to walk away, fully expecting him not to follow me. "TJ, I don't have time to explain the reasons behind my actions. I need you to go home. *Now*," I emphasized.

He jogged to catch up with me, matching our strides. "And tell those two goons stationed outside your bedroom what? That you managed to slip out of the house right under their noses? It would only be minutes before Zane issued a manhunt."

I hated when he was right. "Look, I can't sit around the manor and do nothing. I have to figure out how to fix this. And I can't do that if

I'm worrying about you. I'm trying to keep you safe." It occurred to me that no one knew where TJ or I were. If something happened ...

The smart thing would have been to turn back and take TJ to the manor, and I was going to do just that, but then I heard voices.

Lifting my head, I looked around. The back entrance of Atmosfear was directly to my left. "I can't believe I'm saying this," I whispered. "Stay behind me, and you have to do whatever I say. No questions asked. Agreed?"

He nodded.

Slinking along the side of the club's building, I reached the corner that led to the back door. Crouching down, I poked my head around just enough to see with one eye. There were two people outside the exit door. I couldn't make out their faces, not from this angle or with the lack of moonlight. Not that it mattered. The gleam of a cigarette gave him away.

Crash.

He flicked his lighter, giving a warm glow to the darkness surrounding his face. Alarm jumped into my eyes. I gasped but quickly put my hand over my mouth. And to think I'd been worried about TJ making too much noise.

The other person with Crash was his father, Heath.

Perfect. This was exactly what I was counting on, except for TJ being here.

"You're late," Heath scolded.

Crash blew a cloud of smoke into his father's face. "Yeah, well, my life doesn't revolve around you."

Heath waved the air in front of him, lips turned down. "This isn't a game. You need to start taking your responsibilities as my heir."

"I'm here, aren't I? Each night, helping run this club." Crash had a quietness to his voice I found alarming. Under his I-don't-give-two-shits exterior lived a troubled soul.

"What are they saying?" TJ whispered.

I turned my head from the corner and put my finger to my lips. My original plan had been to mingle inside the club, ask some questions, and do a little snooping in the off limit sections, but this was so much better. And dangerous. I returned my attention to eavesdropping.

Heath's merciless eyes slid over his son. "That's not what I meant, and you know it. There is more to being my son than the club," he spat. "You have duties to uphold now that the veil has been removed."

For the first time, I saw Crash look at his father with distrust and loathing, but only for a split second. He blinked, putting his jaded mask back in place. "Oh yes, your master plan."

"We have too much at stake for your indolence."

Crash gestured toward Heath with the hand holding his smoke. "You mean, *you* have too much at stake." Burning ash fell off the tip, tumbling to the ground. "Don't worry, I know my part."

Heath's face twisted into a fierce scowl. "You don't have half of the strength or loyalty your sister did. At least she had the guts to do what needed to be done."

"And it got her killed. Is that what you're hoping for?"

Heath shook his head. Eyes hard like glass, he lifted them to meet his son dead on. "At least your sister knew her worth," he seethed. "Her sacrifice is what is going to give us what our family has had coming to us for centuries."

Asshole award goes to Heath.

Crash snorted, rolling his eyes as if this was a tiresome conversation he'd heard over and over. "You brainwashed her." He was a glutton for punishment.

Heath raised his hand, and I thought, for a moment, he was going to strike Crash. His hand wavered, but didn't move. "Without her, the veil never would have been destroyed. We wouldn't get the chance to change the balance of power. Why should it fall to only one reaper? It is time we tip the scales. You will follow through with the plan. This is not negotiable."

Crash stood there unblinking, casually lifting his cigarette to his mouth. "Thanks for the pep talk, Pops." He flicked the butt of the cigarette onto the ground at his father's feet and headed this way.

Flattening myself against the building, I had a small panic attack, and then I grabbed TJ's hand. *This better work. Please, please, pretty please.* Zane and I could share abilities; we had done so on numerous occasions to save our asses. This was one of those times I needed our souls to merge. But he wasn't here, and I couldn't precisely scream, alerting the very reapers I was hiding from.

Our bond was strong. I just hoped it was strong enough, because I needed his shadows.

With my back pressed to the cold bricks, I closed my eyes and summoned my power. I murmured his name under my breath. A cold sensation raced through my veins. It was like jumping into a pool of icy water, and then shadows of the night seeped out from the nooks and crevices, blanketing TJ and I in utter darkness.

Crash brushed by us without a second glance. It was the overlord I was worried about it. Heath walked to the edge of the alley, watching his son's back. He paused, and I held my breath. His treacherous, beady eyes swept over the empty lot. My grip tightened on TJ's hand as he glanced over to where we were huddled.

I exhaled. *That was close. Too godforsaken close.*

But as I drew my next breath, we'd traded one disaster for another. Ice cold air and the stench of death filled my nostrils, making it hard to breathe. I'd developed some kind of hallow detector.

TJ coughed.

I got butterflies—the bad ones that made me sick.

Hallows were here.

CHAPTER 11

And they were close. With my luck, there would be a whole gang of hallows.

"TJ," I whispered.

His eyes flashed to mine, beaming with concern, my body language alerting him to trouble.

"We need to haul ass home. Like now." My flight or fight response went into high gear, more so with TJ involved. No place was safe, but *I* had taken the chance anyway. TJ had changed the rules, and I regretted letting him tag along. If anything happened to him … I just had to make sure nothing did.

Stretching out my hearing, I listened for the hissing of ghosts descending upon us. They were coming in fast. Once they caught my scent, it was game over. Somewhere down the alley, a rock skipped, tumbling along the pavement.

No longer shrouded in darkness, we darted around the corner, heading toward the sound of the ocean. My bare feet clattered down the narrow and dark pathway. I glanced over my shoulder to see if we were being followed as the seconds ticked by, each one bringing us closer to danger. No matter how far or how fast we ran, it wasn't fast enough. As I turned back around, I gasped. Our time was up. My feet fumbled to a stop as I came nose to nose with the very things I was running from.

"Little bansssshee, where do you think you're going?" the cold sucker hissed.

I opened my mouth to scream …

A whoosh of stale air whirled around my face as the hallow grabbed the front of my dress, slamming me into the brick wall. Dust and bits of debris rained down over my head. I let out a pathetic groan as black stars dotted behind my eyes, blurring my vision. The hallow turned into two, both staring at me with soulless eyes like I was their next meal ticket.

I blinked. The two figures slowly merged back into one, my eyes readjusting from having the daylight knocked out of me.

"Piper!" TJ screamed in panic.

I craned my neck to the side, peering around the ghost. TJ was cornered. There was only one detaining him, but it might as well have been a hundred. He had no idea what to do. Seeing him in trouble, instincts kicked in. My fist connected with the hallow's chest, and on contact, I summoned my power. Surprise flickered across his pale face. "Suck on this, asshole," I said, my arms covered in ribbons of white.

The impact sent him staggering backwards, a guttural sound erupting from his mouth before he exploded into a blinding blue light.

I pushed off the building, ignoring the blistering burn on my back. Blinded by rage, the usually ingrained thought to call for help never came. With energy filling my veins, I strutted right up to the ghost dumb enough to mess with my brother. He had a hand around TJ's throat, whose coloring was looking a little green. I tapped on the hallow's shoulder. He spun around, his focus right where I wanted—on me. "I wouldn't do that if I were you," I advised.

Teeth bared and hissing, the hallow's cheeks were wishy-washy and sunken. No life reflected in his face, only death and anger. "You should know better than to walk the streetsss alone, Raven," he said, his voice eerie and deep. "If you kill me, I'll take him with me. Are you willing to take that chance?"

His hand was still clenched around TJ's neck, cutting off his air supply. I took a step back. "Blah. Blah. Blah. Talk about original. Tell me something I haven't already heard a thousand times before."

He laughed, the sound lacking humor and life.

I raised a brow. "Come on, I'm really not that funny."

The scrawny bastard shook his head in sharp, jagged movements. "I'm laughing because you're not at all what I expected. There is a lot less of you."

Was that a dig at my small stature? No one insulted my height and got away with it. "I might be short, but I make up for it in other areas, which you're about to find out." The entire alleyway detonated in white light. A pulse of power rippled from my fingertips, crashing into the intended target. The ground shook as I opened my energy, letting it seep into the earth. Sonic shockwave.

Boom. Two down without barely breaking a sweat. Not too shabby.

"Piper," TJ choked.

Our eyes met. "You okay?" I asked, rushing to his side.

He was leaning against a wall for support. "I take it back. You're pretty badass."

A smirk fixed on my lips. "Yeah, I am. Ready to get the hell out of here?"

"You don't have to ask me twice." He rubbed a hand over the red, splotchy ring encompassing his neck.

The action made my blood spike. Steam was coming out of my ears. They had hurt my brother—the only family I had—and I wasn't likely to forget.

TJ and I managed to tiptoe our way back into the manor the same way we had left, but there was a surprise waiting for me in my room. The lights were completely out when I opened the door. Declan was standing erect and alert. "Ten-hut, solider," I said, because teasing Declan was too much fun.

He nodded. "Princess."

I closed the door behind me, leaving Declan in the hall, and threw my shoes, tossing them in the corner. It was good to be home. Being a freaking ninja was hard work. As I started to unzip the little black dress, a voice sounded in the pitch black room.

"I was wondering when you were going to show up."

I jumped, nearly hitting the ceiling and peeing myself a little. I hadn't bothered with a light, but even in the dark, I knew that voice. "Holy crap. You scared me to death." My hand flew to my heart. If I hadn't been so preoccupied and juiced up, I might have sensed the tingles instead of having ten years shaved off my life.

Zane flipped on the table lamp. He stretched, flashing a bit of taut skin. "How was your night?"

"You don't want to know," I grumbled.

The darkness was such a part of him. It had been there when I needed it tonight, needed him. "You're right. I probably don't, but I think I deserve an explanation. You merged our souls. Why?"

Zane undoubtedly wasn't going to like this. It was a given. But how could I blame him? I sighed, plopping onto the edge of the bed beside him. "I went to Atmosfear."

He rubbed his hand over his face. "Why would you do something so stupid? I don't have to tell you who owns the joint."

"Exactly. I went there to get information."

"And let me guess, you found trouble instead? Or it found you."

"Does it matter? I'm here, and as you can see, in one piece. No blood. No cuts."

He shook his onyx hair. "Piper, when are you going to learn? Everything about you matters to me."

My heart squeezed in my chest. "I'm sorry. I'm getting desperate," I said, flopping on my back. "Each day I do nothing, more people are in danger. More people die."

He followed me down onto the bed, lying alongside me, his powerful arms touching mine. "And if you die, we're eternally screwed. My brother died fighting for what he believed in. He believed in you, Piper."

My stomach sunk. The reminder thickened the guilt weaving in my gut. I thought of Zander often: when I went to sleep, when I woke up. His sacrifice was on my mind constantly. I didn't want to disappoint him, not after everything he gave me. I was staring into the face of one of those things. Love. And disappointing Zane would be heartbreaking. "I feel like all I do anymore is apologize. Everyone has their responsibilities. This is mine."

He leaned over me, pressing a kiss to the corner of my lips. "Just know that you don't have to do it alone. I can help, if you let me."

It wasn't that I didn't think he would be there for me; I just wasn't sure he would think before acting. Zane was a guns blazing kind of guy. We both knew each other's strengths and weaknesses. "By help, you mean stop me."

"From getting yourself killed? Yes. But that doesn't always mean I will say no. I might surprise you."

"Are you saying you would have gone with me tonight?"

He shrugged. "Against my better judgment, I would have, just to make sure you were safe. It's easier on my stress levels when I see it with my own eyes."

God, I was in way over my head. "Next time I get an idea, you'll be the first to know."

"Uh-huh," he murmured, pressing his lips to the vein pulsing in my neck. "You're going to have to do a better job of convincing me."

I laughed, looping my arms around his neck. "What did you have in mind?"

His lashes lowered. "I missed you."

My fingers twirled the hair at the nape of his neck that just slightly curled. "We've seen each other every day."

He lined a trail of kisses along my jaw. "It's not nearly enough."

I knew what he meant. "Maybe I should be reckless more often." I said it as a joke, but Zane's eyes instantly lost their gleam of playfulness and flared. "I was kidding. I did learn something, though."

"What? That you like being reckless?" he asked.

"Hardy-har-har." I turned on my side, facing him. "Crash and Heath were at the club tonight. I overheard them talking outside at the back of the building."

His hands dropped to either side of his head. "Princess, you're going to give me a heart attack. If they had seen you …"

"They didn't," I assured him. "That's why I borrowed your shadows: to conceal my presence … and TJ's too."

Zane raised his brows. "What was your brother doing there?"

"The dweeb followed me."

"Unruliness must run in your family."

I rolled my eyes. "Do you want to hear what I found out, or not?"

He wiggled on the bed until he was relaxed, lacing a hand behind his head. "Okay, I'm all ears."

I sat up, folding my legs. My knees bumped up against his thigh. "They were talking about the veil, about how it was destroyed."

"And this surprises you?"

"No, not entirely. I had seen Heath sneaking out of the sanctuary that night. He was telling Crash that there are many ways to thin the veil, but only one way to drop it permanently."

Zane nodded. "Yes, my father has spoken of the myths of lifting the veil. But they were always taken as that: legends. The veil has never been broken before."

My gaze was fixed on his. "There's a first for everything. He implied Estelle's death had something to do with it."

His brows slammed together. "Son of a—"

I whacked him with a pillow before he could finish his colorful expression. "What?"

"Estelle," he stated. "The bastard used his daughter. He wanted you to kill her. It makes perfect sense now. He set Estelle up to kill Rose, knowing how angry you were after your mother died. He used your desire for revenge to push you to take her life."

When I had killed Estelle, I had absorbed her soul. Unlike Zane, being a death reaper, I hadn't destroyed her soul. Estelle definitely went to the other side. "Why would he do that?"

"Because to destroy the veil, he would have to sacrifice someone he loved—turn them into a hallow. Having her on the other side would aid him in being able to drop the veil."

"Wow. I thought I had daddy issues." But that took the cake, though my stepfather had tried to kill me.

"I hate to admit it, but at least it's a start."

"Something we can agree on. It's not much to go on."

"A victory, however small, but don't ever do that again."

I pursed my lips. "You could just say, 'Nice job.'"

He placed his hand on my hip. "I could, but I don't want you to get it into your head that what you did was smart."

I groaned, loud and long. "You're so frustrating. I actually think you're the most frustrating guy I've ever met."

"I live to please," he said, grinning.

I snorted. "You and I have very different ideas of how to please someone."

"Oh yeah? I bet there is one thing we can agree on." His lips pressed to mine. He was absolutely right. When it came to this, Zane and I saw eye-to-eye, or more like lip-to-lip, and all the problems and the nitpicking ceased to matter.

We both treasured these moments not only because we were able to love each other without feeling guilty, but because we both weren't sure how long this freedom would last. Our days were numbered. Zane assured me that the divine would summon me, expecting a new oath to be made between a pure heir and the White Raven.

Gag me.

CHAPTER 12

"Did you just dip your fries into your shake?" Zane asked, eyeing me over his one-pound burger. Soft shadows danced over his face, highlighting the sharp angles of his cheekbone and the curve of his lips.

"Yeah," I replied like he was the weird one.

He shook his head. "What planet are you from?"

"Me," I screeched, smiling. "I'm the most normal person here."

He took a bite into his monstrosity, deemed to be a burger. "If you say so."

I dipped another fry in my chocolate shake. "It feels so … quiet in here," I said, observing the nearly empty café. We were having lunch, doing the normal couple thing for once.

"It's never quiet here. Not anymore."

I lifted my head at the sound of the bell hanging over the door. "Speaking of not so quiet, look what the cat dragged in."

Zoe spotted us immediately. Her raven hair had those beachy waves I could never get—the perfect blend of sexy and messy. She was wearing a flowy sundress, her pale skin luminous from being out in the sun. I watched my casual date with Zane fly right out the door. Parker trailed behind Zoe, looking like he wanted to be anywhere else. His knowledge of the island hadn't affected his boyish charm or his love for worn jeans and manga T-shirts.

He still wasn't talking to me. It hurt. I missed my best friend. This wasn't our first fight and wouldn't be our last, but there was something different this time. I was afraid our friendship might never be the same.

Zane's eyes rotated between his sister and Parker, a frown pasted on his lips. "What? Are you guys dating or something? Every time I see you, you're with *him*."

I picked at my fries, avoiding Parker's gaze. The not speaking to me was getting under my skin. We hadn't gone more than a week without talking ... ever. I still couldn't fathom why he would willingly choose *this* life.

"So what if we are?" Zoe replied, sliding into the booth alongside her brother and plucking a pickle off his plate.

And that left the only empty seat next to me. Parker cleared his throat uncomfortably as he sat as close to the edge as he could manage without falling into the aisle. Ugh. I hated the weird tension between us. Nothing was the same between us anymore. It seemed like the harder I tried to keep him safe, the further we drifted apart.

Zane's icy eyes narrowed. "When did this happen?"

Zoe snatched a fry from me and popped it in her mouth. I guess we were the kind of friends who ate off each other's plate. I really didn't mind. "You've been too busy making heart eyes at this one," she said, pointing a pink nail at me.

Zane looked perturbed. "I do not make heart eyes. I don't even know what that means."

The table erupted into giggles as the three of us all envisioned Zane with little red hearts in his eyes like a cartoon character. It broke some of the tension.

"I can't believe you're dating him," Zane commented, genuinely surprised.

"I could say the same thing about Pipes," Parker voiced.

Nope. There was no hope Parker and Zane would ever be friends.

The world could be coming to an end, and they still gave one another the stink eye.

"How about we don't make a scene for once?" Zoe suggested calmly. I don't know how she did it. She glanced over at her brother and then to Parker, giving them each challenging stares.

Zane relaxed, lounging back in the booth. "We wouldn't be Hunters if we didn't draw attention."

I gave his shin a light kick with my shoe under the table.

His brows rose.

"You gonna eat that?" Parker asked, eyeballing my food.

Did he just speak to me? Was the silent treatment over? It seemed too good to be true. I glanced down at my half-eaten sandwich and pushed the plate sideways—a peace offering. My appetite wasn't what it used to be. Stress. "Have at it."

Zoe flagged down the only server in the locally owned café and ordered a Sprite with no ice and a salad. Parker ordered his usual: a burger. So predictable. "I heard there was some action last night at the club," Zoe said.

The spoon I'd been fumbling with clattered to the table, and my eyes shot forward. "How did you hear about that?" Only three people knew what I had done last night. Two of them were at this table.

"Your brother," Parker chimed in with a mouthful of my turkey club sandwich.

"God, he is worse than a girl," I grumbled.

"He was wired when he snuck past my room, unable to keep what the two of you had done to himself," Parker defended. "I think he needed someone to confide in. The whole ghost and reaper business is still surreal to him. Talking about it with someone on the outside makes what happened real."

I sighed. "I know it probably doesn't need to be said, but this can't go any further than this table."

"We wouldn't dream of it," Zoe assured me. "Did you learn anything?"

"Only that Heath is the scum we always thought he was," Zane said.

"And Crash?" Parker asked, dipping a fry in my milkshake.

Zane shook his head, seeing Parker mimic my choice of fry dip.

I gave him my see-I'm-not-crazy smile and answered Parker. "Undetermined," I replied.

"Guilty," Zane said at the same time.

"Helpful." Parker frowned.

He was accurate. I didn't need information from the past but how to save our future. As soon as I thought I might be getting somewhere, making headway, I realized I was still at square one.

"Since the veil to the other side is broken, where do the souls go?" Parker asked.

Zoe swallowed a forkful of lettuce. "They will still travel to the afterlife, but with the barrier down, if they find the way, they can wander back into our dimension."

"That's what I was afraid you were going to say, but not all ghosts are aggressive," Parker theorized.

Zoe nodded. "Right. Only those with souls who are filled with hate or have unsettled revenge. If a spirit doesn't find peace in the afterworld, it becomes restless."

"What do we do next? How are we going to stop them?" Parker asked, having finished off the remains of my plate and working on his own burger. The boy was, and always had been, a bottomless pit. It made you wonder, due to his lean frame, where it all went.

Zane fidgeted in his seat beside his sister, who stared down at her healthy looking salad.

"That's for me to worry about," I mumbled.

Parker glanced sideways, scowling. "So you alone are going to save the world?"

"I didn't say that," I snapped. There went our truce, the pressure in the air between us rising.

"You might as well have," he argued.

"What is with you two?" Zoe hissed, her dark blue eyes rotating back and forth from Parker to me and back to Parker.

It was a good thing she intervened. I was about two seconds away from lunging at Parker and shoving him into the aisle. Parker and I both knew he was really referring to the fact that I refused to take his humanity and change him into a reaper. "Oh, you mean he didn't tell you he asked me to turn him into a reaper?"

Zoe gasped.

Zane laughed.

And Parker looked like he wanted to throttle me.

Good. If I couldn't get through to him, maybe Zoe could. However, the Hunters never failed to surprise me.

"By the evident tension, I assume you told him no?" Zoe concluded.

"Duh." I took a swig of my melted shake.

"I think Parker would make a great reaper," she announced, smiling across the table.

Chocolate shake went up my nose. "My decision has nothing to do with whether or not I think he could do the job. I don't want him making a choice he might later regret," I pointed out.

Zane remained mysteriously mute over the topic of Parker becoming a reaper, but from our bond, he wasn't as outraged as I was. *Am I the only one who can see clearly?*

Zoe stabbed the fork in her bowl aimlessly, spearing bits of lettuce. I'd never seen her unnerved. "It is ultimately your decision, but I would think, considering your strong feelings for Parker, you would want to turn him. He is human. Death is inevitably part of their nature."

I'd never thought about the flipside to having Parker as a reaper. His life would be prolonged, greatly. Is that what he was looking for—immortality—or did he truly want this for pure reasons? "I have a lot going on right now. I can't deal with another important decision at the moment."

"Have you told your boyfriend about Aspyn's plan for you guys to get married?" Parker's eyes glittered in payback.

"I didn't think you and Aspyn liked each other," I directed at Zoe, dodging Parker's attempt at sabotage. The only way he would have found out was from Zoe, and I'm sure Aspyn planted the seed in Zoe's head in hopes she would join team Knock Up Piper.

Zoe squeezed a lemon wedge into her water. "Oh, we don't, but it doesn't mean I don't hear things. Reapers talk. And Aspyn tends to run hers a mile a minute."

Grand. I slowly let my eyes move to Zane.

He leaned forward and propped his elbows on the table. "What is he talking about, Piper?"

"Thanks, Parker, I appreciate your concern," I muttered.

"Piper," Zane growled my name.

I blinked. He only called me by name when I was in trouble. "I was going to tell you."

His smoky blue eyes were wary. "Tell me what?"

I played with the end of my napkin, tearing little bits off at the corner. "Aspyn came up with this idea that might force the council to accept the idea we could be together."

"And you trust Aspyn?" he asked, sounding leery.

"I do. There are things I know about Aspyn, and we understand each other."

"Then why are you so hesitant to tell me? I can feel your reluctance."

This moment was one of those times it sucked he could sense my emotions. I took a breath, folding my fingers together. "She thinks if you and I have a baby, the council will have no choice but to prolong the pressure of me being wed until after our child is born."

Zane choked. "What?!" he blurted out, shaking the table.

I had played this scene over in my head time and time again. Although Parker and Zoe had never been a part of the equation, Zane's reaction had always been the same. How predictable in some things he could be. I huffed, unhappy to be corralled into telling him before I was ready. "She thinks once our daughter is born, we could prove that she will be a powerful banshee—one strong enough to take my place."

"Wow," Zoe said, tapping a nail on the edge of the table. "That might actually work. I'll never admit it to her face, but it's a fairly solid scheme. If I didn't dislike her from the bottom of my heart, I'd be impressed."

Zane did not share her optimism. "I hope you told her what a stupid idea it was."

Dead air.

"Piper," he prompted, arching his damn brows.

I rolled my eyes. "I don't think it's stupid." There. I'd said it.

"Neither do I," Zoe backed me up.

"Well, I agree with Zane, not that my opinion matters. Piper cannot have a baby. She's only eighteen." Parker sided with the oaf.

Guys against girls. I never thought I would see the day Zane and Parker would side together in anything. I guess they finally found common ground. It should have come as no surprise that it was me. "Why won't you even consider it? What harm would it do to try? If there is a chance at us being together, why not risk it?"

Zane looked as if he was going to flip the table out the little country style window. "I can think of plenty of reasons. The biggest being, what if our child is a boy? What if she isn't a banshee?" The mention of marriage and babies turned Zane green and hulkish.

It made me grin inside. He was worried for a child we might or might not have. He was concerned about me, about what kind of life our baby would have if his bloodline wasn't powerful enough. But he was wrong. Zane was the strongest reaper I knew. I wasn't going to let his sole insecurity ruin our chance to be together. "I never imagined you would let your fears govern your choices."

His eyes flashed a warning. "That is crazy. You can't possibly be pondering an idea so preposterous."

I twirled my straw around in my shake.

"Piper," he growled.

Zoe grinned. "I'm going to be an aunt."

Zane stabbed her with a glare before peering over at me with sooty lashes. "How you can think a baby will fix anything escapes me. The divine could very well shun our child. I won't have it."

"Then what do you suggest?" This was a conversation that couldn't be avoided forever. As much as we'd both love to stay in our blissful bubble, the sand in our hourglass was almost out.

"I don't know ... yet. How about we tackle one crisis at a time? The council isn't pressing you at the moment. They have their hands too full with the increased amount of death and hallows running around on the Earth to think of securing your successor."

I hated when he was so reasonable. "Fine. Don't think you've won. This isn't over." Not by a long shot.

"It's a good thing you're still a virgin," Parker said offhandedly.

The table dropped into ten different kinds of awkward silence. My cheeks betrayed me, infusing with warmth, flaming an unholy red. Super mortifying. I couldn't respond.

"Oh. My. God. You guys did *it*," Zoe shrieked.

Parker was slow on the uptake. "Did what?"

Zoe was all too eager to explain it to him. "Bumping uglies, making bacon, smash, horizontal bop, feed the kitty—"

Feed the kitty?

"Stop," Parker groaned, holding his belly. "I think I'm going to hurl."

Zoe threw her head back and laughed. Dark black hair spilled over her shoulders. "Hearts everywhere are breaking. My brother in a relationship, a serious one at that."

Zane wasn't thrilled at having his dirty laundry aired over lunch. The dark lines linking down his face spread. "Who would have thought—the black sheep and the White Raven?"

"I did," Zoe sung.

I was grateful when the conversation steered toward things that didn't have anything to do with my sex life, hallows, or reapers. Food long gone and drinks watered down, the four of us sat discussing life. Our most embarrassing moments, what our political stances were (Democrat or Republican), what our favorite food was, and so forth. It was as close to a double date and to normal as we would get. It was good, like cleansing the soul. Through all the bickering and jabs, in the end, we were all friends. Maybe not Zane and Parker just yet, but what did matter was we would be there for each other when it counted.

But normal didn't last long. I was a banshee. A day without a dose of weird was unheard of.

"Piper, your wrist," Parker proclaimed, his glasses slightly slipping on the bridge of his nose.

I glanced down, and my heart dropped. The wings of the white raven marked on my inner wrist were flapping and glowing brightly. Zane's shadowy crow behind my raven looked as if it was in distress. A pitching sensation filled my stomach.

Zoe's expression turned ominous, a mirror of her brother's. "You're being summoned."

Huh? I thought I was the only one who did any summoning. "Summoned by who?"

"The council," Zane deadpanned.

CHAPTER 13

My GPS was unable to give me directions to where I needed to go. It wasn't on any map. As my jeep bumped along the rocky road, the wind crackled with the promise of fall. The air was crisper. Summer was coming to a close and so was my freedom. Being a city girl, the island had had a certain charm when I first arrived, hypnotized by the crystal blue waters and green shadows of hills and the dancing of starlight. But now as I drove along the quaint roads, it felt like a straight path to hell. And I was taking Declan with me. Poor sod.

He shifted uncomfortably in the passenger seat, eyes glued in front of him. Sunglasses shielding his golden eyes, I couldn't tell if it was my driving that was making him nervous or where we were going.

Declan and I both would have preferred if Zane had accompanied me. I was comforted only by the fact Zane was never far away. Between my voice and his vow of protection, I shouldn't have been as nervous as I was. But as much as I wished he were with me, the council would feel differently. They were very vocal in their disapproval of my feelings for Zane Hunter. And our soul symmetry.

I was going to walk into the lion's den, uncertain as to why I was being summoned. Did they know a way to seal the veil? Did they have a plan to keep the hallows from taking more lives? Or were they going to make demands of me? Force me into a corner? Insist I must marry?

Heavy stuff.

"Turn here," Declan announced.

I slammed on the brakes and blinked. "Here?" I asked.

"Yes. Look again. Not with your human eyes, but your banshee ones."

Okay, old wise one. But I did as he said, concentrating. At first all I saw was vast, thick trees, their green leaves canopying over the road. Brush and grass covered the ground. Then, as I was about to tell Declan he needed his eyes examined, a vague path began to materialize. The way had been hidden by glamour and from human eyes. It wasn't anything dazzling. A dirt path wound down as a dark tower of trees climbed up the trail and along the slopes. It was a good thing I drove a jeep with some awesome tire traction. We were going off-roading.

Hitting the gas, I gave the steering wheel a turn and entered the road of no return. What an awful thought. I regretted it immediately.

The jeep's headlights beamed down the path, illuminating the way. We traveled a mile or so until we came upon a clearing. The trees gave way, opening to a perfect circular grove. A large medallion was situated in the middle, ancient words and symbols inscribed on it. Magic and power trembled in the air, awakening the banshee inside me. I felt the change, and so did Declan. His eyes were glowing in the dark—a lion's yellow, predatory.

"Have you ever been summoned?" I asked, shifting the car into park.

"Only once," he answered, eyes fixed on the stone circle.

"What was your crime? Eating an apple after midnight?" I joked sarcastically.

Declan was a stickler for rules and order. He let out an uncomfortable laugh. "Hardly. I killed another reaper without a command."

Surprise flickered across my face. So much for his perfect, polished image.

The council was made up of the divine (a skeleton asshole in my book), the elders, and the overlords—the leader for each faction. Roarke. Heath. And Maurice. And they were not my biggest fans. I was disobedient. Troublesome. And free-willed.

From where we were parked, I could just make out the shadowy forms of seven cloaked figures. I'd procrastinated long enough.

My hands were trembling as I stepped out of the car. I don't know why I was so nervous. What was the worst they could say to me? Nothing would change my decision.

A bluish sphere of light glittered over the center of the open stone circle. The air was quiet here, eerily so. Nothing stirred. Not the rustling of leaves. Not the scampering of little critters. The only things living in the area were the trees.

My stomach tightened, and a gross sensation slithered through me. The divine stood a few feet away. He was dressed in long gray robes that made me wonder if he had feet. This guy always gave me the willies. I forced a quick smile on my lips while gritting my teeth. "You wanted to see me?"

With a disdain I didn't fully understand, his beady spider eyes peered down at me. "The council has made a decision regarding the ensured Raven lineage. As you know, it is your duty to assure your bloodline continues. Without a banshee, there is no balance."

I snorted. We had a banshee and the balance was still out of whack. I couldn't believe they weren't trying to impeach me or something.

"Against the council, Death has named his half-breed son as his heir." If I thought the divine held me in contempt, his feelings for me were mild in comparison to how he felt about Zane.

I expelled a breath of shock, my mind working in a hundred different directions. What did that mean? Hope bloomed inside me, spreading like tangled vines, weaving around my heart. I was expected to unify my bloodline with an overlord heir. Could it be so simple now that Zane would one day rule the Black Crows?

"The council will not recognize Zane Hunter as a legitimate heir." The divine's voice held an air of supremacy, and he tipped his chin up, knowing his words were a sword to the gut. "As of this hour, the Black Crows do not have a worthy successor."

My fists clenched at my sides, and I opened my mouth to tell the council to go suck a lemon, but the divine, anticipating my unruly mouth and inability to keep quiet, snapped his fingers and thumb together like a crocodile mouth. A shimmer of purple mist expelled, causing my jaw to lock.

My hands flew to my lips. Oh no, he didn't; he did not just shush me. Shock turned to anger. I was going to go ape shit.

"You have the worst manners," he said, exasperated. "We will continue these proceedings *without* any interruptions, until all has been said."

Declan flinched beside me as he struggled with loyalties. Did he protect me as he was ordered and defy the council? Or did he stay silent as he was trained to do?

I made the choice for him, shaking my head, letting him know I didn't want him to do anything but wait. I stood, knees locked, glaring daggers with my mouth clamped shut, all the while thinking about the different ways I was going to make them pay.

It was a good thing Zane wasn't here. Mayhem would have ensued.

The other elders and overlords stayed silent in the back wing behind the divine, not offering any words or objections. The divine was the almighty voice of the group.

"The bond you have with the half-breed is powerful. Use it wisely. Use it to your advantage. There is no denying he is strong. You will need his strength as well as your own to complete the task in front of you. It is without question, Raven, you came into your position in the middle of a battle we haven't faced in centuries. Not even the elders present can remember days as dark as these. It is due to these perilous times you must pave your future, because without your banshee bloodline, we have no hope to seal the world from the dead."

His words resonated inside me—the importance of what I must do. I tried to tell him such, but all that came out was mumbo jumbo, forgetting my speech impairment.

A twisted smile curved his pale lips. "A new contract has been drawn up between you and the heir to the Red Hawks."

My eyes bulged. I was going to be sick. Knees weak, my heart fell out of my chest for the divine to stomp all over it.

Crash. Crash? Crash!

Were they serious? Heath hated me. I was ninety-nine percent sure he was responsible for the whole destruction of the veil. His daughter had killed my grandmother and tried to give me the same deadly fate. All in the name of power. My power. And the council expected me to marry Crash.

They had another thing coming if they thought I would tie myself in holy matrimony to someone who may or may not slit my throat in the middle of the night, in my own bed, nonetheless.

Declan and Oliver were in the very small circle of people Zane trusted. I wasn't the only one utterly outraged by the council's choice for a suitable husband. Declan rarely showed emotion. Now was one of those rare occasions. His golden eyes darkened, red veins feathering down his cheeks. The combination reminded me of a sunset.

My eyes sought out the snake among the council. The sinister sneer on Heath's lips sent me into a tizzy. I would be silenced no more.

The divine might have power, but it was nothing compared to mine. From the moment he had slapped the restraint on my mouth, I had known I could remove it with a twitch of my nose. I had let him think—let them all think—he could control me.

Until now.

My veins flowed with a tingly warm glow. Lifting my hand, I ripped away the purple mist keeping me from speaking my mind and tossed it to the ground like a wad of gum, and I let my voice find its power. "Did you forget that I am your supreme? I'm not one to be trifled with." I took a step forward, forcing him to take one back. It was I now who stood in the center of the stone circle. "I will not sign the contract. Not today. Not ever."

Disappointment flashed across the divine's face. "It is true; your power is paramount, but your fate is sealed. There is no amount of magic that can change your destiny."

A cloud of whispers from the other council members darkened the divine, but they didn't concern me. "I beg to differ. There is always one power that is greater than all others. Love."

"You are nothing but a foolish girl," the all too thin divine hissed. That was how the council saw me. Just a stupid girl. Their lack of concern for this one girl showed their flaw. Foolish pride.

I stood straighter, keeping my eyes locked on his black alien orbs. "If this is all you summoned me for, it was a waste of our time, which should have been spent on calculating how we're going to mend the barrier between realms." Each breath I spent trying to justify myself was a squander of air. I spun on my heels. Meeting adjourned.

Declan sauntered beside me, his critical eyes watching out for my safety. I bumped my shoulder lightly into his arm. "And to think, Declan, you were worried about me. How cute."

He chuckled, a light dusting of scruff on his face. "I won't make that mistake again, Princess. You can be sure."

I glanced over my shoulder to see the circular clearing had vanished and the council disbanded. "That was one for the memory book."

Crash, huh? The elders had voted my enemy's son to be my husband. It was evident Heath was behind the whole thing, pushing his son into a very high position of power.

Over my dead body.

If I hadn't been rendered speechless, I might have called Heath out right then and there, accused him of disposing of the veil.

We had almost reached my car when Declan stiffened. I stopped in my tracks and swore under my breath. *Oh for frick's sake. Can't a girl get a break?*

"I guess you got the news." Crash was leaning against my jeep, hands shoved in his pockets. His sandy hair was disheveled, and he wore a mischievous grin. "Looks like you and I are going to be hitched."

I relaxed my shoulders. "Don't hold your breath."

He twirled an unlit cigarette between his fingers, rolling from thumb to pinky. "I was hoping you would say that."

I angled my head. "Were you now? I assumed you would be happy with the arrangement. You get to marry the White Raven. Power is all your family cares about."

The slim white stick snapped in half. "Happy isn't an emotion I'm used to feeling."

"I guess with a father like yours, happiness isn't part of your everyday life."

"Ding. Ding. Ding. Give this girl a gold medal. Much like Zander and Zane, I too have a certain reputation to live up to."

Shifting my weight to one side, I folded my arms. "So you had a shitty childhood. That doesn't mean you need to be your father when you grow up. You're capable of making your own choices. Do good, Crash. Help me stop the hallows from destroying everything."

"For someone who is so smart, you can be pretty daft. What do you think I've been doing?" he queried.

If one more person insulted me today … "You can't expect me to believe you have my best interests in mind. How many times have you threatened me? How many times have you broken into my room?"

He flicked both halves of the broken cigarette onto the ground. "At my father's orders."

Declan had heard enough. Muscles bunched under his shirt. "We need to go."

I put my hand on Declan's chest, stopping him from doing anything. "Go wait in the car," I told him. Hopefully, I didn't regret the action, but I was willing to hear Crash out.

Declan looked like he wanted to argue, but after a long stare at Crash, he opened the passenger door and slammed it shut.

Crash's lips pulled back. "I'm not my father."

"You'll understand I can't just take your word for it."

Moonlight sliced through the trees, carving Crash's serious face out with the light. "The way I see it, you don't have much of a choice. I'm the only lead you've got. Am I right?"

He knew he was, but I'd be damned if I said it out loud. "Trust must be earned. You bring me something substantial—that I can actually use—and then we'll see where we stand."

"Such a tough cookie. You've come a long way in three months. About our wedding—"

"There will be no wedding," I vowed. "Mark my words."

He rocked back on his heels. "Oh, luv, the feeling is mutual. I have no desire to be strapped down. A good tumble in the hay, hey, I'm game. Just say when and where. I'll rock your world." The come-get-me grin did absolutely nothing for me.

My face scrunched as if I'd sucked on a dozen limes. "Please. I wouldn't let you touch me with a ten foot pole."

He moved so fast, closing the space between us so he was in my air space. "Come on now," he murmured, running a finger along my jawline. "You know you've entertained the idea of us being together. How could you not? But until death do us part? No thanks. I'm not the marrying type."

I could smell his breath, a mixture of smoke and sweet mint. It wasn't as repulsive as I would have thought but a cool and refreshing combination. Still, there was nothing but curiosity, nothing beyond that. No real feelings or ties. I jerked my chin away from his touch. "Don't lay a finger on me." My veins crackled in a white glow.

He took a step back, a smirk upon his lips. "There's the spark. You're going to need it too, if you plan on rebuilding the veil."

"What do you know of restoring the veil?" I challenged.

"I know who is responsible for deconstructing the only thing that stands between us and the dead."

"Your father and Estelle," I supplied.

He nodded. "Someone's been doing their homework."

I rolled my eyes. "As educational as this knowledge is, it doesn't tell me what I need to know. If I don't figure out how to fix what your family destroyed, we're all majorly screwed."

Crash leaned a hip on the car, still too close for comfort. "That's why you need me. The inside guy."

I resisted the urge to step back, not wanting him to know his closeness unnerved me. "How do I know I can trust you? That this isn't a trap? That you don't really want my power?" There was also the little fact that Zane would never go for it. Us working with Crash? He would go ballistic.

"You don't, doll. You're just going to have to trust me. But I think we'd make an exceptional team."

My arms dropped to my sides. "What is it you want then?"

He leaned down, our lips a mere inch away. "Did it ever occur to you that I want the same things you do?"

Was he going to kiss me? OMG. He was going to kiss me. I was rendered shell-shocked, smoky tendrils wrapping around me.

"Touch her, and I will slap the dog shit out of you," an ominous and fierce voice growled in the dark. It was deep with warning.

Zane.

CHAPTER 14

Crash shook his head, chuckling. "I should have known you'd show up uninvited."

"Zane," I whispered in relief. Then I was moving, closing the space between us. I threw my arms around his neck. "What are you doing here?" I asked, my face buried against his neck.

His body was stiff, but he ran a gentle hand through my hair. "My father told me what happened at the council. I came as soon as I heard, but I didn't expect to find you nearly kissing the leech." His eyes shot over my head accusingly.

Crash kicked off my car. "Let the party begin."

Zane's frosty glare promised lots of trouble. Probably fatal trouble. Scratch that. Definitely fatal. "If they had picked anyone but you, I might have let them live, but not you. There's no way I will let you, of all reapers, marry Piper. Over my dead body." His tone ended on a rather grim note.

Declan stepped out of the car, flanking Crash's other side. Nothing like being sandwiched between two overbearing, protective reapers. Declan might be a Red Hawk like Crash, but he literally had no love for his future overlord.

Crash didn't seem the least bit intimated, a testament to either his bravado or his stupidity. "Who am I to stand in the way of true love? If you had been here two minutes earlier, Death Scythe, you would have heard me tell her that I had no interest in marriage. Not even to the White Raven."

Zane had gone quiet, but anger rolled off him. He didn't look altogether convinced at Crash's admission. "Then why, precisely, were your lips anywhere near hers?"

There was a tinged ribbon of guilt roaming inside me. I hadn't immediately shoved Crash away, and I had no logical answer as to why. The only solace was I could sense Zane's anger was entirely pointed at Crash. He would have felt through our soul connection that I held nothing but neutral feelings toward Heath's heir.

"Curiosity," Crash answered.

Challenge dripped from Zane. "Everything is a joke to you."

"Zane." I placed my hand on his chest, looking over my shoulder into the woods. The scent of death overpowered my nostrils, making them burn. "You better put on your superhero cape. We're about to get some unwanted villains."

He glanced down at me, eyes unfazed. "Piper, how many times do I have to tell you? I'm not the hero."

My hands clutched his shirt. "You are to me." Ice coated my insides. *Hallows.* They were approaching, fast.

The hardness in Zane's expression softened. "Declan, I hope you're ready to unleash your inner Chuck Norris."

Declan cracked his knuckles. "I'm already game. Let's use these assholes as dartboards."

"Should I call ..." for backup, but it was too late. They were already here. A strange, almost prickling of anticipation twisted through me as the hallows emerged from the tree lines. Their eyes appeared first, breaking through the darkness like a dozen lanterns. They dipped and glided along the ground, coming straight for us.

I braced myself as the frightening hissing filled the air. The sight was jarring, and I was so glad to have Zane, Declan, and even Crash present.

The four of us were lined up in front of my car, the clearing quickly filling with the cold mist of the departed. “I love when people come back from the dead. Juices my zombie fetish,” Crash said drily. “You up for this, cupcake?”

I remained in place, trying to control my inner turmoil, and ignored Crash.

Zane, on the other hand, didn’t have my self-control. He pointed a finger in Crash’s face. “By God, if you try any funny business, I’ll kill you with my bare hands. And she’s not your cupcake.”

The sucky thing about being in the middle of nowhere … no streetlights. The only light we had was the measly bit of moonlight illuminating the thick trees and hitting small sections of the clearing. I was going to have to rely heavily on my other senses and instinct.

A strip of darkness filled the center of the glade, and that was where the ghosts came from. Straight down the middle. As they drew closer, so did the scent of decay. It was a noticeable smell I’d never detected before, but as my banshee abilities strengthened, so did my other senses.

“Game on,” Crash said and stepped out of his body, emerging a wolf. He let out a howl, long and high.

Instantly, the air became degrees cooler, more so as Zane cloaked himself in his shadows and my veins flowed with a bright light. If things went haywire, Zane and I always had our secret weapon. No use going in all guns blazing, not until we knew how many we were dealing with.

The fight was on.

Three hallows descended. Being typical guys, Zane, Declan, and Crash engaged before I had a chance. Crash took a wide gash out of his target’s calf, an action that wasn’t a fatal wound but would merely disable him until the final blow. Declan spun and delivered that hit to the screaming hallow.

Zane took a different approach—one clean swipe, removing the head. It rolled over the dirt before detonating into nothing. I wasn’t sure if it was on purpose, but the guys seemed to take care of the hallows before they had a chance to reach me.

“Impressive,” said a voice to my left. It was a voice that haunted my dreams, one I wasn't likely to forget. She was the first person I ever killed.

Estelle.

This bitch just keeps coming back.

I angled to the side to get a better look. Besides being abnormally pale and her glossy eyes, she looked like … Estelle. "I thought I killed you. For good." I gritted my teeth.

She smirked. "You thought wrong. That's the great thing about being dead. It's full of surprises."

"Your timing sucks, as usual." My eyes slid sideways to Crash. I needed to know that he was with me. This was his sister; she was the very thing reapers trained to fight, but could he send her back to the other side? Could he do what must be done? He harbored some not-so-friendly feelings about how she died. Would seeing her ghost instill his flame for revenge?

I knew what it was like to have to face someone you cared about, what it felt like to stick a blade through their heart, to siphon their soul dry, and I didn't wish it on anyone, not even Crash.

He stood, no longer a wolf, but as Crash, his eyes roaming over the figure who was his sister but at the same time wasn't. "Estelle?" His voice cracked.

"Fancy meeting you here," she greeted him. "With *her,* nonetheless."

Obviously there was no love lost between Estelle and me. "How many times am I going to have to kill you?" I snapped before I thought about how Crash might feel about me killing his sister again. He had to know it must be done.

She grinned. "You still don't get it, do you? Priceless."

"Estelle, you don't have to do this," Crash pleaded.

I could all too well imagine what was going on in Crash's head. Seeing someone you loved turned into a vicious being was a knife to the heart.

Her movements were jerky as her eyes acknowledged her brother. "You know I do," she hissed. "She deserves it after what she did to me."

Snapping out of his daze, Crash sadly shook his head. "What Piper did? Correct me if I'm wrong, but it was our father who made you do it, not Piper."

She gave a twisted laugh. "Nice play. Father would be proud."

The corners of Crash's eyes crinkled. "Have it your way, sis."

If Estelle's plan was to dig her own grave, it worked. "How do we know this isn't a setup?" Zane's voice thundered over the chaos.

Crash reached in his back pocket and pulled out a pack of cigarettes. "You don't. I guess you have to trust me." His gaze slid sideways to me, and for a second, I thought he might attack me. His hazel eyes flared crimson—his wolf eyes.

But nope. It wasn't him that leapt forward but the pack of hallows dying to get their pasty grubs on us.

Crash and Zane backpedaled, moving in opposite directions as they surrounded us from all sides. We each took a corner, making a square, protecting each other's backs. The guys took on the mob of hallows led by Estelle, and that left me with crazy-pants herself. I leveled a hard glare at her, and my anger faded into determination.

She advanced on me. I stalked forward. We met in the middle, and I wasted no time. In the moment, I didn't know anything but blind rage. I was sick of people thinking I was weak. I was tired of being disregarded. But mostly, I was done being attacked by the dead and seeing them kill innocent souls. No more.

I increased my speed and threw a punch laced with power, but she sidestepped me, avoiding impact. Arching back, I narrowly avoided having my eyes clawed out. She recovered in a rush, nails slicing and swinging, teeth snarling. Her almond-shaped eyes no longer twinkled. She had been the first friend I'd made on the island, or so I'd thought.

"Can't you do better than that?" she taunted.

I grinned. "Oh, we're just getting started." I swiped my fist through the air again. Boom. Contact. Unfortunately, she returned the gesture, a tit for tat. She nailed me in the left temple. The force of her hit had me stumbling backwards, but I'd learned a few things since our last match and was back on my feet. As I approached, I whipped out my glowing blades, the tips slashing into the sides of her arms.

Some people got off on drugs. Estelle got off on trying to kill me.

She ignored the cuts that oozed black goo down her arms and threw an elbow toward me. I sliced downward, blocking her blow with my blade.

"Incoming," Declan hollered behind me.

Zane was suddenly beside me, solid and formidable. A hallow had snuck in close, preparing to rip me to bits. Darkness ate the ground at my feet, wrapping me in a cape of shadows. Gloom sprung from the pores in his hand, quickly disposing of the ghost.

Zane's eyes met mine. A thousand emotions and words transpired, our bond making it easy to decipher. *Be careful. I love you.* My eyes blinked, and he shot forward, onto the next hallow, leaving me with the queen of crazy sauce.

Panting, I circled her. We parried. She went left. I went right. And vice versa. On a subconscious level, I was aware of the fighting around me. Hallows. Hallows. Hallows. They were everywhere. Swarming and buzzing like killer bees. Crash, Zane, and Declan moved through them, one at a time.

When she made her next move, I was ready. Forget honor. Estelle fought dirty, and so did I. Bending a knee, I kicked out with my other leg, catching her in the gut. As she doubled over, I elbowed her in the back of the head. "If you know what's good for you, you'll stay down."

Fighting had become ingrained into my blood. I couldn't say when it happened. Maybe it had been there all this time and coming here, training with Zane, had unlocked some badass part of me I hadn't known existed. It sounded good.

The last person I expected to see popped up on the other side of Estelle. Crash grabbed onto his sister's arms and forced her to her feet. "Do it," he roared painfully at me.

Estelle screamed and in an oh-so-not-pretty way.

No hesitation. I lunged, arms glowing brightly, and lit her ass up. Her mouth dropped open in a silent cry. "Say hello to the other side," I said drily. I hoped to never see her face again.

Her body didn't explode in the usual burst of shattered light but slowly shriveled up until the only thing left was the drab and tattered dress she'd been wearing.

Well, that was new.

I didn't think much more of it as my eyes drank in the scene around me. If I hadn't witnessed the fight, I never would have known something horrible had occurred. Crash moved soundlessly to my side. "If we're keeping score, that's a point for me. I know you still don't trust me, but I think my actions today say something."

Zane frowned as he came to stand on the other side of me, his gaze staring out over the field. He was troubled.

"What is it?" I asked, moving closer to him

His body was still tense and firm for battle. "I don't know. Something's not right."

Joy.

I wasn't about to stick around and find out. Tugging on the end of Zane's sleeve, I let him know I was ready to skedaddle. It didn't take a whole lot of convincing once he looked down at my face and saw the exhaustion. "Come on. I'll drive," he said.

No argument from me. I gladly handed him the keys and sunk into the jeep, and I didn't bother to ask why we were heading in the opposite direction of the manor. It didn't matter as long as wherever he took me had a bed and him. All I needed was a couple of solid hours of sleep, but when we got back to Zane's, my restlessness made it difficult. My body was spent, but my mind was swirling with questions, buzzing and persistent. With my hand resting on Zane's steadily beating heart, I finally felt myself pulled under just as the sun was rising over the water.

CHAPTER 15

That night I dreamed.

I stood alone. The world surrounding me was barren, a wasteland. Dead bodies littered the grounds where trees, flowers, and grass once all grew and thrived. The air was dusty, stale and vile. It made my nostrils burn and my stomach pitch.

There was nothing to indicate I was in danger, yet my skin prickled with unease. I could have sworn a hundred pairs of eyes watched me, stalked me, hunted me. I was the prey, and the stampede was about to begin. Survival of the fittest.

My fight or flight response kicked in as I spun in a circle, eyes sharpening and taking in every detail, searching for any signs that I wasn't alone. Barefoot, my toes sunk into the burning sand. The unpleasant sensation brought my attention to my attire. *Why am I barefoot, and what the heck am I wearing?*

This had to be a dream, because I would never be caught dead wearing the one-shoulder white goddess dress that floated around me as the balmy breeze picked up. The flimsy material was like silk on my skin, such a stark contrast to the world around me. Bone fragments, sand, and dust swirled in the wind, embedding in the delicate fabric and tangling in my hair.

I shoved wisps out of my face, wishing for a hair tie, and began to walk. No matter how many steps I aimlessly took or how many minutes went by, the scenery never changed. It was like strolling in a loop. My frustration grew to anxiousness, turning to a bubble of panic inside that grew at an alarming rate. I closed my eyes and squeezed my fingers together, telling myself to wake from this nightmare.

When nothing happened and the sweat was still beading over my flushed skin, there was only one option. Unable to take the solitude a moment longer, I screamed.

The release was exhilarating, and with it went my edginess, my doubt, my uncertainty. I was calm. If something was out there, let them come. I could handle it.

I opened my eyes.

Nothing had changed, but it was as if I could see clearer. The sky was a weird orange, lacking any true sunlight, but the heat was insufferable. The windstorm waged on around me, but no longer hindered me.

"I wondered how long you would last," a feminine voice said. From within the sandstorm materialized a woman with long, wavy, flaxen hair. She was hard to see at first, her skin and hair blending with the sand, but as she emerged from the flurry, I was struck by her beauty. She pursed her rosebud lips. "You're stronger than you appear."

A goddess. It was the first thing that came to mind as I stared at the mystery woman. "I get that a lot," I replied, sizing this newcomer up. Was she a friend or foe?

Her laugh was sensual and inviting. "I'm glad to see the reaper wit hasn't been diluted down the line."

"Who are you?" I inquired. She chatted like we were old friends.

"Do you not recognize your own blood?" Her eyes studied my face. There was something very otherworldly about her—a glow to her skin, a familiarity I couldn't explain. "Huh." She commented in a way that made it sound as if she might have misjudged me at first glance.

The longer I stared at her, the better sense I got about her. There was an energy surrounding her I identified. "You're a banshee," I guessed.

Her facial expression changed, as if I had gravely offended her. "Not any banshee," she said with an air of importance. "I'm *the* banshee. Celeste."

I let her words soak in. "You're the original banshee?"

She gave a small bow, her skirt flowing and rippling out behind her. "In the flesh, daughter of my daughters."

I'd been able to converse with the dead before—Rose and Mom—but this was taking mediumship to a new level. "How is this possible?" I asked.

"Surely you know it's one of your gifts to communicate with White Ravens of the past."

I had known, but I'd assumed it was only banshees I knew in the world of the living, plus it never hurt to be overcautious. As far as I was concerned, anyone I didn't know was a threat. However, I couldn't deny a sense of kinship. "I only recently found out what I am. My abilities are just revealing themselves, but I knew it was possible to communicate with other banshees. I never expected to receive a visit from the original."

"Ah yes, that's right. You were brought up in the mortal world. No knowledge of who or what you are." She brushed a piece of hair off my face, sympathy and regret shining in her emerald eyes. "And I thought I had it bad. You've got your work cut out for you."

"What happened?" I asked, my gaze returning to the barren state of Earth.

She took a step back, spreading out her arms. "This, my daughter, is a warning, a premonition, if you will, of things to come if you do not seal the wards between realms. Your world will fall prey to the dead and, in the process, no longer exist. No mankind. No life. No reapers. Only death for all."

Talk about a Debbie Downer. Celeste didn't sugarcoat it; she laid it all out there. This was what we had to look forward to. Death. Destruction. Desolation. Doom. If there was even a sliver of a chance that this could be our future, I had to stop it. No ifs, ands, or buts about it. This couldn't be the future outcome of my world. "How do I prevent this?" I mean, there had to be a reason she had appeared to me in a dream. To help me, right?

In the back of my mind, a voice was telling me that would be too easy. Saving the world was rarely ever that simple. I wanted to tell that little annoying voice to jump off a bridge.

"If only I could tell you what must be done. It is forbidden by the laws of nature for the past to interfere. I can tell you restoring the veil will take a great sacrifice, just as it does to remove it, but the sacrifice is different for each. Mine would not be the same as yours."

What a relief. I wasn't willing to turn Zane into a hallow, as I suspected Heath had done with his daughter. But what did I have to sacrifice if not love? I couldn't believe that was all she had. Her information was basically useless. "There has to be a way," I insisted, refusing to wake up without something tangible. "Tell me what I must sacrifice. My firstborn child? What does the universe want?"

Celeste was petite like me, but the fact that she floated gave her an inch or two over me. "You know it is never that easy. Power doesn't come without a price. It is your blood that makes you capable of this trying task." Death knocked. But there was no one home. Earth was no longer a place for the living.

"I've given up my entire life. My mom. The father I grew up with. A friend. Rose. What do I have left? Nothing about being a banshee has been easy," I grumbled. *Didn't I deserve a break before I cracked?*

Pressure escalated in my chest, almost to the point of being unbearable. I was having something worse than a panic attack, and all I could think was this was entirely my fault.

"Don't fret. You have what many of us never did."

"What's that? Foolishness?" I was feeling particularly snarky.

She laughed. "I was talking about the death reaper, the other half of your soul."

My chin lifted at the mention of Zane.

"He offers you love, power, and courage. You will need all to defeat what is to come," she said softly.

Those were things I already knew. I was stronger with Zane. He had an aura about him that made me think I could do anything, even save the world. Chill bumps flew across my skin, and I grew cold. "What's out there?" I asked.

Her eyes followed mine beyond the horizon. "A graveyard. No hope. No happiness. No laughter. Nothing of life. Can you sense it?"

I nodded.

Tears glittered in her bright green eyes. "The ground is littered with the blood of millions and the tears of a million more. You might be feeling dejected and desperate, but Piper, daughter of my daughters, you have the strength to restore not only the veil, but also the broken order. I believe in you."

CHAPTER 16

I woke up to the drumming of rain on the roof. Feeling like one of the walking dead, I rubbed my bloodshot eyes, digging out the crusty eye boogies that had gathered at the corners. Not pretty. But that was nothing compared to what was going on inside my mouth. It tasted like something furry had crawled inside and died.

My first thought was to scamper out of bed, rush to the bathroom, and brush my teeth with a gallon of mouthwash. Anything to remedy the rancid taste on my tongue. Except as I pulled back the covers, I sensed something was wrong. I scanned the room. The walls weren't lavender and white, but gray and black. There was no cluster of makeup, no clothes haphazardly tossed on the floor, and the room smelled distinctively of male, in a very, very good way—the kind that had my ovaries buzzing.

Only one person gave me that butterfly, excited feeling.

A sleepy mumble drew my attention to the other side of the bed. In the light of day, he looked appealing, his hair rumpled from sleep. The tattoo of his reaper's scythe peeked out from under the covers that hung down by his waist. There was an old scar that ran down the center of his chest.

Memories rushed in. The attack. Estelle. The council. Crash. The dream. Celeste. I'd spent the night with Zane at the Hunters' house. There was something oddly reassuring about sleeping under the same roof as the Grim Reaper.

After the council meeting and the fight with Estelle and her ghostly gang, Zane had insisted I come home with him, where he could keep an eye on me. He wasn't taking any chances that Crash might make another unexpected visit, whom he'd promptly told to get lost. Crash seemed to be able to get around every defense Zane set up. It didn't bode well with Zane. If Crash was on my side, why was he continually cornering me alone? I had a feeling Crash was playing both sides.

Zane had sent Declan to the manor to watch over Parker and TJ. It was a relief; however, it had done little to quiet my overactive mind. I didn't know why he'd chosen his house over the manor. Maybe he wanted to sleep in his own bed, but since the night we slept together, neither of us could bear to sleep alone.

An indisputable fact: I loved Zane. All-encompassing. All-consuming. Now and forever. His love was going to protect me. Save me. Save us all.

I just didn't know how, yet.

As my brain became less jumbled and foggy, I remembered the vision of the future. It wasn't a memory I wanted to retain. The rain tapping against the windowpane made the dream that much more depressing.

Zane stretched beside me, pulling my eyes back to him. I no longer wanted to climb out of bed and would much prefer to stay snuggled up to his cool body, forget my problems, and forget the dream.

My hand was still resting over his beating heart, and I was comforted by the steady sound. He was alive. The world was spinning, but for how long? How much time did I have?

I thought about all we had been through to get here, causing a smile to cross my lips. It had been a bumpy road, and we hadn't always been civil to each other. There had been multiple times I'd wanted to drown him in the ocean, but he did have a few award-winning qualities.

He was a keeper.

I lay on my side, tucking my hands under my cheek, and watched him like a total creeper. The sheets were twisted at his waist, and his face looked almost angelic. Thick, black lashes fanned over his cheeks. It was hard to believe that I had bagged and tagged Zane Hunter. *Sigh.* If anything happened to him …

The fluttering of anxiety came back just as Zane's eyes began to move.

And then I was lost in a sea of deep blue. "Morning." His voice was raspy from sleep.

A smile swept across my face. "Hey, sleepyhead."

He roped an around my hips and pulled me to him. "I was almost afraid you wouldn't be here."

"Where else would I be?"

His lips drifted over the arch of my cheek. "It doesn't matter. You're here."

"I am. And there's nowhere else I'd rather be."

His eyes searched mine. "How are you dealing?"

"I'm not," I admitted, unable to stop staring at his lips. It took all my self-control to concentrate on what he was saying when all I wanted to do was kiss him. I wanted him to make me feel alive. I wanted him to evoke all the emotions my dream had lacked. Human emotions. Love. Pleasure. Desire.

His eyes darkened as he ran the pad of his thumb along my bottom lip. "Maybe I can help you … focus." He brought his lips to mine in a kiss that was sweet and tender.

It reached me everywhere. "Hmm. Things are starting to get a little clearer." I snaked my fingers into his rumpled hair. "Another kiss?"

"Anything I can do to help." He planted his lips on the hollow of my throat.

I shivered, pressing my forehead into his shoulder and inhaled deeply. The scent of him never got old—beachy, like my own personal island. "What would I do without you?"

"Let's never find out," he murmured.

"I like the sound of that." I drew him to my lips again, lingering over the taste of him. Things quickly went from hot to knock-your-socks-off hot. Needing to get closer, I climbed into his lap. I couldn't help it. He was so darn addicting. Wrapping my legs around his, I arched up, pressing myself against him, and a shudder rolled through Zane.

The kiss spun wildly out of control, and I was totally okay with it. His name tumbled from my lips as his fingers slid under my shirt.

He hissed in a breath. "I love hearing the way you say my name."

I rained kisses on his face, softly whispering his name between each, before fully pressing his to mine in a kiss that had my nerve endings humming. *I love you, Zane,* I said in my head. *So much it scares me.*

"Me too," he whispered in my ear.

My nails tightened on his neck. It was easy to forget our souls naturally aligned, especially with our guards down or when we were caught up in each other, as we were now. We could transmit our thoughts to one another through our soul connection. I must have done so without realizing.

Kinda hot and a tad frightening. Thank God all I had done was confess my love, instead of telling him what a delectable butt he had and how sometimes I wanted to just take a bite.

He brushed our noses. "Thanks, I think." He grinned, one side of his lips tipped up.

I buried my head into his shoulder. Voice muffled, I said, "You weren't supposed to hear that."

"I gathered as much." He planted a kiss on top of my head. "But I'm glad I did, and that I can hear what you're thinking. I want to know everything about you."

"Being with you makes me happy."

AT PRECISELY ELEVEN-THIRTY, I had my first cup of coffee in the Hunters' kitchen. I sat at the breakfast bar, feet dangling from the stool, watching Zane work magic in the kitchen. He was making us breakfast, or more like brunch. *How many other talents did he have?*

I was enthralled. His dark hair was freshly showered, and his blue eyes were bright. I could feel the happiness sparking off him, and it warmed my heart to know I was the cause. Sipping my sweetened coffee, I didn't want to dampen his spirits with an ominous dream.

He expertly flipped the omelet with one of those chef pan tosses you see on television. "I hope you're hungry."

"I don't usually eat breakfast," I replied.

The Hunters' kitchen was straight out of *Better Homes & Gardens*. There was this homey quality I missed: the smell of home-baked goods and the clutter of pots and pans hanging from a rack.

The toaster popped up four pieces of golden, slightly crispy toast. Just how I liked it. Before Zane had finished smothering on the butter, Zoe strutted in. She snatched a piece as she went to the fridge and poured herself a glass of orange juice.

Zane didn't even blink, adding four more pieces to the toaster.

Zoe was rockin' a messy bun on top of her head and a pair of purple skull boxer shorts. She had just rolled out of bed and looked super cute. I hated her.

"Someone have a sleepover?" she asked, taking a bite out of the whole wheat toast.

My cheeks colored. "I needed a change of scenery."

"Heard you had a rough day."

"Rough doesn't cover my days anymore. How's Parker?" I asked, tapping a nail on the side of my mug.

She swiveled in the stool beside me. "Mopey. Lost. Stubborn. Adorkable."

It was still weird thinking about Zoe and Parker being an item. He thought I was against their relationship because Zoe was a reaper, but that wasn't the case. It didn't matter who or what Parker dated. Sharing him wasn't something I'd ever had to do. I guess this was sort of how he had felt seeing me with Zane. I loved Parker, not in the way I loved Zane, but knowing Parker cared about someone as strongly as he did me, or stronger, was unsettling. I didn't want him to get hurt again, and maybe a small part of me was jealous. In my head, I knew there was room in his life for both of us, but my heart was afraid. "You really like him," I said, staring into my coffee.

She took another chunk out of the side of her toast. "What's not to like?"

Zane snickered. "I could think of a few things."

I shot him the stink eye. "I agree with Zoe; Parker has many redeeming qualities. You, on the other hand, have many questionable qualities."

He leaned over the counter, a smirk on his lips, and kissed me. "Those qualities are why you love me."

"Maybe."

Zoe made a gagging noise. "Gah, not while I'm eating."

I smiled. If only every day could be like this. My phone buzzed on the counter just as Zane placed three plates down. I picked it up, eyes narrowing at the name flashing on the screen. It was Crash.

We need to talk. Alone, the text said.

I'm not sure that's a good idea. I quickly responded, praying that would be the end of it. I wasn't so lucky.

Zane won't let you come out and play?

He was such an instigator. ***I just don't trust you.***

I have information that might be of use.

Do you know how impossible alone is these days? I texted back.

His response was immediate. ***Meet me at the docks in two hours.***

I sighed, knowing I was going to take the bait. Damn him. ***Fine. Don't make me regret this.*** The screen blinked to black.

CHAPTER 17

Not a single tourist among the boardwalk shops of Raven Hollow had any idea reapers were in their midst. If they did, if the truth of my origin was revealed, fear would radiate in their eyes. Mothers would keep their children close. People would avoid touching me, afraid of instant death. There were many fables surrounding reapers, good and bad, but what none of these people knew was the real terror wasn't us but the spirits who walked silently in our realm. At every corner, I expected to turn and come nose to nose with a hallow. I seemed to attract them like flies to horse shit.

It must be my perfume.

I meandered through the crowd, blending in to keep from drawing attention to myself. The last thing I wanted was to be recognized. I was safe within the crowd. Meeting Crash in such a public place was risky, but until I knew what team he was on, precautions must be taken. I was already putting myself in danger by leaving the manor unaccompanied.

I imagined Declan was having a shit fit right about now. The image brought a half-smile to my lips.

As I walked, the sun glittered on my skin, and the air smelled of cotton candy and classic hot dogs. The sights and sounds were lively and colorful, just like my life. Trotting down the rickety wooden stairs to the beach, I headed to a spot just under the docks where the boardwalk was still visible, yet offered privacy.

But as I rounded the corner, I came to a complete stop. Someone was following me.

A girl stood on the beach a few feet from where I'd come from, her head tilted skyward, soaking up the rays. It was her hair I recognized, even before my banshee sonar ability kicked in. The red strands glowed in the sunlight.

"Venus?" I said suspiciously. What was she doing here? I might have thought it was only a coincidence, until her gaze fell upon mine. Venus and I had never really had a proper conversation. Regardless, there was a mutual dislike between us that had everything to do with Zane.

Her almond-shaped eyes were encompassed in webs of black. "I followed you."

At least she was upfront about it—slightly disappointing. I'd sort of been looking forward to calling her out. "Why?"

She moved forward wordlessly, and the vibe coming off her was not friendly. "To warn you."

I didn't take too kindly to warnings, and I was just about to tell her so when she attacked.

She body-slammed into me with force, taking me by surprise. We went down into the low tide, the wet sand cushioning our landing. My brain hadn't caught up to the turn of events, and she was already moving on to phase two—the hair pull. She grabbed a wad of my hair and yanked my head back. I yelped. Not thinking clearly, I tugged in the opposite direction, making the pain amplify. *Smart move.* The sting brought tears to my eyes.

Christ, she had octopus arms.

No matter what I did, I couldn't get a grip on her, and to make matters worse, the tide was sucking us farther into the water. "What the hell is your problem?" I yelled right before an icy wave tumbled over us.

I drew in a sharp breath, but it was cut short. Her hand landed on my head, and she shoved, holding me under the cold water. I opened my mouth to scream and ended up swallowing a gulp of saltwater. My arms flailed against the cold, fighting to break free to the surface.

Shrieking, I clamored to stand up. Looking like a drowned cat, my clothing clung to my skin and water dripped down my face. "I'm going to kill you," I seethed, getting my feet secured in the sand. Waves continued to hit me from the side.

My threat on her life didn't faze her a bit. "I had to get your attention."

I shoved the hair sticking to my face to the side. "By attempting to drown me? You're freaking crazy."

"Thank you," she replied in all her supremeness.

I squeezed the water from my hair, not bothering to tell her that hadn't been a compliment. It would have been like talking to a brick wall. My hands shook. "You better have an exceptional reason why I shouldn't slap the reaper out of you."

Her long legs glistened with water, and even soaked to the bone, Venus looked beautiful. "Are you ready to listen?"

My eyes bounced from the water to Venus. Being wet and cold pissed me off, almost as much as being jumped for no good reason. "Not until you get out of my way."

She stepped aside, but I could feel her eyes stabbing me. Her cheeks were crimson with rage.

For a brief moment, I contemplated popping her right in her perky little nose. I wanted to draw blood almost as much as I wanted to get out of these wet clothes. I lumbered my way through the rocking waves caused by the nearby boats. The bottoms of my feet were raw, and I'd lost my flip-flops somewhere in the struggle. I could have kissed the shore, but even on steady ground, my heart wouldn't stop pounding.

She smiled sweetly, holding me with her stare. "Consider that a warning. Stay away from Zane. Do us all a favor: marry Crash."

I thought I was going to lose it right then and there. *Is she serious?* That leech had gone completely over the edge because she wanted Zane. Newsflash: he was never hers. Maybe for one hot second before I arrived, but the moment I'd stepped on the island, it was over. She couldn't hope to have a fragment of what Zane and I felt for each other. Our souls were intertwined. My response was a no-brainer. "I can't do that."

Her eyes snapped up as water lapped at her ankles. "Then you've issued your own death sentence."

Was I supposed to thank her for the gracious warning? "Did Heath put you up to this?" I asked, unable to disregard the facts. I had received a text from Crash to meet him and ended up getting ambushed by a jealous lunatic demanding I marry Heath's son. The whole thing stunk like the low tide.

"Does it matter?" she countered.

"You know I could strip you of your abilities for this."

A faint snicker sliced through the crackling air between us. "You don't have the guts."

Oh, boy. That was it. Underestimated once again. White-hot fury encompassed me. "The hell I don't." I snatched her wrist, and her eyes went wide with shock. Enjoyment filled my veins, joining the power trembling inside, cold and terrifying.

She swung her tormented gaze to mine and let out a feline yowl, but it did nothing to waver my command. There was only so much I could take, and Venus had made her choice, as I had mine. It needed to be known I wasn't going to be manipulated or disrespected. I wasn't an outsider any longer. They needed to accept that. It was my responsibility to maintain order, and that was exactly what I was doing.

Venus was a death reaper, but not a very good one. The soul power I drained from her was minuscule compared to someone like Zander. It still gave me a buzz as white lightning raced over my skin from head to toe.

When she was completely tapped out, she ripped her hand from my grasp, the silver charm at her wrist tumbling into the sand. Her eyes were bright and filled with angry tears. If I thought Venus hated my guts before, she despised me with a vengeance now.

I tipped my chin, meeting her violent gaze head-on. "Leave my island. And don't ever come back. If I see you, I will take more than your powers. I will make you beg for mercy until your throat is raw."

Cold anger crept into her eyes, turning them black. "You bitch." Her hand rose in the air, prepared to crack me across the cheek.

I caught her forearm inches from my face and kept my expression blank. "I've been called worse. You have twenty-four hours before I come looking for you. Is that clear?" Without any reaper abilities, she was weak—no match for me. Not that she ever was.

Venus collapsed to the ground. Those emotions of fury shattered into sparkling tears as the reality of her fate seeped in. She was no longer a reaper. She no longer had a home. And she most definitely didn't have what she came looking for. Zane.

Dropping my hands to my sides, I exhaled, my fingers tingling with energy. I turned around and stormed off the beach, leaving Venus on her knees, crying in the sand.

The sand squished between my toes as my legs carried me in purposeful strides toward the boardwalk. The hustle and bustle of the crowd hit me all at once as I trudged through the boardwalk's parking lot, water dripping from my clothes and cursing Crash under my breath. The happy-go-lucky vacationers thought I was nutso. Not only did I look like a drowned kitty, hair flat and soppy, I was mumbling to myself.

"Are you playing parking lot spy again?" said a familiar husky voice, cutting through my bleak thoughts.

Crap-a-cola. After my run-in with the jealous mongrel, I thought for sure Crash wouldn't have the balls to show his face. Obviously, I was wrong. So much for our undercover operation.

Ignoring the sharp pebbles digging into my feet, I turned around. There he was, shaggy hair the color of straw blowing with the ocean-front breeze. His Irish green eyes were sparkling with humor. My gut reaction was to throw a bunch of accusations at him for double-crossing me, but something held me back. "I don't *play* games," I replied, not in the best frame of mind. It wasn't lost on me that he'd implied I'd done the spy thing before.

"Why are you soaking wet? If you wanted to take a dip, you should have at least lost some of the clothes first. Not that I'm complaining. This look has a certain …" his eyes roamed over my body "… allure."

He would make the situation into something perverted. My clothes were plastered to my skin, revealing every curve. "Don't be an ass. I'm so not in the mood."

"I can see that. Care to share?"

"With you?" I snorted. "I'll pass. But more pressing, tell me, do you have a car?"

He leaned causally against the pier. Everything about Crash was lazy and carefree. "I might. Are you asking me for a ride, Princess?"

I bit my tongue. I wanted to tell him to go screw himself. Unfortunately, that wasn't going to get me where I wanted to go. Home. "Look, you say you want to help me, so this is your chance. I just got into it with that hood rat, Venus. And right now, all I want to do is go home and get out of these wet clothes."

He smirked. "Fine. But with one condition."

I frowned. "What's that?"

"You tell me what happened between you and Venus."

"Like you don't know."

His hand went to his chest. "Ouch, you wound me. What did I supposedly do now?"

"Shut up. You don't have emotions," I said.

He angled his head. "True dat. So, do we have a deal?"

"Just take me home, and then you're going to tell me why I should believe anything you have to say."

The look in Crash's eyes was bleak. "The manor isn't safe."

I crossed my arms. He was right, too many ears and eyes. "Okay," I agreed. "We'll go out."

The smile on his lips spread so fast. "Are you asking me on a date?"

He was the only guy I knew who could go from serious to flirty in a blink. "I'm two seconds away from planting my fist in your gut.

Another suggestion like that and I'll follow it with a kick to the balls." I flipped my hair in his face.

Crash's laugh was husky. "I love it when you talk dirty."

I shook my head, searching the lot for a car that had Crash's name written on it. Just what kind of vehicle would the rule-breaking, mellow, irresponsible Hawk drive? My bet was on the flashy red Scion.

He was suddenly at my other side, holding the door open for me. It wasn't the little sports car, but a black truck that had seen better days. The rust and dirt collecting on the bottom reminded me of my jeep. "Your chariot awaits," he said, leaning over the door. "Any chance you brought a towel? The seats are leather."

I glared and plopped my soaked butt directly onto his seat.

"All right then." He looped around the car and got in. "Buckle up, doll."

"Cut the cute nicknames. We're not a couple."

"Not yet," he said as the engine ripped to life. "But if my father gets his way, we'll be doing more than hand-holding and making out in the backseat."

I wrinkled my nose. "Don't make me vomit."

"So ..." he prompted, hanging an arm out the window. "What's the big to-do with you and Venus? She got her thong in a bunch because you're encroaching on her territory?"

"Are you *spying* on *me*?"

"Don't flatter yourself. I heard Venus ranting the other day at the club about you moving in on her man. She has a reputation for being delusional and clingy. Not to mention confrontational."

"Thanks for the heads-up. It would have been nice to know there was a psychopath plotting my demise. Might have come in handy," I mumbled.

Crash drove one-handed, a sly smirk on his lips. "God, I can't believe I missed that. If only I'd been five minutes earlier. There's nothing better than a chick fight."

He was warped. "You should try being on time for once."

Blink. Blink. Blink. The turning signal chimed on repeat as he waited for a break in the oncoming traffic. "Story of my life."

I fumbled with the rings on my fingers as he drove us to the west side of the island. It was a quiet affair. He stopped outside the gate leading to the manor. I was borderline shivering and never so happy to see the pristine palace. Before he could put the truck in park, my hand was on the door handle. "Hey, Crash," I said as I was about to swing my feet outside, "don't breathe a word of this to anyone. She won't be a problem anymore."

He cast me a look of intrigue. I hadn't admitted what I'd done, but Crash understood. His eyes said and comprehended too much. "My lips are sealed," he assured me.

Call me crazy, but I didn't believe him. Shaking my head, I made a beeline toward the back of the house. I didn't get very far before the ranks swarmed me.

Declan shadowed my steps. "Where have you been?"

A crow squawked over my head, a message to the others. I was no longer missing. "I went for a swim."

"In your clothes?" he asked, calling me out for what it was: a bold-faced lie.

I rolled my eyes. "It was a spontaneous decision. Don't you ever have them?"

"You know you're not supposed to go anywhere without an escort."

"Sue me. I needed some space." I stopped and spun around. "And Declan, since you need to know my constant whereabouts, I'm taking a shower. Think a girl can shave her legs in peace?"

The mere mention of any body part made Declan squirm. I found it hilarious and used it to my advantage. He stared at me. I started shedding clothes, wiggling the button on my jeans. That was Declan's cue to exit. He grumbled some response about being in the hall if I needed anything.

As soon as the door clicked closed behind him, I dropped my pants and peeled the shirt off my back. Being wet sucked. My skin looked like a raisin, wrinkly and purple.

Tearing through my dresser, I grabbed clean clothes. After a quick towel-off and a bathroom visit, I stood in the bedroom with the shower running. There, that should give me a few minutes. I never thought I would have to sneak out of my own house. Tiptoeing across the room, I grabbed my backpack and slipped it on. A jab hit me in my stomach: guilt for running out on Declan a second time. It couldn't be helped. If there was a chance, even the slimmest, that Crash knew something, I needed to hear what it was, because currently, I had nothing.

Flipping over the side of the balcony, I felt like a thief in the night. I used the impending nightfall to my advantage, as well as borrowing a bit of Zane's shadows to disguise me from the ground's guards. Zane would feel me link our souls, but I would deal with the backlash later. He wasn't the only one who acted first and left the consequences for later.

I climbed down the trellis, careful not to miss a step and plummet two stories in the most epic fail of my life. I breathed a sigh of relief when my feet touched the ground. Boom. Home run. I disliked breaking promises, but with the world's future at stake, I didn't see how I had much of a choice.

Staying flush against the exterior of the manor, I inched my way to the rear of the building. There was a section of rocks, more like small cliffs, that dropped off to the beach. The bluff was about a six-foot jump, but it wasn't the first time I'd taken the plunge. It fulfilled the hidden daredevil inside me.

I didn't wait around. Once my feet hit the sand, I was gone, backtracking to where Crash's truck was idling. The lights were killed. A part of me expected him to have flown the coop. It was easier to believe the worst in him than to believe he had a heart or a conscience. Yet, for reasons I could not explain, my intuition was to give him a chance.

I slipped into the passenger seat and dropped my bag onto the carpeted floor. The radio was on low, and Crash was thumbing the steering wheel in beat with the drum solo to "Cherry Bomb." His gaze slid to mine. "Are you sure you weren't a ninja in another life?"

"I can't tell if you are being serious or a shithead. I'm going with both."

"Since the docks have been compromised, where to?"

Throwing my hair into a messy bun, I said, "Anywhere that serves hot coffee by the gallons … and no one knows me," I added.

He hit the gas. "I like a challenge."

CHAPTER 18

I gazed out the window, watching the sun sink behind the water's edge. No matter where you were on the island, the sounds of waves could be heard, along with the cawing of crows, sparrows, and hawks. It was the elusive White Raven that was a sight to behold. Rare. Beautiful. And mysterious.

I didn't ask Crash where we were going. Instead, I sat back in the seat, took a moment to close my eyes, and let my mind wander. As it normally did when I wasn't stressing over saving the world, I thought of Zane. The strain of the extra work was starting to wear on everyone.

"Mind if I smoke?" Crash asked, interrupting my worry-fest.

I folded my hands in my lap. "Since when do you ask?"

"Very true." He pulled a box out of the cup holder and lit up a cigarette.

"You should quit, you know."

"Cancer?" He took a drag and blew out a ring of smoke. "Don't worry. Reaper benefit."

"That's not what I meant. It's disgusting. Girls don't want to suck face with an ashtray."

Crash grinned in the rearview mirror as he checked traffic behind us. "Does this mean you're rethinking my offer?"

I gave him a funny look.

"To sleep with me," he said, filling in the blanks.

My knee-jerk reaction was to hit him. So I did, on the side of the arm.

He winced, flicking his half smoked cigarette out the window. "You don't hit like a girl."

"Good. Maybe you'll remember that the next time you think to open your mouth and say something that has anything to do with sex."

He opened his mouth, and then closed it.

I couldn't help but smile. In a jerky way, Crash was fun. Zane wouldn't agree, and remorse wormed its way in me for having a second of small, senseless fun. "Where are we going?" I sighed.

"Keef's Reef."

"Never heard of it."

He grinned. "That's the point, lu—" His voice cut off, clearly thinking twice about calling me another endearment that would have earned him an added bruise.

Keef's Reef was a dive, and that was putting it nicely. I don't know why I expected anything less from Crash. The two-story building was weathered and definitely not a place I would have ever ventured to on my own. There were missing pieces of blue cedar shakes on the rundown house turned bar. The parking lot was gravel, and there was a sand pit in the back with a volleyball net on the verge of falling over. Motorcycles lined the front of the building, forming an L shape along the side.

"You brought me to a bar."

"Yep. You won't find a single reaper here besides us."

"Maybe, but our chances of being mugged or assaulted are probable," I mumbled. I knew joints like this. The crowd was rough, and it was no place for an eighteen-year-old girl. I was beginning to regret my decision to trust Crash.

His lips moved into a barely-there grin. "You're a banshee with more strength in your pinky than these guys have in their entire bodies. Don't ever forget it."

His words resonated inside me. As much as I thought I had moved on and accepted who I was, a piece of me was still holding onto my old life. The fears and worries of being human were no longer of my concern. *Tell that to my brain.*

I wiped my palms on my jeans, taking an almost steady breath. "This better be worth my while," I said, staring at Keef's Reef.

Dim track lighting lined the edge of the ceiling and went over the multiple pool tables. Cigar smoke as thick as the early morning fog clouded the low ceiling. The room reeked of dirty men and booze, a combination that made my stomach turn over. Nestled on the outside walls were rows of bar stools, most unoccupied.

I followed closely behind Crash as he weaved between the pool tables toward the rear corner. If the patrons thought it odd that we by chance stumbled into their establishment, they didn't show it. My guess was that Crash was a frequent visitor.

With a tilt of his head, he motioned at an empty table. I boosted myself up onto the barstool and crossed my legs. The accommodations might not be a five star restaurant, but the service was quick. A waitress shimmied over to our table. She had saggy boobs, a shirt too tight and too short, and red heels that made my feet hurt by just looking at them. Jackie, her crooked nametag revealed, winked at Crash. He gave her a half-cocked smirk and ordered us each a Long Island Iced Tea.

"I'll just have coffee, black, no cream or sugar," I corrected. I needed a stiff drink, but not one that would make my brain fuzzy.

Jackie lifted a brow. "How about I bring both? Just in case."

As she turned toward the bar, I rolled my eyes.

Crash tipped his head sideways as if to study me from a different angle. "I pegged you for a party girl."

"That was in the past," I replied firmly. "I'm not that girl anymore. I hope your plan wasn't to get me drunk."

"I wouldn't dream of it," he said around a smile.

Keeping my expression impassive, I cut to the chase. "What have you learned?" I asked firmly.

He dropped a bombshell. "I think I know how to reestablish the barrier."

I was afraid to hope. This was Crash, after all. We hadn't exactly been on the best of terms, always yo-yoing between flirting and fighting. "If this is one of your games, I'm not interested in playing."

Any smirk left on his face slid away. "As hard as it is to believe, I can be serious when it counts."

I gave him a droll look.

He dragged a thoughtful hand across his jawline. "Fine, but unless you have another plan up your sleeve ..."

He knew I didn't, otherwise I wouldn't be sitting here drinking bad coffee. "I'm listening, but it better be worth my while."

"My father was at the club, holding one of his typical long, boring meetings. He was yammering on about the injustice of his position and how he is tired of other reapers regarding him as less than the shit on their shoes—his standard complaints. No one respects him. He isn't given enough credit. He deserves to be more than a low man on the totem pole. Blah, blah, blah. Normally by this time, I've completely checked out of the lecture."

"Is there a point to this long, drawn-out story?" I interrupted.

Jackie had returned with our drinks. Crash downed half his glass before continuing. "I heard him speak about a relic."

My ears perked up. Finally, we were getting somewhere. I leaned forward on the table, not touching my so-called tea, but going straight for the good stuff.

His voice lowered into confidential levels. "He believes the banshees have kept this relic hidden for centuries. Before now, there had never been a need for such power, no reason to seek it out. It has been secret for so long many don't give any value to the story—that it even exists—but my father is leaving nothing to chance. If it does exist, it is in the manor."

"And he wants you to find it," I added. I was afraid I knew just how Heath planned to ensure his son access.

Crash nodded. "If we marry, it would give me the perfect opportunity to search the estate."

Son of a gun. I ignored the queasiness tap dancing in my belly at the mention of Crash and I tying the knot. "What does he plan to do with this relic if he finds it?" I didn't bother mentioning there was no way in seven hells I was marrying him. The council was going to have to kidnap me, drug me, and cuff me to the altar.

"I don't know. Nothing maybe. I think the goal is to make sure you can't get your hands on it. It's important enough for him to go to great lengths to guarantee it doesn't fall into your hands."

"If this is true and it does exist, what will he do if he finds out you helped me?" The impulse to protect poured through me.

"Ahh. That's sweet. You're worried about me."

I sat back in my chair. "I did not say that."

"You don't need to. I've always been the family screwup. It was Estelle who was my father's protégé. He told me at least once a day how he wished Estelle had been his firstborn, and it was her who could be his successor."

"I'm sorry." The words left my mouth before I thought about what I was saying. I had a bad habit of apologizing, even when I had nothing to be sorry for.

"I told you not to feel sorry for me. I don't want your pity." Crash tipped back the remaining half of his drink. "To make matters worse, he is right now pushing the council to insist we marry before the end of the month."

I gaped. "That's in … two days. He can't possibly be serious."

He dropped bomb after bomb. "Father doesn't believe in procrastination. Once an idea takes root, he expects immediate action. He's petitioning the council to forego the traditional engagement period due to the grim situation the world now finds itself in."

What bullshit. We wouldn't be in this grave predicament if it weren't for Heath. "Do you think the council will agree to what he's suggesting?"

His somber eyes said it all. "I do."

My heart dropped as the ground slipped out from underneath me.

I planted my hands on the table to keep from falling out of the seat. Everything was moving too fast, spinning out of my control. As soon as I thought I had a handle on being a banshee, things went south. I was going to pass out. "No," I breathed, forcing my lungs to work. "We can't let that happen."

His eyes engaged in concern, and he laid a hand over mine. "You okay?"

Okay? *Okay?* I didn't think I was ever going to be okay again. I let out a manic laugh. "I haven't been okay in a long time."

"Welcome to the real world, Princess."

My gaze went to his hand resting over mine. His touch was light, but sturdy. Crash didn't have the physical strength Zane did, but he wasn't someone I'd regard as weak. He was more calculating in his moves.

"You going to drink that?" he asked.

I shook my head and pushed the untouched Long Island across the table.

He took the straw and dunked it up and down, mixing the drink. Ice clanged against the glass. "I keep expecting the Death Scythe to come barreling through the doors and threaten to end my existence for merely being in the same breathing space as you."

"You and I both." I uncrossed my legs, letting them dangle, and snuck a glance at the door. "So now that we know about this relic, what do we do?"

"Well, I figure we have two options. We buy us some time. You and I get married, and I continue to let my father think he has an inside man as we hunt for the relic."

I made an ugly face.

Crash gave me an eerie stare. "Or you have two days to find it before the Kraken descends on us, forcing us both into a commitment neither of us wants to make."

Either way, we had to find the relic before Heath got his hands on it. I shuddered to think what he might be capable of with such ancient power. We had no idea if it was even capable of restoring the veil, but I was leaving nothing to chance. I picked through the tangled thoughts in my head, trying to piece together what I wanted to say. "I choose option C."

Crash leaned back. "And what might that be?"

My jaw twitched. "I haven't figured it out yet. Hell, I haven't figured out if I even believe you, but when I do decipher this mess, you'll know."

He tapped on the black band covering his wrist. "The clock is ticking."

"Thanks, captain obvious." The back of my neck tingled, growing with each passing breath. I opened my mouth to let Crash know we were no longer alone when a dark shadow towered over the table.

Here comes the fireworks.

CHAPTER 19

Crash kept his eyes fixed on my face. "Care to join us for a drink, Death Scythe?"

A whoosh of air blew past my face. I blinked, and the chair where Crash had been sitting was now empty, but not for long. Two seconds later, it was occupied by an extremely menace-looking Zane.

His dark eyes were flaming hot. "What are you doing here?"

"Uh, drinking coffee," I replied, taking a sip from my cold mug. *Smooth Piper.* I wanted to kick myself. This was Zane. Pissed off or not, he was the one person I trusted most in the world. I should have told him that Crash contacted me. Knowing that he was going to be angry was a whole lot different than seeing it … feeling it.

There was a phantom quality about him tonight. "What happened to not ditching your guards? Twice in one day, Piper?"

I flinched. "It was critical."

"So is keeping you alive. I thought we'd been over this and you agreed," he reminded me, though it was unnecessary.

I sighed, hating the disappointment in his voice. "I did. I don't do well with boundaries."

"She's fine," Crash intervened, appearing at the side of the table. "No need to slap her wrists. Not a hair out of place."

"Shut up," Zane and I said in unison.

Crash dusted off his jeans, scowling. "You guys really are in sync. Cute," he said drily.

"Leave," Zane advised in a low threat. "Before I make a new exit with your body."

Green eyes narrowed. "So much hostility. Forever is a long time, Piper."

Zane growled, and the chairs surrounding us began to shake.

Luckily for everyone here, Crash didn't push his luck. He grabbed his keys and the last half of his drink from the table. "I'll be in touch," he said to me and left.

The thick cords of muscles in Zane's back bunched with tension, waiting to be unleashed. He was throwing off waves of power that distorted the air between us. I wrapped my fingers with Zane's, bringing his piercing eyes to me. "Let him go," I murmured, watching Crash saunter out the front door.

It wasn't until the door swung closed that Zane's body loosened. "I hope you know what you're doing."

Me too. I cleared my throat. "We might have our first lead."

Zane went rigid. "Why in the world would you trust anything he has to say?"

I swallowed, knowing Zane's reaction was going to be epic. As quickly as I could, I relayed everything Crash had told me.

"It sounds like a trap" was the first thing out of Zane's mouth when I finished.

"I know, but it's worth checking out. Have you ever heard of such a relic?"

His lips slipped into a frown. "No." Curiosity replaced his expression. "He's probably sending us on a wild goose chase to keep us from finding a *real* solution."

"Could be, but what other choice do we have? I can't disregard it." *And here comes the kicker.* "He wants to help us search."

Zane's head whipped up so fast, I thought he was going to fall out of the chair. "Say what?"

I leaned back. "I get that it's not an ideal situation."

"You mean, he wants us to do the dirty work so he can take all the glory when he double- crosses us and hands it over to Heath."

"I've got two days, Zane. I don't care if the devil himself wants to help. Unless you *want* to see me married to Crash."

Zane's eyes turned feverish. "Don't go there. You know how I feel."

I did. And that's what made this so hard. The last thing I wanted to do was fight. I needed him. More than ever. "I'm scared," I admitted, wrapping my hands around my coffee mug. I needed something to do with my hands, because despite my awesomeness and Zane's killer instincts, there was one thing we hadn't been able to do, and the failure was tearing me up inside. Neither of us wanted to trust Crash, but what else did we have to go on?

Since the dream with Celeste, I couldn't shake the feeling the worst had yet to come. It wasn't going to be pretty. Each second that went by was wasted time I couldn't afford.

Zane's chest rose and fell. "If you weren't afraid, I would question your sanity. There's only one thing to do."

I turned my head to the side. "And what's that?"

He thrust his fingers though his hair, but his expression was a blank mask. "I'm getting to it. My father told me about the emergency meeting."

"Oh." Death was one of the council members. He would have been summoned. "And?" I was dying to know the outcome but at the same time scared out of my mind. I tried to convince myself it didn't matter what they decided. Nothing anyone could say would make me go down the path of arranged marriages again. Been there. Done that.

The depths of his sapphire eyes darkened. "Majority ruled you would marry the Hawk's heir in two nights."

The air in the bar was already thick with smoke, but it became unbearable, pressure clamping down on my chest and my lungs overtaxed with the simple effort of taking in air.

"I. Can't. Breathe," I gasped.

Zane was at my side in a blink, murmuring my name. "Hey, I'm not going to let that happen." His fingers ran down my hair, pulling my face against his chest.

There was an instant stream of tranquility flowing through my veins, the mounting panic attack receding. I wanted to lose myself in the comfort he offered and the outdoorsy scent of his shirt. Steady as a rock, he wasn't going to let me fall apart. He wasn't going to let anything happen to me. I tipped my head back, staring at him. "You're not, huh?"

He reached over, threading his fingers with mine. "Never. I'm going to spend every second of every day of every year with you. The only person you're marrying is me. You got that?"

I rolled my eyes, not taking him seriously, but it didn't stop my heart from cartwheeling. "Whatever you say."

He tugged at the end of my hair. "You're adorable."

I bumped our noses. "You're weird."

A lopsided grin appeared on his face. "True, but I was being serious." A glint of purpose lit his eyes. He was up to something, and it was a welcomed distraction: figuring out how Zane's mind worked.

"Are you-u …? Did you-u …?" The words wobbled from my mouth. There was a different kind of heaviness elevating in my chest.

He tipped his head to the side, silky strands of dark hair falling across his forehead. "Piper?"

Time stopped. Even my heart seemed to have halted. Was he asking what I thought? I wasn't sure. All I could do was stare at him with my mouth dropped open. No way did Zane Hunter just ask me to marry him. Did he? The idea had come out of nowhere, not that I hadn't thought about him asking me to marry him a hundred different ways. "What did you say?" It hadn't been a question, but more of a thought, or a statement. I needed him to clarify what he meant before my heart leapt out of my chest.

His lips curved, and he dropped down to one knee, right there on the bar floor along with the discarded peanut shells and dried spilled beer. "I never imagined I would be proposing in a place like Keef's Reef."

I blinked. "Proposing?" I echoed, my heart doing a series of flips.

He stood, tossed some money on the tabletop, and tugged me to my feet. "Come on. We can do better than this."

"Where are we going?" I asked as he dragged me out of the bar and ushered me outside. A million stars dotted the sky like sparkling diamonds. I lifted my face, letting the brisk breeze cool my flushed cheeks.

I got the silent treatment.

Two could play that game. He couldn't dangle something like marriage in my face and then go all mysterious. I planted my feet, digging them into the ground. Zane threw a glance over his shoulder, and I angled my head. "I'm not going anywhere until you tell me where you are taking me. What was that back there?"

He shook his head. "You would make this difficult." Dipping his shoulder, he planted his hands on my waist and hoisted me over his shoulder.

Oomph. The air rushed to my head, my hair fell out of its bun, dangling near the floor. I struggled, making it harder for him to keep his hold on me as his long strides ate up the ground. "Have you gone mental?" I couldn't understand his actions.

He gave my bottom a swat. "If you'll just settle down ..."

Oh, I was past reasonable and had leapt to full-fledged crazy. "I might, if you put me on my feet."

"No can do, Princess."

We'll see about that. A chill circulated through my blood and shadows shrouded us from any prying eyes. He couldn't possibly get around the island like a normal person. Why would you when you had shadows to do your bidding, shadows that could shield you and transport you from place to place?

After everything I'd learned tonight, my emotions were running high. It was the only reasonable explanation for my actions. Energy accumulated at my fingertips, and I sent a jolt of power through his clothes, like an electric shot. Mild, of course. Not enough to hurt, only to get his attention.

He chuckled and set me down on my feet but kept my hand in his. "Did you just zap me?"

"You weren't listening," I replied and then took a moment to look around. We were in a small chapel, beautiful stained glass windows casting rainbows of light over the hardwood floors. White pillar candles scented the air in vanilla and lit the dark corners. "What's this?"

Our fingers were still intertwined, and he turned my hand over. "There's one way to prevent you from marrying Crash. We're getting married," he stated, like it was any other day of the week.

CHAPTER 20

My chest squeezed. Holy moly. "You're serious?" I replied. "Do I need to give you a Breathalyzer test?"

His grin widened. "I'm not drunk, Princess. I'm in love. With you."

I wasn't dreaming. This moment was real. He'd gone from on his knee to sweeping me away to a church. "And you want to get married? Right now?" My voice came out in a squeak.

"Not this second. Five minutes good for you?"

Five minutes? He wasn't joking, but he was crazy. I glanced down at my attire. "I can't get married like this!" Ripped jean shorts and a white lace halter was not the beaded gown I'd always envisioned. "I look like a hot mess."

Slowly his hands went around my waist. "You look beautiful to me."

My heart melted. And what did it matter how I looked? I'd never wanted a big, flashy wedding. I had everything I ever wanted standing in front of me—someone who loved me unconditionally. Someone who vowed to always protect me. And now he wanted to give me his love forever. It honestly couldn't have been more perfect, even with the caveman style he had brought me here with. Zane had flare—his own—and it worked for me.

"You know you didn't have to drag me to the altar. I would have come willingly."

His lips tilted at the corners. "Yeah, but this was more fun."

I rolled my eyes.

"Now we have an interesting story to tell our children during Thanksgiving dinner."

This was really happening, and my heart was going super fast. "What about the council?"

"We need to act immediately," Zane replied. "The council can't get wind of our marriage, not until after. The less people that know, the safer we are. If the council found out ..."

He didn't need to say anything more. The council had been very adamant in their displeasure at my marrying someone without pure reaper blood. How could something so right be wrong?

I might be young, but I knew what I wanted. And I'd wanted Zane since the moment I'd laid eyes on him at the docks. It was a memory I'd never forget—the way the sunlight hit his face, the smirk that crept over his lips. But mostly, the feelings he enticed. I didn't know it then—how deep our connection was; I only knew he made my knees weak and my body feel things it had never felt. "Will it be enough? Will it be legit?" I asked. "Make no mistake, there is nothing I would love more in this world than to be your wife. I need to know that it will be for real. If I lost you ... I couldn't handle it."

The pad of his thumb ran over my bottom lip. "You'll never lose me."

Easy to say, and I only hoped it would be true. Life constantly threw curveballs when you least expected. Like me getting married today. I couldn't believe we were having this discussion, rationally talking about getting hitched. It was a contract, in essence, to love, to honor, and to obey. I wasn't sure about the obey part, but I would love him with all that I had. "Does this mean you've thought about Aspyn's idea?" *The one where you knock me up,* I silently added.

"I've thought about it," he said softly. "You still haven't given me an answer. Piper, will you marry me?"

A ridiculous grin crossed my lips, and I looped my arms around his neck. "I thought it was obvious. Yes, I'll marry you, Zaney." If given the opportunity, we wouldn't be rushing into this, but the outcome would always be the same. What did it matter if it was this week or next year?

"We're getting married," he said, wonder and bewilderment in his voice.

Now that was more of the reaction I expected from him. Emotions clogged my throat. "I love you. I will always love you."

I glanced around the room, memorizing the shape, the smell, and the feeling inside that I'd never be able to duplicate. "What do we do now? Don't we need an officiant or something?"

"It's all been taken care of. We have the two most important ingredients: you and me. And a marriage license."

I buried my face into his chest, hugging him. "That was so cheesy. I loved it."

An amused smile lit his face. "I have my moments." He bent down and brushed his lips along my temple before holding out his arm. "Ready?"

I hooked my arm through his. "Lead the way, fiancé." Wow. That was weird on the tongue, and in half an hour, I would be calling him my husband. The quickest engagement in history.

As we started toward the altar, Death walked into the room.

Of course. It made perfect sense. Zane's father was an overlord. He had the station to perform the sacred ceremony as well as the traditional one. How many people could say the Grim Reaper married them?

His white beard was trimmed neatly, and his blue eyes sparkled with mischief, a look I'd seen in his son countless times. "I was beginning to think you weren't coming."

"Well, he did have to carry me here," I said.

Death let out a belly-shaking laugh. "Oh, Piper, welcome to the family." He opened his arms wide.

It was a bear hug like no other, gruff and tender. That pretty much summed up Zane's father. "Thank you," I replied.

Roarke cleared his throat and gave me a pat on the back. "We should begin," he encouraged us, moving to stand directly in the center of a circle painted on the floorboards.

The details of the room came to my attention. I had failed to notice them before. There were glowing rune-type markings covering the raised platform and up on the pillars lining the aisle. My hand tightened on Zane's arm as we took our places in front of his father. In a few minutes, we were going to be husband and wife. Come hell or high water, this marriage was happening, and damn anyone who stood in our way, who tried to separate us.

"Tonight we celebrate," Roarke said in a booming voice.

Zane and I both burst out in laughter. It must have been the nerves, because I was having a hard time taking Death seriously as an ordained officiant.

Roarke looked at his son. "I guess we can skip the traditional ceremony and get straight to the vows. We are, after all, under a time restraint. Take her hand."

We didn't have any vows written, so we were winging it. Zane appeared a little nervous for the first time tonight. He took my hands, but not before he blew out a breath.

I looked into Zane's eyes. Oh my God. This was really happening. I told myself not to cry.

In a velvety voice, Roarke began again. "You will each say the vows of commitment."

"I, Zane Hunter, promise to stand by your side and sleep in your arms. I will risk my life for yours. I will die for you. There are only so many ways I can tell you how much I love you, but I vow to show you every day. We shall bear together whatever trouble and sorrow may lie upon us. You will never be alone. Even in death, our souls will find each other. I let you go once; I won't do it again, Piper. I can't lose you. Never." His accent came across, punctuating his words, heavy and lyrical. It was beautiful. He was beautiful. "I marry you and bind my life and soul to yours."

How was I supposed to top that? Silent tears slipped down my cheeks. These weren't just words. He meant every one of them from the bottom of his heart. This was one of those moments I wished I had on videotape. Too bad I didn't vlog. I wanted to capture every second, bottle these feelings inside me.

I swallowed, tightening my fingers on his. *No more tears.* It was my turn. "I, Piper Brennan, promise to be your partner in crime. I promise to share hopes and dreams with you as we build our lives together, assuming the world is still standing."

A laugh escaped Zane, and Death only shook his head.

"I marry you with no hesitation and with my whole heart. My commitment to you is absolute."

Death pulled out a slim blade. "Now we will join your bloodlines."

I looked at the sharp tip of the knife, and my stomach got a bit queasy. *You are not going to faint at your own wedding.* "It's a good thing I don't pass out at the sight of blood," I said right before Roarke poked the tip of my finger with the end of the blade. I jumped, but the sting was gone and forgotten when I lifted my gaze.

We pressed our fingers together, mixing our blood. There was an instant jolt of power, followed by a cool tingle. I stared mesmerized by our joined hands. I'd seen our veins glow together before, especially when our souls merged, but this … it was something truly magical. It made me dizzy with happiness.

"Together you will repeat after me," Roarke said. "From this point, we form an eternal and sacred bond. The promises and ties made today will greatly strengthen our union and will cross into this life and the next, bound by our souls."

In unison, Zane and I stared into one another's eyes as we recited the words of our blood oath. I had never felt closer to anyone as I did in this moment, not even when we had joined bodies. This was a different kind of intimacy.

"You are now bound eternally to each other. Do you have the ring?" Roarke asked.

Zane reached into the pocket of his jeans and pulled out a platinum band. He slid the ring onto my not-so-steady finger and lingered. The look on his face was almost bashful, but his voice was smooth. "With this ring, I vow from this day forward that your love is my anchor, your trust is my strength. May my heart be your shelter and my arms be your home."

Tears blurred my vision. "You had this planned, didn't you?" I whispered, unable to take my eyes off his. For a spontaneous wedding, he had all the elements.

"Let's just say I was optimistic. It crossed my mind a time or two since the council made the foolish decision to join your bloodline with Crash's. I can't bear to see you with anyone else. You've turned me into a jealous maniac. We've got nothing to lose and everything to gain."

I turned my hand from side to side, admiring the beautiful scroll wrapping around the ring. I had no idea what it said, but it was the most exquisite piece of jewelry I owned, and I would treasure it always. "What took you so long?" I asked, lifting my damp lashes.

He wiped a tear from my cheek. "Some things need to age, like good wine."

I couldn't stop smiling. "See, I knew you were drunk."

He laughed, tucking my hair behind my ear. Zane's gaze was locked on me as he leaned down and pressed his lips to mine. He had kissed me a hundred times before, but none was like this. Fireworks exploded inside me as his kiss reached farther than just my lips. I swore he branded my soul, and he might very well have, considering our unique connection.

Death cleared his throat a second time. "I don't think I said you could kiss your bride yet."

"Well, hurry up and say it, old man," Zane murmured, his lips hovering over mine.

"I now pronounce you husband and wife. You may kiss your …"

Zane's lips were already on mine, and I'm pretty sure my heart exploded.

"… bride." Death sighed.

My arms were secured around him with a permanent smile on my lips. I was floating on air, never so elated in my life. I was someone's wife, not just anyone's, but Zane's. With misty eyes, I gazed up at him and whispered, "I love you." We. Actually. Got. Married. No one busted through the doors to object.

His hand lingered at the curve of my neck. "Let's go home, Mrs. Hunter."

I almost tripped over my feet. *Home.* Oh God. Zane was moving into the manor. "We need to tell TJ and Parker."

He leaned down and pressed his cool lips to mine. "We will, after," he murmured. "The rest of the night is about us."

Oh man. I liked the sound of that. If only he had been right.

CHAPTER 21

The Red Hawk overlord stood before me, arrogant in his stance, silver eyes hard as steel. He wore a long black coat that billowed behind him, accenting his pale skin and emphasizing the crimson veins glowing under his eyes. Like the devil himself, he stalked toward me, murder shining in the depths of his treacherous gaze. Greed coiled around him like the wings of a fallen angel, spreading wide as his lips curled.

I lunged forward, thinking this was it. This was the moment I'd been waiting for: the chance to avenge the asshole that had killed my entire family. As we moved, his arms mutated, making them tentacles of sorts, like an octopus. He wrapped them around me, holding me off the ground.

"You came," he crooned in a smooth voice that gave me goose bumps. "I didn't think you had the guts."

I frowned, tipping my chin. "I want my brother." I also wanted to gouge his eyes out.

"He is yours for a simple trade," he replied, running a hand through my hair in a creepy, old dude vibe.

My feet dangled in the air, but otherwise I was motionless. "What is it you want?"

He moved closer. "I only want one thing. Power. Your power."

I shook my pounding head, trying to fight against his binds, but the tentacles held me fast. "No! I can't do it. This is wrong." Something was off. I couldn't pinpoint what, but I didn't feel right. Beside the thumping temples, my head was fuzzy, as if I'd been drugged.

"You've just issued your brother's death sentence," Heath said.

The words *go to hell* were on the tip of my tongue when something pulsed in my hand. It was a blade, radiating white. With a banshee cry, I raised my arm and plunged the tip into Heath's chest, sinking the knife into his heart.

The overlord staggered backwards, his mouth open in shock and horror. Only … as I stared into his eyes, the satisfaction of killing him turned my blood to ice, for it wasn't Heath's eyes I was looking into. It was Zane's bright starlight blue. Cloaked in darkness, the shadows surrounding him faded as he swayed on his feet.

"Christ," I whispered. "Zane … oh God." I repeated the phrase of sheer shock and disbelief a few too many times.

"Piper," he murmured, his shaky hand reaching out and his eyes beseeching me. Thin droplets of blood trickled from his mouth. The blade was still stuck into his chest.

I stepped back, shaking my head back and forth. *No. No. No.*

"Why?" he wheezed, wrapping a hand around the hilt of the knife as he fell to the ground.

I thought I was going to die, right alongside him of a broken heart. Never in a gazillion years would I have hurt him. This had to be a trick. My heart was roaring in my ears as I sunk to the ground and that was when I noticed the blood covering my hands. Zane's blood.

"Don't die," I told him, running a hand over his forehead. He was cold, way colder than normal.

"Why did you …" He lay on the ground, struggling to get the words out. I felt the life leaving his body, rapidly, piece by piece each second. "… betray me?" he managed to utter before his eyes went blank.

Betray him? I would never. Tears were rapidly streaming down my cheeks. "Please, don't leave me," I sobbed, cupping his face with my bloody hands.

Nothing. His mouth was pale, and his eyes were closed, unmoving. Damp bits of hair clung to his forehead and temples. I pressed my mouth to his blue cold lips, tasting my own salty tears. "I'm sorry," I murmured over and over again. "I'm so very sorry."

The depth of my despair was so overwhelming that all I could do was scream.

I JOLTED AWAKE, eyes wide open, staring at the ceiling with the sharp taste of fear in my mouth. My room was cold. Or maybe it was just me. The reality sunk in as I caught my breath, forcing my lungs to breathe in and out. It had only been a dream, but a dream like that left a mark on my soul nonetheless. Zane was fast asleep beside me. I watched the steady rise and fall of his chest, reassured by the movements.

Quietly, I slipped out of bed and tugged on one of Zane's hoodies, but it did little to rid the chill that had taken up residence inside me. Cold air prickled over my skin. I stood tall, searching the shadows, but I saw and felt nothing. How could I, when I was still rocked to the core by the dream? Was it a premonition? Could this be my fate? To kill the one I loved?

Giving up any notion of going back to sleep, I wandered to the window seat. I hugged my knees to my chest, laying a cheek on the cool windowpane as I glanced out into the vast waters—sparkling as a bit of sun crested, casting crystals on the surface. I shivered and glanced up at the sky. A flock of dark birds fluttered in the shape of a V, wings glistening in the sky.

"Hey," Zane said from behind me. "Can't sleep?" he asked.

I lifted my head off the window. "Sorry, I didn't mean to wake you."

He laid a hand on my shoulder. "Why didn't you? What's wrong?"

I rubbed my cheek on top of his hand. "You looked so peaceful; I didn't have the heart to disturb you." It didn't make sense that both of us should lose sleep.

"That's why I'm here. If something is wrong or something has happened, I want you to tell me. It doesn't matter what time or what I'm doing. I'm here for you."

I scooted forward a tad, making room for him. Without hesitation, he moved to sit behind me and drew me into his arms. I leaned my back against his chest. "I had a dream."

"You're freezing." He noticed and rubbed his hands up and down my arms. "What happened in the dream?"

"I stabbed you. I killed you."

"It was only a dream," he murmured in my ear, making my stomach flutter.

If anyone could thaw the ice in my veins, it was Zane. "And if it wasn't? What if I hurt you or worse?"

"It's going to take more than a knife to do me in."

I nudged him with my elbow. "This isn't funny."

"I know, but there is nothing we can do about it now," he said softly. "Come back to bed."

Things were tumultuously spinning out of control, but when Zane pulled me into his arms, for a short time, I found peace. He played with my hair, twisting strands around his fingers. "You're not relaxing."

"I know." I sighed. "I'm sorry. Every time I close my eyes, I see your blood on my hands."

"Maybe we can find a way to distract you." His hands moved over the flat planes of my belly, melting my icy skin.

My lips curved. "That might work." I needed to do more than know he was alive; I needed to feel he was alive.

At the first touch of his lips, fire licked in my blood and roared in my belly, warmth shooting across the back of my neck. My fingers yanked him closer, digging into his hair as his arms held me close, like he wanted to merge more than our souls. Our tongues swept in a dance as old as time. This was what I needed—the quick and wild, almost desperate need. I wanted to forget the dream completely. There was no room for thought, only feeling.

Mission accomplished.

Zane was above me, pressing his body against mine, his lips

suddenly at my neck, tracing a line of flames along my skin. My breath hitched. I knotted my hands into his shirt, pulling his face back to mine, and bit down on his lip, making him moan. I drowned in the sound, in Zane.

My hand slid over his cool chest, feeling the hard muscles of his stomach and chest. He made my entire body tingle, senses buzzing in a rainbow of emotions.

He pulled back slightly, eyes bright in the darkness as he stared down at me. His breath was cool on my face as he murmured, "You're beautiful, you know that?" The soft tip of his thumb brushed along the end of my chin, just under my lip. "I know I don't tell you often enough, but I want you to know. I've never met anyone who can stop the air in my lungs. You turn me inside out."

My pulse fluttered. "I don't need sweet words. I just need you." The emotions between us swirled in the air as if almost a tangible force. I closed my eyes, and I swore I could see the colors of our souls merging together.

Afterward, I held onto him, murmuring how much I loved him. More than anything, I wanted to cling to the honeymoon high, but the day seemed to be a chain of extreme ups and temperamental lows.

And the emotional roller coaster didn't end there. The day was only beginning.

CHAPTER 22

The only noise that sounded was the howling of the wind and tree branches hitting the side of the house. Our first night as husband and wife was turbulent, as was the weather. August was coming to a close and fall was creeping up on us, along with a shit storm of problems.

One of those problems was Parker. He refused to leave the island, whether it was because of Zoe or me, it didn't matter. I didn't know what excuse he'd given his mom for not returning for the start of his senior year, but I was sure he'd used me as an excuse. There was no other rational explanation for why his mom hadn't come here and dragged Parker back to Chicago by his ear.

His resolve, however, made me take his request to become a reaper a little more seriously. I wasn't saying I would do it, only that I thought about it more. The idea had settled and wasn't as atrocious as it had initially been.

I cuddled closer to Zane. His goal had been to keep me all night doing wicked things that had blood rushing through my body and left me breathless. I dozed off and on, but sometime around four a.m. I woke with the eerie feeling of being watched.

Using more than my eyesight, I surveyed the room, but nothing was out of the ordinary. The storm must have me on edge when there was no need. Tonight was my wedding night, yet it did nothing to quiet my racing heart. Someone was out there—a reaper. I was sure of it, and it was not one of my stationed guards.

Zane jerked away, sitting up so fast I almost fell out of the bed. His expression was tense. "We're not alone," he whispered.

I pushed the hair out of my face, clutching the covers to my chest. "What?"

"Don't move."

I wasn't sure if he was talking to the intruder or me. "Zane," I hissed, but it was a waste of breath. He was already out of bed and creeping toward the balcony. The moaning winds blew the white curtains. I sat up too quickly, rapping my elbow on the wall. The thump echoed through the room, followed by my string of curses.

"That doesn't sound like a happy bride," said a husky voice. "I hear congratulations are in order." Crash stepped into the stream of dim moonlight.

Zane disappeared, cloaked in shadows. Lightning struck, illuminating the room, and that's when I saw him. His hands were wrapped around Crash's throat as he confined him to the wall. "We're going to get a deadbolt for that door," he growled.

I scrambled off the bed. "Zane! Let him go." If he had given me a moment, I could have told him who it was.

"Why should I?" he protested, shirtless, his muscular back gleaming in the rising sun streaming from the glass doors.

"Because it's our wedding night," I replied, standing behind him. I placed a hand on his shoulder.

His fingers held steadfast, and I thought he might not listen. Seconds gave way to minutes of him staring into Crash's smug face. His muscles trembled under my hand, barely restrained. "This is the last time you come into this room uninvited. Is that clear?"

"We've done this dance before, Death Scythe," Crash said with a bored look. "You threaten me, and I don't give a rat's ass."

I put my hand to Zane's chest. "Crash, shut up for once. Next time I won't stop him."

Zane let go, and Crash fell to his feet. He huffed, and ran a hand through his unruly sandy hair. "I came to warn you, but I'm thinking I should have stayed home. Being the good guy doesn't suit me."

Zane scoffed. "No, it doesn't. So, why are you here? I won't believe anything that comes out of your ashtray mouth."

"I might not always be a model reaper, and my methods might be questionable and self-serving, but I am useful, as you will find out."

"This better be good." Zane shot him a pointed look.

I had to agree. What could possibly be so important for him to rush over here at the ungodly hour of four in the morning?

"I figured you guys wouldn't be sleeping," Crash said, brows raised.

The insinuation in his tone made me roll my eyes. I didn't know if it made the disruption better or worse. "How did you find out?"

"About your undisclosed wedding, or your secret love child?"

Okay, now I wanted to punch him. My fingers clenched at my sides. "Crash, just tell us what's going on." My patience was thin.

"After I left Keef's Reef, let's just say I didn't go straight home."

"You followed us," Zane concluded.

Crash shrugged, leaning against the wall in his usual nonchalant way. "What's the point of being a phantom reaper if I can't be a fly on the wall? It comes in handy."

"You're an ass," Zane said, taking the words from my mouth.

I crossed my arms, annoyed that Crash had invaded our privacy. "He's worse than an ass. He's an asshat."

"What she said," Zane added.

Cool air washed over us. Good thing. Things were getting heated in my room, and we were going round in circles. I exhaled. "How about we all take a chill pill?" I didn't think that was actually going to work, but it was worth a shot.

"What do you want?" Zane asked.

"The honeymoon is about to be cut short. My father has caught wind of your holy matrimony."

"How?" I screeched.

"The fly on the wall," Zane interposed.

I glanced from Zane to Crash. "You told him?" I threw the accusation at the one person who made sense.

"Would I be here telling you if I had?" Crash countered.

"To throw us off your scent," Zane theorized, and I was beginning to agree with him.

Crash sounded impatient. "I'm starting to doubt your saving-the-world skills."

And I was doubting Crash could ever be trusted. "Fine, say you didn't tell him. What is your father planning to do then?"

"What else? Tell the council. He doesn't like being outfoxed. And you, my pretty, are becoming a thorn in his side. We need to find the relic. Now. There is movement on the other side. Something big is brewing, and before you ask, I don't know, but it's going to be universally epic."

"Helpful," I mumbled.

"Enough," Zane spat. In two long strides, he was in front of Crash. "It's time for you to go." Zane wrenched the door open, and a blast of lightning struck, glowing in the sky. Rain pelted the balcony in a bittersweet symphony.

I stared out the doors thinking Crash was lucky he still had a pulse. A little rain couldn't hurt. It could have been worse. Much worse. And Crash had given me ample things to ponder, as did most of his unexpected visits.

Zane was getting ready to toss him out into the storm when a series of knocks pounded on my bedroom door. Apparently, Crash wasn't our only visitor today.

"Saved by the bell." Crash was in no position to be a smartass, but it didn't stop him.

"Oh, I'm still planning on tossing your ass out of here." Zane's voice had gone soft and dangerous.

Almost afraid to turn my back on the two of them, the impatient rapping of knuckles gave me little choice. "Behave," I warned and then padded across the floor. I flung open the door, expecting to see either TJ or Parker coming to harp on me about being in bed all day. Hell, even Dean Winchester would have been less of a surprise than seeing the Hunter twins.

"Hey, sis," Zoe squealed, enveloping me in a hug. Her sweet floral perfume transferred onto my wrinkled, oversized tee. "You have no idea how long I've waited to have a sister. Growing up with three brothers, there was always too much muscle, testosterone, and general guy stinkiness in my house."

I loved that girl.

The passing mention of Zander grouped into her three brothers gave me a quick, sharp pang of sadness and guilt.

"What are you two doing here?" Zane asked the twins.

"What are we doing here?" Zoe echoed. "What is *he* doing here?" she asked, pointing a slim finger directly at Crash.

"It's a par-tay. I see you got the invite." Crash's voice hinted at amusement.

Zoe frowned. Her and Zach brushed past me as if my bedroom was their second home. Zach was grinning from ear to ear like he was up to no good. And probably was.

"Speaking of invite, big brother." She poked Zane in the chest, ignoring Crash completely. Neither her nor Zach batted an eye at seeing Zane holding Crash by the scruff of his shirt. I was shocked my room was still in one piece. "Where was my invite?" she asked. "It's my sisterly privilege to see my brother get married." She pouted and looked cute doing it. Her hair was straight and flowed down her back like a waterfall. I bet even her cry face was attractive.

Zane unfolded his fingers, letting Crash go. "Unbelievable," he mumbled, combing a hand through his tousled hair. He looked adorably disheveled. "You know we would have had you there if there had been time," Zane replied, the lines softening on his face.

Sucker.

He had a soft spot for his sister. It was one of his endearing qualities. The family dynamics between the Hunters had always fascinated me. I didn't know another family like them. They were close knit despite all the drama. Maybe it was all the death; it made the infidelity, the revenge, and illegitimate child small in comparison to all the lost souls. Regardless of their dysfunction, I was happy to be a part of their family. I needed it—to feel loved again.

She gave a little shake of her head. "That's what Dad said, but a quick text wouldn't have killed you."

"You're here now," Zane said, dropping an arm over her shoulder and giving her an award-winning smirk.

Zoe turned her sad sea-green eyes up a notch. Girl had skills. "I really wanted to be the maid of honor. It's not every day we have a royal wedding."

I cringed inside at the word "royal."

Zoe and Aspyn were the only girl friends I had. It sucked that they hated each other with a passion. It was better for everyone I hadn't had a big splashy wedding. The catfights I was envisioning were enough to make me glad for my private little ceremony.

"She'll get over it," Zach said, his aqua eyes sparkling. "Congrats." He gave Zane one of those masculine hugs where they bumped shoulders and patted each other on the back. Then Zach turned that boyish troublesome charm on me. "Welcome to the fam, sis."

The Hunters were huggers.

"Thanks," I replied, trying not to be weirded out by the fact I was in my jammies and there was a quickly multiplying gathering in my room. But Zoe had no shame; so I figured neither did Zach. If they didn't feel awkward, then neither would I.

Zach bent down and picked up Zane's discarded shirt off the floor and threw it at his brother, who caught it in midair with one hand. "Get dressed, stop showing off your pecs, and let's celebrate. Where do you keep the booze? There's got to be champagne somewhere in this castle."

"We can't." Zane shot him down, frowning.

"Whoa, I thought marriage life would agree with you. It's one little drink. I'm not saying we have to get drunk. It's five o'clock somewhere."

"Funny. That's not it. We've got a situation." Zane glared at Crash from the corner of his eyes.

"Obviously, because when don't the two of you get yourselves into sticky messes?" Zoe said, staring at Zane and me before rolling her eyes.

"I think we figured out a way that might save all our butts from extinction," Crash announced.

The room was silent for about two seconds before the questions exploded.

How?

When did you figure it out?

Why aren't we doing something?

What's the plan?

"Okay, everyone chillax," Zane ordered. "Maybe a drink is a good idea, because now I could really use one. Or ten," he mumbled.

As if my stomach agreed, it growled like Godzilla. All eyes stared at my vocal belly.

"Jeesh, don't tell me my inconsiderate brother has kept you captive in this room without thinking you might need to eat." Zoe gave a cat-like wink.

"Or drink," a grinning Zach added.

"She needs food, not alcohol," Crash said. Somehow in the commotion, he'd stuck an unlit cigarette into his mouth. It dangled from one side of his lips.

The edges of Zane's eyes started to darken. "Don't presume to know what my wife needs."

Energy crackled through the room. "You guys are going to drive me to *drink*. And you," I said to Crash, "don't think about lighting that thing in my house."

Zach was relentless. "Then it's agreed. Mimosas and breakfast. Perfect. I can eat."

Zoe elbowed him in the side. "Duh. You're a bottomless pit."

What I thought was going to be a quiet day in bed, turned into a three-ring circus. Our hush-hush marriage wasn't so top secret. Why not take a moment and celebrate what was supposed to be a joyous occasion? Or we could stay here and watch Zane and Crash kill each other with dirty glares.

The wise thing to do was for the five of us to head to the kitchen, eat, and brainstorm. Maybe, just maybe, we'd come up with a solid plan. It was iffy to include Crash, but it was also an opportunity, and I was an opportunist. Kill two birds with one stone and all that mumbo jumbo. It was time to find out whose side he was really on.

Zane tossed on a T-shirt, and I slipped on my fuzzy zombie slippers. Still, I felt underdressed.

The halls were dark due to the overcast sky, making the usually bright and airy stairwell gloomy. It didn't hinder us as we made our way downstairs.

Zane and I walked holding hands, both of us needing the contact. His skin was cool against mine, but even though my heart was happy, my mind was plagued with uncertainty. The three musketeers' chatter echoed off the high ceilings. I needed to do the day-to-day things, like eating, but all I could think was there wasn't time. Shit was about to get real.

My mind was computing and compartmentalizing all the decisions I needed to make when I felt the presence of a reaper. Relying on Zane to make sure I didn't face-plant into a wall, I reached out with my abilities to identify who it was and whether I should be concerned. My detection skills were getting better, and after a second or two, my shoulders went lax, recognizing Declan's signature. It wasn't a Red Hawk assassin. Someone call the Vatican, because an honest-to-God miracle had occurred.

It didn't hurt to be overly cautious. I was uptight, always poised for the next hallow attack. I was sure everyone else was as well. So when Zane stiffened, I didn't think much about it, not until the collision happened.

CHAPTER 23

Parker rounded the corner, nose tipped down like he was known to do while reading a comic. My heart jerked in my chest, unable to stop the crash. Parker smacked into Zane. The comic fell to the floor, and Parker's glasses slipped down his nose, green eyes brimming with surprise.

He scrunched his nose, nudging his glasses back into place. "Uh, sorry." He bent and gathered his rumpled comic. As he straightened up, his eyes passed over me and landed on Zoe. His whole expression changed. "Hey. I didn't know you were here."

"Just got here." She grinned.

I was getting more comfortable with the idea of them dating. It didn't make my insides all topsy-turvy.

"Oh." He shuffled his feet. "Something going on?" He glanced to the small party behind me.

"Parker, what are you doing up?" I asked. Parker had always been a morning person, but this was early even for him.

He shrugged. "I couldn't sleep, so I thought I would read, and then I got hungry. What's this all about? A reaper convention?"

"Better." Zoe beamed. "They got married."

Parker was rendered motionless. They only thing that moved was a stray piece of straw hair slowly falling over his forehead. I thought he was going to go into cardiac arrest. "Married?" he echoed.

Zoe nodded vigorously.

He shook his head as if he was clearing the cobwebs. "What? When?"

"Last night," Zoe sung.

"It just happened," I clarified. "There wasn't time to tell anyone. Zoe and Zach only just found out. I'm not even sure if it is safe for you to know."

His peepers, not so disoriented anymore, flashed to mine. "That's something you tell your best friend, no matter what time of the night."

Zoe slinked between us to stand beside Parker. "That's what I said."

"Whatever. Who cares?" Crash interrupted.

My eyes narrowed in his direction, and Zane's jaw clenched. *How hard was it to go and grab a bite to eat?*

Zach laid a hand on Crash's shoulder. "Don't worry. I got my eye on him."

Crash snickered, clearly not worried.

Zoe weaved her arm through Parker's. "You hungry?" she asked in an enchanting tone that suggested something other than food.

"I guess," Parker replied, his head still reeling over my marriage.

Crash thumped Parker on the back of the head. "What do you mean, you guess? When a lady asks you if you're hungry, always say yes. We're going to need to work on your game, man."

Zane snorted.

Poor Parker. He had no idea what he had gotten himself into. Breakfast with reapers. It should be a movie.

Zoe laughed, her heels tapping along the hardwood as she led Parker along. "You're too cute for words. I could just eat you."

"I'm about to lose my appetite," Zach groaned.

Since there was no need to work in the dark, I flipped on the kitchen lights, and the large room came to life. As expected, it was as orderly as the rest of the rooms in the manor, excluding TJ's and mine. Stark white floors shined under the soft lights, looking so clean I could see my reflection. The dark granite counters were speckled with flecks of silver, sitting on top of ivory cabinets identical to the ones lining the walls. The appliances were top of the line and no doubt industrial. Zane headed for the fridge to take stock.

"Can I help?" I asked. Zane was an exceptional cook, when he had the time. I lucked out in that department, but I wasn't half bad. The last year, feeding TJ, had stretched my skills. I couldn't care less if I ever made mac and cheese again. TJ would agree.

Zane glanced at me over his shoulder. "I got this. You take a seat. Eggs? Or French toast?"

"Both, pretty please." I grinned.

"Coming right up." He reached in the fridge, grabbing eggs, milk, and an armful of other ingredients.

"So, when am I going to be an aunt?" Zoe asked, making herself at home in the kitchen beside Parker.

Zane's head whipped around so fast, I thought he was going to pull a muscle.

I choked. The thought of getting pregnant had never crossed my mind, but after the things we'd done last night, anything was possible.

Zach slid us a cheeky grin, rocking back on his heels. "Uncle Zach. Hmm. It has a nice ring to it."

"Uncle Parker, huh. I like it."

My mouth dropped. Parker too? When did he become Team Zanper? "It's been like six hours," I reasoned.

"Plenty of time to get a bun in the oven," Crash supplied, grabbing two cans of soda.

"Girl, I missed your wedding. There is no way I am missing the birth of my niece. Got it?" She pointed a pretty fuchsia nail in my direction.

I leaned my hip on the counter and rolled my eyes. "I pinky swear you will be the second person I tell."

Zane was shaking his head as he cracked eggs into a bowl. Bacon was already sizzling on the stove, flooding the air with salivating scents. "No more talk of babies. Not until my stomach can handle it. We have more pressing matters, anyway."

Coffee. I needed a caffeine kick. Pushing off the counter, I went to the cabinet to pull down the coffee. We were going to need an econo-sized pot. "And we will get to them as soon as I've had my caffeine jolt," I said.

"You got dark roast?" Crash asked.

"I'm a coffee connoisseur. Asking is an insult."

The kitchen began to fill with all my favorite scents of breakfast. There was something homey about having a full house of people. It made the manor feel less cold and formal, more like a home. Conversation was kept light while Zane finished cooking, and it made me wish it didn't have to end. I sighed. The only way I could ensure there would be many more breakfasts like this was to find the relic ... if it existed.

There was so much wrong with everything, but sitting in the kitchen, eating French toast and bacon with family and friends, was the only good thing in my life. A dose of reality was a bit sobering.

Since everyone was here and I was on my second cup of coffee, it seemed as good a time as any to devise a battle plan. Zane, Crash, and I caught the group up to speed, mostly. "Okay, so now we need to figure out what our next step is, what *we're* going to do."

"Simple." Crash smirked, forking a piece of French toast. "We search the manor from top to bottom, leaving no cushion unturned, no room unscathed, and no pantie drawer untouched."

I snorted. "You go anywhere near my pantie drawer and I'll zap you."

Zane cut Crash a dark look.

"Then we grab the relic, reenergize with a shot of Red Bull, and save the world. Boom." Crash threw his hands up in a makeshift explosion.

"What I think Crash is trying to say," I said, shooting Crash a frown, "is we need to start by finding the relic. Then we can worry about what to do with it."

"Is it powerful? Will it really restore the veil?" Zoe asked, taking dainty bites off her plate, unlike her twin who wolfed his food in two minutes flat.

"Let's find it first. We can figure the rest out later. *If* this thing is real and at the manor, we have to find it," Zane voiced, again casting doubt that Crash could be trusted.

Crash leaned back in his chair. "Okay, but there is one problem, sunshine. Where do we start? Have you seen the size of this joint you live in?" The manor was like a museum. It would take hours, days even, to leave no room unturned. We didn't have hours or days.

"You're the expert." Zane pinned Crash with a glare. "You tell us."

I sighed. *We're doomed.* As soon as the fleeting thought left my mind, something happened. And not a good something.

CHAPTER 24

The kitchen wasn't the kitchen. I blinked, but there was still nothing but darkness. No light. No sound. Gone was the chatter and the sarcasm, and in its place was the serene sound of nothingness. For a moment, I did absolutely nothing, and then I freaked. Zane's name tumbled from my lips, my eyes darting around, trying to make sense of what happened—desperately searching for something … anything.

Then I saw it.

A speckle of gray, growing as the darkness faded, revealing I was no longer inside the manor, but outside. *Had I transported myself?*

It was foggy, hindering visibility and covering the ground in wispy mist that curled in the cool air. Calm waters, deep, almost black, surrounded me on either side. I spun slowly in a circle. In the distance, the manor was disappearing into the sweeping mist. There was no way for me to make my way toward home. Straight ahead lay only one path … away from the manor. Guess I was meant to go that way. This was more than a dream, or me day walking, but it had yet to reveal its purpose.

I followed the dark trail, my breath clouding the air as I walked.

Thick trees with long weeping branches lined the walkway. The ground was cushioned in moss, muffling my footsteps. I kept my gaze directly ahead, but out of the corner of my eyes I caught glimpses of movement—flashes really, like faeries drifting between the branches.

Cautiously, I walked, unsure of where I was going or what I would find, but I didn't stop. Something pressed me to move on. That something called my name. The soft voice carried in the wind, whispering and summoning me.

A flutter of light caught my gaze, standing out in the otherwise drab environment. It was familiar, oddly comforting and lacking any sense of danger.

Piper. Again, I heard my name. Going with my gut, I sought the direction of the voice.

The pathway abruptly dead-ended, opening into a massive glade, where spheres of glowing blue light dangled in the air. They lit the treetops. The only thing I could compare it to was the northern lights. It was beautiful. I hadn't expected such beauty to live in the middle of nowhere. Take away the otherworldly glow, and it looked eerily like the circular grounds of the council.

A tingle skated up my spine right before a voice said, "Welcome to the Grove."

I recognized the voice at once. "Mom?"

"Hey, sweetie." Her voice was the most tender sound in the world. She looked regal in a silky dress of plain white, but she didn't need anything flashy to be beautiful. Her beauty was all natural.

Relief crossed my face. I wasn't alone, thank God. "The Grove?" I repeated. "What is this place?"

"It is the sanctuary for those who have passed on," she explained. "Only a person with a pure heart and the power of a reaper may pass through the guards."

"How did I get here?" I wasn't dead. At least I didn't think I was. That would be my next question.

Her dew-colored eyes softened. "Real power is inherited from women. You know by now our bloodline is supreme. To walk between realms is one of your gifts."

What did she mean, 'walk between realms'? "I thought I could only summon the banshees of the past, my ancestors? It doesn't explain how I'm here."

"I know this is a lot to absorb. We didn't want to overwhelm you all at once." Translation: they had withheld information, leading me to believe something that was false. "It's you who comes to us. Prior to the destruction of the veil, we could not pass in any form to the living, but you, Piper, are able to pass over to the other side—not with your physical body, but with your mind."

Say what? My eyes glanced left and right, seeing my surroundings in a different light. "I'm in the afterlife?" I asked, staring at her.

She nodded. "You are."

My time in the otherworld was like a dream, hazy and ethereal. I finally understood. Rose, Mom, Celeste, they weren't coming to me on Earth. I was traveling to them. Not physically, but with my mind. I bridged the gap between here and the other side.

It was like *Inception*.

I glanced down, checking out my form. "So this really isn't my body?"

"It's the form you gave yourself."

Hell's bells! Why hadn't I made myself taller with bigger boobs?

She laughed, seeing my distressed expression. "You are beautiful just the way you are."

"Don't tell me you can read my mind," I muttered.

"No," she said, brushing the hair off my forehead. "I just know how your mind works."

"Lovely," I muttered. "So, this place, is it made up as well?"

"The Grove is never the same, for it is not a substantial place. It's what you create, pulled from a memory or important place that may have impacted you." She gazed around, seeing the stone circle where the council met. "By the looks of it, you've been summoned by the council. And I can guess why."

I bit my lip. "Uh, yeah. They're very persistent in their attempts to marry me off."

"Oh, Piper, it's so good to see you." She pulled me in, wrapping her arms around me tightly. I'd forgotten what her hugs were like. "How's TJ? I want to hear about everything. Are you okay?" she rambled.

I opened my mouth and then closed it. If I started unloading now, I wouldn't be able to restrain the emotions threatening to spill. It was the mom complex. Seeing her broke down my walls. Besides Parker, Mom had been my confidant—the person I leaned on to make everything better, the one who wiped my tears and kissed my scuffed knees. Maybe what I needed was a good long crying jag. But as I looked up into her slim face, I stiffened my lip and took a breath, forcing back the tears and willing them to freeze inside me. She also gave me strength. There was no room for useless tears, not today. I needed to be a tough chick. "I'm still alive," I said with a lame laugh.

"I can see that." She smiled. "And TJ?"

"He's with me at the manor. I'm doing everything I can to keep him safe."

"You were always such a protective big sister. I know you will take care of him." She reached out, picking up my left hand. "What's this?" she asked, running a finger over the silver band. "I thought the council wasn't getting its claws in you?"

A quick smile came to my lips. "They aren't. I did get married, but to someone they will never approve of."

"To the other Hunter?" she guessed. "The half-breed?"

My nose wrinkled. I disliked the name "half-breed." It didn't matter to me who his parents were or how pure his blood was. "Yes, Zane. His father has declared him his heir."

A low chuckle scampered from her lips. "I bet that went over well with the council."

"The *council* thinks I'm incapable of making decisions on my own. They had the nerve to assume I would follow like a dog and drew up a contract between Crash and me." The idea still made me shiver. "So I went behind their backs and wed Zane. I hope you're not disappointed in me. I just couldn't be forced to marry someone I didn't love."

"You can never disappoint me. I would be more upset if you didn't fight for what you believe in, including love. You, Piper, behind all the sarcasm and tough-girl shell, are a romantic. Just like me."

I don't know how she figured, but it was true my mom had been a hopeless romantic. She'd married a painter, for criminy sakes.

"Crash?" she repeated, trying to place the name. "He is the son of Heath, overlord of the Red Hawks?"

I nodded. "The son of king douche."

"He was a baby when I left, but Heath has always been a slimy tool. He used to give me the creeps as a little girl."

Her comment made me smile. "Same," I agreed.

"And his son?" she inquired, wondering what kind of reaper he was—like his father or someone I counted on.

I shrugged. "Crash is a wild card. I don't know if I can trust him. I definitely couldn't marry him. Actually, he claims there is a relic at the manor that could mend the boundary between us. Do you know anything about that?"

Her goldish-white locks shined through the mist, but it was the seriousness of her mouth that caught my attention. "I do."

"I can't believe it's real," I mumbled.

"I didn't say it was real, only that I've heard of it. The ground the manor sits on is sacred. It was the sole reason Rose chose to have her grand home built on that part of the island. If the relic does exist, it won't be inside the manor but located somewhere on the land."

"But you have no idea where?"

She shook her head, regret clear in her gaze. "I'm sorry, honey."

"What about Celeste?" I offered, eager for any information.

Skepticism crossed her brows with a pinch of surprise. "Where did you hear that name?"

I shuffled my feet over the stone slab I was standing on. "I saw her. Here, I guess, but at the time I didn't know it."

She lifted my chin with her gentle fingers. "This is why you will be a great leader, Piper. You're smart. You know what you want. And you're so strong, more powerful than you even know. I couldn't stay and face my future. I ran away and only made a bigger mess of things. But you, my daughter, are going to restore the balance."

I swallowed a lump of emotion churning inside me. "You did what you thought was best," I said, needing her to know I wasn't angry anymore—just the opposite. "I understand why you left, why you never told me. I might not have a few months ago, but I'm grateful. You gave me a life. You gave me Parker. And TJ."

"What of Parker?" she asked. "Is he nursing a broken heart?"

I snorted. "Um, maybe for a hot minute. I think we both realized we're better as friends. He's sort of dating Zane's sister, I think."

"You think?" She gave me one of her secret, all-knowing smiles. "I thought you guys told each other everything."

"A lot has changed," I muttered, *including Parker,* I added silently. "He wants me to make him a harbinger of death."

She looked at me squarely. "Why haven't you?"

I stared at her, seriousness lining her forehead. My eyes widened. "Mom!" I thought she would have been on my side, not for turning my best friend into a reaper. "It's dangerous."

"So is him knowing. Maybe more so."

I twined my fingers together. "I've been thinking the same thing."

"Sounds like, to me, you've already made your decision," she mused.

My heart twisted as I looked at her face. I knew what I was going to do, what I should have done already, but I was exceptional at procrastination. Like now. There were a million things I should be doing, but being in the Grove gave me a quiet calm I hadn't felt in a very long time. I closed my eyes.

"Princess," whispered a voice, heart-wrenchingly familiar, drawing me out of my moment of Zen. There was something sad and painful, bordering on desperate, and it tugged at my soul.

Zane? Was he here? With me? But even as the thought ran through my head, I knew he couldn't be here. Zane was alive. This was a place for the dead. I opened my eyes, seeing the mist had swelled, eddying around me from toe to head.

"Come back," he murmured, his deep and lyrical voice cutting through the thick layers of fog. "I need you."

I was torn, my emotions split down the middle. I wasn't ready to leave my mom, wanting to treasure the rare moments we were able to see each other, but I couldn't stay here forever. No matter how much I longed for the solitude and the quiet. Really though, how much could a few more minutes hurt?

"You can't," he pleaded. "If you don't come back soon, you'll be lost forever, drifting in the afterlife. Fight, Piper, please."

All I did was fight. I was tired of fighting. Nothing but pain and death waited for me back home. Here, I didn't feel the agony. I didn't feel the pressure. All I felt was … nothing really. And that's what made it so blissful. Emotions tangled everything up. Without them, life was so much simpler.

"You have me," Zane reminded me, urgency lacing his words.

What was the big rush? Five more minutes with my mom wasn't going to kill me.

"I'm waiting for you. Don't leave me, Princess." His voice broke off in a shaky sob that rocked me to my core. It was so unexpected, the sheer despair. A trigger went off inside me.

Leave Zane? I would never leave him. I loved him. Why would he think I would leave?

"He's right, Piper," Mom said, softly sweeping a pale strand of hair off my shoulder. Hair so like hers. Sometimes it scared me how much I'd grown to favor her. When I looked in the mirror, for a brief second I saw my mom. Then my world would crumble, remembering she was gone, and my reflection was the closest I would get to her … except for moments like this. "You must go back, now," she rushed, her eyes becoming frantic. The mist grew angry, coming between us. "You've been here too long. Time isn't the same here as it is in the living. If you stay any longer, you'll risk losing your soul."

"I'll be dead?"

Her face was solemn and beautiful. "You'll be trapped, neither living nor dead."

There was always a catch. Blood drained from my face.

"Please, Piper," Zane murmured. "Don't leave me. Not yet." The raw emotion hit me, breaking through the mist to reach me. So vital and gut-wrenching, it almost brought me to my knees.

Tears clogged my throat and burned my eyes. My heart lurched. I had to say good-bye. "I won't see you again, will I?"

She shook her head, smiling sadly. "Go home, honey. You don't belong here. I love you." Her voice trailed off.

"Mom," I called, but it was too late, my surroundings had begun to shimmer, blurring the stone circle. The mist broke, stirring to darkness. An eternity passed, or maybe it was only a few seconds before the void gave way.

When it did, I blinked. Zane's voice calling my name slowly sharpened, until the room around me focused. I latched onto his eyes.

His hand grabbed me, solid and very real.

The journey back to the living had been swift, leaving him a little unstable. I leaned on him, knowing he wouldn't let me fall. Seeing his bright cobalt eyes and how pale his skin was, I understood how much I had to lose here. My mom might be gone from me, but Zane was right here in front of me. Keeping me anchored. Keeping me sane. Keeping me focused. Keeping me strong. He was my future. I needed to stop looking to the past and concentrate on making sure we had a future.

I could never go back. I would never see my mom again. Rose. Or Celeste. It was too dangerous. I'd already crossed over with my mind one too many times, to do so again would push the laws of nature. It didn't stop the sharp ache that overtook me, leaving me gasping for air.

"Breathe, Princess," Zane murmured, his lips brushing against my temple as he held me to him.

"Don't let go. Not yet." My voice was weary.

"I wouldn't dream of it," he said softly.

What I'd learned today—about myself, about the relic, and all that I had to leave behind—was like losing my mother all over again, an open wound that would only heal with time. I suspected Zane's love for me would dull the pain. He was my road to recovery.

"Are you all right?" he whispered, his hands framing my face.

"I think so." I had to push my personal emotions aside. We had work to do, but first, I was going to monkey hug my husband.

His arms automatically went around me, and he dropped a kiss on my forehead. "Don't ever do that to me again."

My eyes glistened as I looked up at him. "I won't," I promised.

"Good, because you took ten years off my soul."

"Is someone going to tell me what just happened?" Zoe demanded, a frown deepening her dimples.

I let my heels touch the ground again, but didn't move completely out of Zane's embrace, and turned slightly to see everyone staring at me, their faces ranging from concerned to baffled. "I think I know where to start looking for the relic," I announced.

"How?" Parker was beside me, leaning against the counter.

I bit down on my lower lip. "I crossed over."

"To the afterlife?" Zane stated in a way that said he was hoping I was joking.

Sorry, Zane. No joke. I nodded. "The one and only."

"Piper," he scolded. "Do you know how dangerous that is?"

I rolled my eyes. "I didn't do it intentionally. It just happened."

He stared at me, and I stared back.

Knowing what *that look* meant, the furrowed brows and hard set of his jaw, I caved, sighing. "Anyway, you pulled me out. I could hear you," I said, in an attempt to diffuse his overprotective nature.

His eyes lost a degree of sharpness. "Keeping you alive is a full-time job," he muttered.

"But you're so good at it." I flattened my hands on his chest. "Something worthy might have come out of my little trip to the veil. My mom was there."

"Did she know anything about the relic?" Zach asked what everyone was wondering.

"She never saw the relic but remembered something about the grounds of the manor being sacred. If the relic is here, it won't be inside the house but somewhere on the grounds."

"Well, that narrows it down," Crash drawled in a snide voice.

Zane cut Crash another of his famous dark glares.

If I didn't step in, things would only escalate between them. "Before we go on a scavenger hunt, I've got to do something. Come on," I ordered Parker, grabbing his hand and dragging him out of the kitchen, leaving a room of people scratching their heads.

CHAPTER 25

"Okay. I'll do it," I said as soon as I closed the door to the library behind us.

Parker adjusted his glasses. "Do what?" he asked, looking utterly confused, disorientated, and adorable.

I took a breath. A faint hit of saltwater teased my senses. Dusty books that probably hadn't been opened in years lined the shelves all the way to the ceiling, and it was a helluva ceiling. An old-timey ladder was propped in the corner to reach the top shelves. *Here goes nothing.* "I'll change you." The words were like lead in my gut, heavy and metallic. I had agreed to make Parker a reaper, but that didn't mean I wasn't scared. This was Parker. What if I screwed it up somehow?

He'd been running a finger along the edge of a book spine and then suddenly whipped around. "Say what?"

I thought he was going to knock over the bookshelf. "If it's what you really want, I'll make you a reaper. You'll be a Blue Sparrow—a reaper who has been made."

"Are you serious? This isn't your idea of a joke?" His hand pressed into the side of the shelf.

I shook my head. "Of course not. I wouldn't joke about something like this. You're way too important to me, and this isn't something I take lightly." I'd never turned anyone into a reaper before. It seemed fitting for my first to be my best friend.

He paused, his eyes bulging behind his lenses. "Pipes, I-I don't know what to say."

I wiped my clammy hands on my shorts. "I just need to hear you say it. I need you to tell me this is really, really what you want."

"It is. What made you change your mind?"

My shoulders lifted. "I don't want to lose my best friend, and right now, I can use all the help I can get. You're smart, Parker. The smartest guy I know. I need someone like you on my side."

"I didn't think you'd change your mind," he said honestly.

I crossed my arms. "Well, I was hoping *you* would change yours. You ready?"

"We're doing this right here? Right now?" he squeaked, glancing around the room.

A smile tugged at my lips as I readjusted my bun, tucking the stray pieces back in. "What's wrong with the library?"

"Nothing," he assured me, scratching the side of his temple. "I just thought there'd be a secret lab in the basement or something."

I rolled my eyes. "It's now or never. If I have time to overthink what I'm about to do, I'll chicken out, and with the end of the world looming around the corner, this might be our only shot."

"No second thoughts. I want this, Pipes. I swear it."

I nodded with a heavy heart. "Okay, let's bring you over to the dark side."

Parker grinned. He stepped forward and straightened his shoulders.

"Um, maybe you should lie down," I suggested.

"Okay, sure." There was only one chair in the room, an oversized chaise just perfect for curling up in on a cold winter day with the book of your choice. It was nestled in the corner under a large picture window. He lay on the chair as I drew the curtains closed, drowning out the sunlight.

I plopped down on the edge of the chaise, breathing in the scent of leather and old books. The room fell silent, but in the distance, my friend's voices traveled down the hallway. Declan, my faithful shadow, stood outside the door.

"You sure you know what you're doing?" Parker asked, staring me in the eyes.

I could see his assurance in me, but that didn't mean he wasn't a bit tense. "What do you think? I haven't had many willing participants to practice on."

He gulped.

"Nervous now?" I winked.

"Only that you're going to turn me into a donkey with glasses."

I chuckled, losing some of the stiffness in my shoulders. "Close your eyes," I instructed.

He shifted his head on the cushion, finding a comfortable spot. "Why?"

"Because I can't concentrate with you staring at me."

"Why?" he repeated.

Smartass. I pinched him. The *why* game used to be something we played to annoy each other when we'd been kids. "Just do it."

He smiled, but promptly shut his eyes.

Deep breaths, Piper. You got this.

Flexing my hands, I lifted them in the air, preparing to work up my mojo. An intense tingle began at the tips of my fingers, just below the skin. I grabbed both his hands and let my lashes drift over my cheeks.

"Wait!" he yelled, eyes popping open.

"Parker!" I breathed, pinning him with an exasperated glare. He'd almost given me a stroke.

"I couldn't resist." He chuckled, settling back into the chair. "I swear I'll behave," he promised, eyes resuming their closed position.

"You better, or you might turn into that jackass after all," I muttered.

Other than his lips curving, Parker lay as still as a board. Once again, I claimed his hands with mine, letting the power residing inside me swim to the surface. It came quickly, channeling throughout my body. I took souls, absorbing their essence, sometimes without batting an eye. Making Parker into a reaper, I deduced, would be a reverse process. The plan was to fill his veins with my power, infusing him with enough to alter his soul, but not kill him.

No sweat.

I was surprised how calm I was. Clamping my fingers together with his, glamour poured off me in waves. My head buzzed furiously, and I could taste the glow of energy on my tongue. A ripple went through the air as I sent a stream of my power into his veins. If there was a ritual or words, I didn't know them, relying only on instinct.

I felt a surge of cold fire. It started with a crackle, a blue light burning behind my eyelids as my core banshee power flooded into Parker's vessels, offering him a chance at a different life. His lashes twitched, and his fingers held mine, but other than that, I couldn't tell what he was feeling. Pain? Pleasure? Nothing?

I, on the other hand, felt too much. Every nerve in my body came alive, and anticipation I hadn't expected blazed in me. The whole shebang only took a few minutes. When the last ribbons of electricity returned to me, I sat back, fingers still tingling, but it was done. No more stressing over whether or not I was going to turn the person who knew all my secrets into my biggest secret.

Parker's eyes fluttered open, and the first words out of his mouth were, "Did it work?"

For the barest of seconds, I wasn't sure, but then a fleck of cool blue shimmered from the corner of his eyes over his cheek. As I studied him, my banshee recognition registered, sensing Parker as something other than human. "I'm so sorry, Parks."

He stared at my face, unblinking, though his eyes dimmed with disappointment.

I laughed. "I'm kidding. Welcome to the dark side. You should see your face right now."

"That seriously wasn't funny. I should be mad at you, but wow," he said, turning his hands over again and again. "I feel incredible."

I folded my fingers in my lap. "It's weird, huh?"

He pushed himself up in the chair, keeping his legs extended. "I never knew. I mean, I knew you could do things, but I didn't understand how powerful you were. I felt it inside me."

"It's a rush; that's for sure," I said, removing my hair from its bun and shaking it out. We cast bemused glances at each other. "I can't believe I did it," I said.

A slow grin pulled at Parker's lips. "That's it? I'm a reaper?"

"Yep. How do you feel?"

"Cold, actually, but not uncomfortable, just cooler."

I nodded, standing up. "That's normal. You'll get used to it."

"Anything else I need to get used to?" he asked.

"We don't have enough time," I replied, tugging a handful of his *Berserk* manga shirt and pulling him to his feet. Parker stepped forward and hugged me, pulling me close with desperate relief. I slid my arms around him and squeezed tight. "Friends forever—literally."

He laughed. "I wouldn't have it any other way."

My eyes watered, and I brushed aside the tears before they could fall. "I love you."

"Ditto." He grinned.

I was happy to have Parker on my side, but the celebration would have to wait until later. I wasn't feeling so hot, and if I wasn't so dizzy, I might've puked.

Parker grabbed me on either side of my shoulders, steadying me. "Hey, you okay?"

I leaned on him, shoulder to shoulder, praying the room would stop whirling. "I will be. I just need a minute. Turns out, making a reaper is exhausting." It took more out of me than I'd anticipated.

"Should I get Zane?" he asked, concern lacing in his eyes.

Slowly, I stood straight. "Nah. I can make it back on my own."

And I did. Together we made our way to the kitchen. All the while, Parker kept a watchful eye on me with Declan guarding my back.

"Everything okay?" Zane inquired, seeing the serious lines on my face.

I weaved my fingers through his, drawing some of his strength. "Yeah, Parker and I had some unfinished business."

Zane arched a brow.

I laid a hand on his chest. "I'll be okay," I murmured.

"Parker?" Zoe's eyes were zeroed in on him. Then she was flying through the kitchen. "Ohmygod," she squealed as she threw her arms around his neck. "She did it, didn't she? You're a reaper." Zoe must have sensed the change. Just looking at Parker, there was no outward difference—same shaggy hair a tad too long, same cute nerdy quality, same lean build.

"Well, this is an unexpected turn of events," Crash said. "Any other surprises up your sleeve?"

"Guess you'll just have to stick around and see."

Zane snorted, not keen about the idea of having Crash hanging around. "Or not."

I nudged him in the side. If we were going to restore the veil, he was going to have to learn to play nice, at least until the world was once again in perfect harmony.

Zach put his hand on Parker's shoulder. "Time to suit up, reaper boy, we got work to do."

"Do I get a badge for this?" Parker asked.

"If we live past the next twenty-four hours, I'll get you a goddamn gold medal," I offered.

"As heartwarming as this moment is, we have a relic to find." Leave it to Crash to ruin a bit of happiness, but he was right. The honeymoon was over. We had work to do.

CHAPTER 26

Tick. Tock. Tick. Tock. I hadn't noticed the noise of the clock before today, but now, each annoying click echoed in my head, reminding me I was almost out of time.

I dressed in black jeans, a black halter top, and a black leather jacket. Yeah, I felt badass. If I was going to restore the veil in the next twenty-four hours, my jammies and zombie slippers weren't going to cut it. As I laced up my black boots, Zane walked into the room.

He blinked. "Wow, you look …"

"Ready to kick some serious hallow ass?" I supplied.

"Uh-huh, that about sums it up."

Together we left the safety of my bedroom. Downstairs, the entryway was bustling with excited and restless energy. Everyone was tired of sitting around; they were ready for action, ready to restore the universe's balance. There had been a shift in the air since the veil dropped, and because reapers were so in tune with death, our awareness was sharper. It made them antsy.

Crash was leaning against the wall, an unlit cigarette dangling from his lips.

Zane gave Crash a slit-eyed, dangerous smile. "Let me guess, oral fixation?"

Crash remained bored. "There are worse fixations to have."

"I wouldn't know."

We were going to get nowhere if we started this again. "Guys! Focus." My voice rasped. "Let's split up into groups of two." Seemed simple. Zach and Crash weren't thrilled with their pairing, but they were going to have to make do. Just in case, I sent Declan with them as a mediator to make sure they stayed on track. Zach wasn't as hotheaded as his brother. If anyone could deal with Crash's rude behavior, it was the easy-going Hunter.

Parker divvied the estate into sections, assigning one to each group. If anyone found something suspicious, they were to text "911" before doing anything else. It was agreed we would inspect any possibilities together as we couldn't afford any careless mistakes.

No one knew anything about the relic other than it might be able to close the veil. We had no clue what it looked like, if it could be dangerous, or how to activate the ancient device. That was too many unknown factors in my book, and I wasn't willing to jeopardize the life of anyone in the group. Together we would assess the relic. Seven heads were better than two.

I looked over my shoulder one last time at Parker, my brain still processing the monumental change in his life. I wanted to protect him from all this, and I doubted that feeling would ever go away. The further I tried to keep him from this world, the deeper he immersed himself in it. Maybe it was fate. Didn't matter, he'd gotten what he wanted. I only hoped it made him happy. His happiness meant a lot to me.

"He'll be okay," Zane said, sensing my worry.

I huffed, my feet dragging over the grass. "Will he though? Will any of us?" I countered, sounding like a negative Nancy.

"I don't have all the answers. Sometimes you have got to trust everything will work out, even when all hope seems lost." He slid a hand to the small of my back, helping me up an incline. "Besides, he's with Zoe. Have you seen what she can do with a whip?"

I laughed. "I have. It's frightening. You always say the right thing."

"Remember that after we've been married for ten years."

I sighed, glad that at least TJ was tucked safely in the manor, oblivious to the scavenger hunt just outside his window. We walked the southeast corner of the lot, closest to where the beach bordered the property. "Any ideas what we should be looking for?"

"Something old, out of the ordinary, and utterly foreign. Trust me, you'll know when you see it."

"Wonderful."

"If this thing has power and a connection to the banshee line, it's possible you might be able to feel it," he suggested.

Oh, I was getting a feeling all right, but it had nothing to do with the relic and everything to do with my distracting, drool-worthy husband. His arm occasionally brushed against mine as we walked, making me forget why we were outside and not between the sheets. "When this whole saving the world business is over, you and I are going on a proper honeymoon," I said as my eyes searched the ground.

Zane grinned. "Just name the time and place."

An hour went by and with it our sunlight. There had been only one false text from the three stooges. Larry, Curly, and Moe (aka Crash, Zach, and Declan) had found a mysterious looking urn; turned out it was just an ordinary flowerpot and nothing supernatural.

I gazed out over the courtyard, the breeze ruffling my hair and clothes. We'd been over this part of the yard time and time again. "This is useless," I complained.

There was a long silence before Zane answered. "Maybe, but so is doing nothing. At least we're trying."

I thought about Earth fading away bit by bit, dying at the hands of the hallows. "I just hope it's enough."

"Don't tell me you're giving up."

A sharp wind hissed off the coast, making me shiver. "I never give up." I let my gaze wander. "Look at this. How can I close my eyes and pretend the world is okay when people are dying?"

"If this doesn't work, we'll find another way."

Will we? In time? He was so confident. I wanted some of that self-assurance to rub off on me. Each second my resolve weakened, making my stomach twist and my hope diminish.

The remaining groups trickled back to the courtyard, waiting for direction, uplifting words of wisdom, or a new plan. I had none of the above.

"Where's Crash?" Zane prompted.

The devil himself miraculously morphed with a smirk on his lips.

Any other time and place, Zane would have knocked that cockiness off Crash's face.

Parker scratched the back of his neck. "We've been around this place ten times, searching from border to border, and we've found jack shit."

Crash shot Zane a sideways glance. "What now, big shot? We're no closer than when we started."

"Makes me wonder if the relic is nothing but a farce or a distraction," Zane spoke up, firing accusation daggers at Crash.

"Stop," I whispered, my lip trembling. A burst of emotions assaulted me, tears of frustration threatening to spill.

Zane's eyes thawed when he looked at me. "I'm sorry. Maybe we need a break."

"No," I sniffed, wiping my nose and surveying the grounds. "It's out here. We're just not looking in the right spot." I refused to give up.

Zane sighed and raked a hand through his hair. "If you say so, Princess."

Even though I was as tired and discouraged as the rest of them, something in the darkness pushed me. "One more sweep, and if we don't find anything, we'll call it a night," I conceded.

"Sounds like fun," Crash said grimly.

Zane eyes glared furiously, looking like he was going to blow a gasket. "You don't have to be here, you know. I don't recall inviting you. If you got a problem, leave."

"Too bad, Death Scythe." Crash smirked in a way that only ever infuriated us. "I live for this kind of drama. Tormenting you in the process is the icing on the cake."

"Fine," Zane growled. "Stay out of my way, and if you double-cross her, you won't live long enough to feel a second of satisfaction."

I leaned against a big old oak, shaking my head, thinking maybe I should just let them duke it out. *What the—* I jumped forward off the trunk with a yelp. The tree had ... *zapped me?* I turned around and scowled at the wide trunk.

"What is it?" Zane asked, coming to stand behind me.

"I don't know, probably nothing," I said, rubbing the back of my shoulder. "But I think this tree just shocked me."

All eyes flashed to me, beaming the same look. Hope.

"I wonder," Zane breathed, putting his hands on the big old tree at the heart of the courtyard. "Could it be?"

I felt silly waiting for something to happen. It was a tree. A very tall, ancient tree. "Do you feel anything?" I asked, cradling my arm against my chest. It pulsed with a strange tingle, almost like when your fingers fell asleep.

"Give me your hand," he instructed.

My immediate reaction was to say no and give him my are-you-cray-cray glower. The idea of subjecting myself to another bolt of tree mojo wasn't the least bit appealing. Hesitating, I curled my fingers with his while he still had his palm flattened against the trunk. There it was, the electric sting radiating down my arm. Zane's eyes widened. "This has got to be it."

I unfurled my fingers from his. "If this tree zaps me one more time, I'm going to chop it down and use it for firewood," I said, frowning.

"That wouldn't be wise," Crash said, his eyes sweeping up the length of the trunk. "I doubt you could if you tried. This isn't just a tree, but a capsule. It is protecting something."

When did I ever do anything wise? And we all knew what that *something* was. "How do we get it out?" Zoe asked, not getting too close. Parker was at her side, inspecting the tree like we'd all lost our minds.

"It's obvious. Princess here has to work her magic." Crash touched the bark, running his fingers along the bumpy texture, testing to see its effects. "It's nothing more than an ordinary tree for the rest of us."

"As much as it pains me to agree with douchebag, he's right," Zane said.

The idea of having to touch the thing again filled me with dread. I didn't like subjecting myself to the voltaic jolts and would prefer to avoid singeing the hair on my arms. "Why does it always have to be me?" I grumbled, regarding the tree with scorn. A brisk breeze blew in from the north, cooling my face and causing the leaves to rustle. Because I'd never uncovered a relic before, I didn't know where to start. Did I blast it with banshee sonar or hit it with a glowy ball of light?

None of those seemed appropriate. I needed to get to the roots of the tree. I sunk to my knees at the base of the giant oak, fighting the urge to wince like a little girl for fear of being shocked. There was no time for fear anymore. The world was getting dark, and I had to do this, for I could no longer ignore the throbbing in my gut. Trouble was coming, and it was getting close. I could pick up faint traces of death. *Hallows.*

We were on borrowed time.

Closing my eyes, I reached out with my power, letting it rise up around me like a force field. With caution, I dug my fingers into the ground where thick roots were slightly exposed and let my power seep into the deep cracks of the dry earth, wrapping around the tree at its hub.

A shudder went through the tree, shaking the branches over my head. Leaves tinged with the beginning colors of fall rained down on me. The air smelled of fall, damp grass, and earth. To my great relief, there were no more tiny bolts of current.

I opened my eyes as a cool mist coiled around me. My skin was glowing in a hazy white. It hadn't occurred to me before how quiet and calm the atmosphere had been, but as I pushed to my feet, the whisper of my friends traveled through the wind. Leaves crinkled under my feet as I stood under the great oak. I blinked. A small outline of a narrow door was etched along the trunk.

"Congratulations, Princess," Zane murmured. "I think you've done the impossible. You might have just saved the world from utter darkness." It creaked open as Zane gave it a push. The old wood groaned as it lifted.

A hush descended upon us. The interior of the trunk glowed softly and had a sweet musky smell, like a dusty trunk in the attic filled with your dead great-great-aunt's perfume bottles. But there, nestled deep within the tree, was what we'd been searching for. The relic.

Boom-shacka-lacka!

I wanted to do a happy dance, arms flailing and screaming like a goat, but I managed to squash the urge and smiled instead—the biggest, brightest grin.

Inside, the relic pulsed with a soft amber radiance, as if sunlight had been captured and bottled. It reminded me of a scepter the kings and queens used to carry, decorated with vines trailing up the handle. The carved head of the scepter encompassed a clear glass ball that at the top came to a needle prick point.

A halo of awe filled the courtyard as we all gaped. "It's beautiful," I murmured, reaching out, the glow washing over my face. Mesmerized by its ancient and otherworldly refinement, it aroused something inside me, beckoning me.

"Princess, don't," Zane warned, reacting quickly and pulling my arm away before I could touch it. "Not until we know it's safe," he reasoned.

"And how do you plan to determine that?" I asked, unable to take my eyes off the relic. I swear it sang to me, a song as luring as a siren's.

"There's an inscription," Crash said, eyes glittering as he moved to get a closer peek. He too seemed to be in some sort of trance, but as my eyes narrowed, I saw what he was talking about. There were indeed markings carved elegantly up one side of the handle like nothing I'd ever seen before. Enthralling scroll and swirly shapes that obviously meant something. A warning? An instruction manual?

Again, I had the urge to trail my finger over the etchings. "What does it say?"

"Parker," Crash said, stepping back. "You got some kind of ancient reaper decoder in one of those books you always got your nose in?"

"Right in my back pocket," Parker answered drily.

Zoe shoved Crash in the shoulder. "Don't be such a jerk."

"I was being serious," he mumbled, as if any of us believed him.

"How do we know this tree isn't a booby trap?" Parker asked, shrinking back from the tree.

Zoe gave him a reassuring smile, linking her fingers with his. "I've got killer reflexes. I'll make sure you don't get swept up in a net or peppered with arrows."

Crash snorted.

"So we think it's safe?" Parker again prodded the million dollar question. "It did shock Piper when she touched it."

Zane sent Parker a look. "There's only one way to find out."

Declan, my stealthy shadow, stepped forward. "Maybe someone other than Piper should extract the device." He was so military in his thought process.

I shook my head. "No, it has to be me," I proclaimed. A tiny seed of hope flickered inside amongst all the mounting anxiety and fear. Maybe I could do this: really save the world. All I had to do was take hold of the relic and activate it. I had managed to reveal it without a hitch; here's to hoping using it wouldn't be any different.

Story of my life: things never go smoothly.

Parker wasn't having it. "I have a nasty feeling about this."

I patted his chest. "I'll be fine." Not mentioning that the nasty feeling he was talking about was an ambush of hallows headed straight here. I sensed them. They were moving quickly, threatened by the relic. I had to get my hands on it. Now.

With no expectation and a fire under my butt, I stuck my arm into the little door, half expecting there to be an intense heat. As my fingers grazed the top, sliding to the handle, an arctic chill amplified through my arm, up my shoulder, until my entire body was encompassed in a cold that made the air in my chest crisp. In my hand, the scepter flared, a golden aura shooting up the staff and over my face. *Holy macaroni.* I felt a sudden dizzy spell.

"I told you it was real," Crash said with a small degree of victory in his voice.

Zane said something in response, but I didn't catch it, because the ground began to twirl beneath me and another wave of dizziness made my head spin. I fought the darkness threatening to take me into oblivion.

It wasn't Zane's voice that kept me from going over the edge. Nope, it was Heath's.

CHAPTER 27

H*eath.* My brain echoed his name as my eyes tried to deny what was right in front of me. Heath approached, flanked by two Red Hawks whose names I knew, thanks to my banshee roll call abilities, but I'd never seen them before. He stood before me, a satisfied smirk on his dry lips, as if he was the cat who had caught the canary. I should have been afraid, but the relic pulsing in my hand gave me courage, and I stayed unwavering under his glare.

Heath gave a jerk of his head, and his two goons circled behind us, boxing us in. Then the artillery showed up, covering the perimeter of the manor, bearing hollow eyes and anger strong enough to kill. My confidence dipped. Okay, it more than dipped. It plummeted, and my fear spiked.

I had known Heath would bring an army, but knowing and seeing were two very different things. Never had I seen so many hallows in one place. As I surveyed the sheer volume of ghosts, not all of them were vengeful spirits but had joined the bandwagon in promise of a chance at life again. They probably hadn't been given the disclaimer. If I didn't succeed in putting back the barrier, this place wouldn't be inhabitable, so a chance at a life was a farce.

Zane whirled around. In one smooth motion, he drew his sword from the shadows. "How did you get in here?" he hissed. The grounds of the manor were heavily guarded; reinforcements had been added since the night Zane and I married, in anticipation of trouble.

Several dark forms emerged from behind the shrubs and peonies. Four wolves growled, teeth bared as they made their way through the bushes. Eyes glowing, their growls turned to snarls.

Zach tipped his head to one side, his aqua eyes shining. "Looks like he brought the wolf pack."

Shit buckets. Things kept getting more interesting and not in a good way. No, this wasn't sketchy at all.

Heath had breezed into the courtyard with no warning from my security. In that guileless way of his, he seemed to know what I was thinking. "It helps to have a man on the inside."

Zane had Crash slammed up against the tree in three seconds flat. "I told you what would happen if you stabbed her in the back."

Crash didn't bother to struggle. "It wasn't me, you blockhead."

Zane flashed a black dagger at Crash's throat. "Sorry if I don't believe you."

Heath laughed, not concerned for his son's safety. He was the king of douchebags.

"What are you doing here?" I demanded.

"You're in possession of something I want." His voice held power, echoing over the courtyard. He looked at me with slitted eyes. "I knew you could find it, *your highness*. You just needed a push in the right direction." His slimy gaze moved to his son.

"Okay, that I am guilty of," Crash unabashedly admitted.

Zane's eyes went steely, and the shadow binds he used to keep Crash from morphing into another form tightened. "You son of a bitch. I'll kill you."

A wry grin appeared on Heath's face, but Zane was too focused on Crash to notice. "Understandable. He served his purpose. And now it's time for you to serve yours."

I couldn't agree more. Giving my lungs a workout, I screamed, a beacon to every reaper, summoning them to my aid. The battle between reaper and dead had begun.

"You shouldn't have done that." Heath tsk-ed.

My skin prickled with disgust. "You left me with no choice."

He chuckled weakly. "I'm not the only one who doesn't abide by the rules, *Mrs.* Hunter."

"I'm nothing like you," I spat.

"This can all end. All you have to do is give me what I came for."

"Don't do it," Zane blurted out.

"We've got your back," Zoe added.

"And he's out of time," Declan said, glancing upward. Reapers were coming, answering my call.

Heath stared stonily at me, daring me to act. "They're right. Time's up. You should have just given me the relic and saved them all from bloodshed. We both know my numbers are greater than yours."

I quelled my fear. "And let you win? No thanks. Didn't anyone ever tell you size doesn't matter?" This was one of those moments I was proud of my filter-free mouth.

"So be it."

My throat dried.

Zane's face went cold and blank. He shoved at Crash's chest, releasing him. "I'm gonna kill you in a minute." And then he spun around, throwing out his hand, and a bolt of darkness expelled from his palm. The arc of the shadows split in half, striking both of Heath's goons in the chest. The two Hawks went down, a blast of light erupting from their bodies.

It kicked off from there.

"Well, that's one way of taking care of things," Zach said. "No turning back now."

"Hold off as many as you can while Piper figures out the what-cha-ma-bob," Zane instructed.

No one needed to be told twice. Zach threw out his arm, hitting a wolf in the nose. The hound went up in the air, ears flapping like wings before he smashed into the ground. "Already on it," Zach said, grinning.

Parker swung around. "They're coming."

"Zoe!" I yelled. "I need you to keep Parker safe. If anything happens to him ..."

"I got this," she replied, unraveling her glittering black whip. "I can keep him out of trouble."

Parker's mouth dropped open, but there wasn't time to argue. Fire exploded down the stone pathway leading up to the courtyard, thrashing and twisting in a maelstrom of heat and fury. It shot straight for us. Zane wrapped me in shadows, tackling us flat to the ground as flames shot over our head, singeing my back as I lay gasping on the grass.

For a few seconds that felt like minutes, I lay there with Zane's body covering mine, feeling both hot and cold at the same time as the shadows warded off the fire. Through the crackling and hiss of the inferno, I swore I heard Heath laugh.

Declan was the only one on his feet. He made a sweeping motion with his hand, dousing the flames with a gust of icy wind.

"Oh, man, tell me someone brought the marshmallows," Crash blurted out.

Zoe and Parker struggled to their feet, muttering curses and groans, but they were unhurt. They moved beside Declan to block the entrance of the courtyard, but their eyes glanced upward, pulled by an enormous cluster of dark bats that seemed to move with incredible speed, blocking the moonlight. The feeling that rolled through my gut told me those weren't bats, but reapers.

Yes, they were.

As the cluster got closer, it broke apart. Reapers edged along the perimeter of the manor, coming up behind the army of hallows. They were a welcomed sight. Aspyn and Oliver were among the reapers who had arrived. We were no longer ridiculously outnumbered, but pandemonium followed.

The hallows gasped and hissed, preparing to tear into us, kill us one by one, setting free the souls collected. They zipped in like a mob, darting and dashing over bushes and landscaping, destroying everything in their path.

"Now, this is more like it," Zach said, throwing back one attacker and whirling to meet the next. Zoe was at his side, her whip slashing through the air like a viper, poisoning her targets to their end.

Zane's mind moaned. *Princess, stay close.*

My eyes sharpened, glinting as our souls merged. There was no reason to hold back, no reason not to use the power we possessed together. A dry laugh escaped as I steeled myself. It was go time.

Crash knocked a strand of hair out of his eyes and smiled. "Let's do this," he announced in a raspy voice.

Zane shot him a look that was purely predatory.

"You guys, stop this!" I cried. "We got company." The hallows went berserk, howling, hissing, and screaming in the night.

Lean and dangerous, silhouetted in all black, Zane's hand went to his sword. With a flash of black, his shadowy blade breezed past my face before cutting down a hallow in one clean sweep. He burst into a thousand pieces of shattered light. Zane arched a brow at me.

"What?" I said innocently. "You told me to stay close."

At least you listened.

Crash slipped into his wolf form, sleek and lean, with a sly twitch to his lips and a troublesome glint in his silver eyes. I had to say, he was a whole lot scarier as a wolf. Snarling and fangs shining in the moonlight, he leapt at his fellow hounds. One let out an inhuman sound as Crash sunk his canines into the scruff of its neck. Another with gold eyes and a thick, dark, scraggly coat jumped on Crash's back. They rolled, jaws snapping and paws lashing.

My name echoed in warning from across the yard. "Piper!" It was Parker.

Company was coming directly at me. With my soul aligned with Zane's, electricity crawled throughout my body. White energy burst from me, smacking into four hallows and tossing them back into the stone wall.

Zane lunged at me. I tensed, my heart hammering in my chest. He pinned us up against the garden wall as the air was peppered by lethal darts of fire, shielding me with his body. They flew through the air, thunking into the stone walls and pinging off the metal gate to clatter to the ground. Oliver took a direct hit. He jerked, spinning to the left, and came face to face with a gleaming hallow. Oliver, hugging his side, tried a detour to no avail. His assailant slammed his fist into Oliver's chest.

Panic sliced through me.

I started to race forward, but a pair of strong arms circled around my waist, lifting my feet off the ground. "It's too late, Princess," Zane whispered in my ear, confirming what I already suspected. Oliver was dead.

My stomach twisted and churned.

Zane whirled away from me, his arm moving upward in a vicious slash. After he took out two hallows, he turned to me, framing my face. "Piper, you can do this. We can do this."

"I-I can bring him back," I stammered, frozen in place.

Zane shook his head." You can't save them all and save the world, Princess. You're going to need your strength."

And I was going to need his. I understood sacrifices must be made; I just hated it was those under my protection, those who put their lives on the line to defend me.

Together the reapers must stand. Or one by one we would fall. The world would cease to exist as we knew it. Scary shit. And a fairly compelling reason to fight. In my head, I knew war was inevitable, but seeing my reapers fall to their death made my common sense tingle. The power I'd learned to accept, even embrace, wavered like a candle under hot breath. As I stared around, a thousand scenarios raced through my mind, each more horrifying than the last.

"Piper," Zane called—the only voice that could bring me back from the brink of a meltdown.

As much as it devastated me, I needed to press on. All I could do was strive for the best but plan for the worst. I nodded, gaining conviction from the look in his eyes. Then as one, Zane and I leapt out. His shadows wrapped around me, acting as a barrier against the war surrounding us.

Shit went colossal.

A chorus of hisses filled the night. It was a horrible sound that made me want to curl up into a ball and cover my ears. The hallows advanced. Beams of light slammed into the ground, flashing into the sky. Streaks of red and white clashed with my reapers, knocking several of them into the ground. I caught a glimpse of Aspyn just as she was grabbed by a hallow and tossed over a bush like her life meant nothing. We weren't going to win this battle by fighting only. As hard as it was to watch, knowing many would die tonight to save millions, it was time for me to do my part.

I tore my gaze from the horror and turned around to find Heath blocking my path. His eyes bored into my skull, yet I refused to turn away. I desperately wanted to back down, making myself stand my ground.

"Go," Zane instructed, stepping in front of me, a shadow of darkness. "I'll take care of the traitorous overlord. Be careful," he pleaded.

"Back at you," I told him, wishing there was time for at least a good luck kiss.

I looked over my shoulder, seeing Declan and Zach shooting off blasts of energy like there was no tomorrow. Adrenaline burst inside me in tumultuous waves. All around me chaos ensued as I fumbled with the relic.

Another series of lights went over my head. "Come on," I mumbled, turning the device to inspect it from different angles, desperately searching for a button, a trigger, anything to bring the contraption to life.

I felt a pang of disappointment as time elapsed, pressure mounting, but I inhaled and exhaled a deep breath, squashing the frustration. *You can do this. You have to do this.* At the end of the day, if I survived as a victor, I was going to need to replenish my reapers—a rebirth. Those who didn't stand beside me would die, but to give anyone a chance, I had to crack this sector.

I took a second to see how we were faring. The good news: my friends were still alive; the bad news: I couldn't find Heath. Zane leapt off the ground, flying directly at a hallow, and slammed into the ghost in midair. They collided, light and darkness, rolling until they hit land like a bomb, shaking the ground and lighting up the sky.

A movement caught the corner of my eye just as a hand wrapped around my throat. "If you scream, I'll snap your neck." Heath's breath tickled the back of my collar.

"Shit," I breathed, going still. On the up side, I'd found Heath, or I should say, he found me.

He shifted around, so that we were inches apart, so close I could see my reflection in his iron eyes. "Bravo, Princess, bravo. You've managed to give me what I've dreamed about for a decade: power to rule. Nothing can stop me now."

I wanted to spit in his face, but I was partial to having my neck and shoulders connected. "The night is still young."

"True, but I'm guessing you don't know how to use the only weapon to stop me." His breath was cold on my cheek. "Sweet justice."

My heart slammed into my rib cage, fingers digging into the relic handle. "Perhaps not, but I can shove it up your ass."

He threw his head back and laughed, a haunting sound of a mad reaper. "That won't be necessary. I'll just take this off your hands." His free hand moved down my arm in a sensual caress that churned my stomach and creeped me out. Big time.

I shouldn't have given into the urge, but it was too late. I'd spit in Heath's face. A second later, I was on my back, pain spiking and the air knocked from my lungs. I was staring up into Heath's triumphant face as my breath faltered, and for a moment, my mind went blank.

Then I remembered. The relic. My head thrashed to the side, and everything came crashing down. It was gone. The darkness I embraced came rising up to take me to oblivion, and I did nothing to stop it. What was the point?

Heath laid his hand over my chest, his lips leering as I closed my eyes. I didn't want Heath to be the last face I saw, but I didn't have the strength to move. Serenity overwhelmed me, erasing all the pain and suffering, all the hurt and failure. The world would end, and I with it. What did I care what happened if I wouldn't be there to see it?

Because you care, Zane spoke through the shroud of blackness. *Your humanity and growing up apart from this world is what makes you better.*

You mean weaker, Heath mocked.

Don't listen to him. Zane reached for my hand. He was bathed in shadows, eyes blue as sapphires. *Take my hand.*

But I couldn't. Something snarled and snapped behind me. No matter how hard I tried, I couldn't manage to lift my hand. Didn't he see I couldn't move?

Yes, you can. Don't look back. Just take my hand.

If only I could. The slightest movement hurt, sending shooting pain down my arm. There was nothing wrong with me, not physically. They were projections. I just needed to lift my hand.

Letting out a raw scream, I raised my arm, reaching out for him. Our fingertips touched, and that was all it took to break the illusion.

I've got you, Zane assured me, his eyes never leaving mine. *I won't let you go.*

The pressure clamping down on my chest exploded, like a cork out of a champagne bottle, shooting into the air.

My eyes snapped open, glaring up at Heath from the floor with narrow eyes. His palm was fastened to my soul, but Zane had given me the strength to fight. This war wasn't over yet.

"Bastard," I croaked out, my butt still stinging, making my words sharp.

A slow, unnerving smirk twisted on Heath's lips. "Ready to give up?"

Smoky shadows billowed behind Heath, huge and imposing and familiar. Zane looked as daunting as ever: lean, powerful, dynamic. "I'd like to see you try that crap on me."

Heath didn't even flinch. "You're not worth my time." He disregarded Zane like an ant under his shoe. Big mistake.

"That's what you think," Zane snarled. "My blood might not be pure, but I don't need to hide behind an army and have them do the grunt work. I don't mind getting dirty."

Exasperated with the disruption, Heath finally turned to face Zane. "You'll never be your father."

Zane's expression stayed unyielding and fierce. "Too bad you won't live long enough to see." His eyes flicked over Heath's shoulder at me, a blaze of blue fire. "It's your time to shine, Princess." Then Zane attacked the overlord.

CHAPTER 28

I dashed for the relic, thinking of nothing but getting my hands on it, and this time I wouldn't fail. My feet flew over the ground, ears buzzing, and lunged for the scepter, snatching it up by the handle. Knowing I was probably breaking a hundred sacred rules, I spun around, getting my bearings. The cold seared my hands, and I gasped, nearly dropping the relic on the ground. The coldness wasn't painful, but a shock all the same. It wasn't going to deter me. I circled back around toward the tree, dodging hallows as I went. It was hard to keep my eyes from checking on Zane, validating he was still on his feet. I resisted the urge, pushing on and rushing into the circular clearing.

Something caught my eye, something I had missed before or never paid attention to, but I understood now. A section of the courtyard was a replica of the stone circle. How had I missed that before? My feet slid over the dirt as I came to a screeching halt, narrowly avoiding being clotheslined by a large tree branch. I exhaled when I saw the little door nestled in the trunk of the big oak. My fingers were firm on the scepter, tingling as I held it up.

"Keep them away from her!" Zane ordered, trying to give me the time I needed.

The hallows had scattered, descending from all directions and swarming the courtyard. Slivers of moonlight provided our only light in the fight against darkness. Cursing, I looked up and saw two familiar silver eyes glowing at me in the dark. For a stomach-dropping second, I thought it was Heath, but then I saw the stupid grin. Crash. The last person I'd expected. He had ditched the wolf form. "What are you doing?" I snapped.

"I'm watching your back," he replied.

I snorted. "Because that panned out so well before. I'm not a sucker."

"I was in a precarious situation. If I hadn't convinced my father I was loyal to him, do you think he would have confided in me about the relic?"

He made a good point, but too little too late. Eyes scanning the area around the tree, I searched for a clue on what to do with the scepter. "So you're saying you betrayed me for the greater good?"

"I wouldn't go that far. I'm not a saint," he answered and then twisted to the left and planted his fist into an incoming hallow.

"It doesn't really matter whose side you're on at the moment. The only thing that does matter is getting this thing to work," I said, shaking the relic. I was starting to sweat.

"Just say the magic word." Crash mocked.

"Blow me."

He chuckled. "I don't think that's it."

Hell, what did I have to lose? For shits and giggles, I mumbled, "Abracadabra," and waved my hand over the globe. I knew I was being ridiculous, but I was willing to do anything, even something as absurd as that.

Shocker. Nothing happened, other than Crash folding his arms and smirking. "It was worth a shot."

I wanted to sucker punch him. "I don't have the liberty of time. If your father gets his hands on this ..."

"It's all over," he finished. "I know." Crash's eyes were suddenly alert. He frowned, scrunching his forehead. His hands flexed at his sides as he moved forward, ramming his fist into the belly of a girl not much older than me. "Somebody test this chick for steroids," he said, opening and closing his fingers.

She hissed, running her tongue along her teeth. "Is that all you got?" Crash's hit had no effect on her whatsoever, other than pissing her off more. Nails swiped in the air toward his face. She managed to get a scratch or two on his cheek before he scurried out of her reach.

"Damn, you're feisty. Good thing I like a challenge." And she gave him one. This hallow had skill, making her a hell of an opponent. Crash wasn't Zane but had been trained to fight his whole life. I had to keep reminding myself of that.

Using her weight and brute strength, she barreled forward like a freight train, hands extended. Crash shot to the left, shoving her back a step, before spinning her around and pinning her wrists together. "Geez, I normally don't mind when a girl is all grabby, but you, honey, are not my type."

She sneered, trying to break her arms free. "It's laughable that you would think that. I don't want your body; I want your souls."

"Oh, in that case, Piper, a little help," he prodded, shifting the hallow so she was directly in front of me. She didn't make it easy, and I thought any minute she would break free.

I rolled my eyes and lifted my free hand, attaching it to her chest. A burst of white light followed, and poof, steroid chick was gone. "Happy?"

Crash dusted off his jeans. "Took you long enough."

I shrugged, blasé. "I wanted you to suffer."

"Fair enough."

"You got no qualms about hitting a girl, I see."

He smiled tightly. "Hey, I just saved your hind end."

"Whatever. I saved your ass." My chest rose slowly as I diverted my attention back to the task. "Now what?"

"Did you try giving it some juice?" he offered, attempting to be helpful.

I didn't want his assistance, but with everyone otherwise occupied with the battle, I didn't have much of a choice. Zane would only be able to keep Heath busy for so long.

One-handed, I revved the energy inside me, allowing it to seep into the handle as I had with the tree to unlock the relic. It radiated inside me like a wave of light. After a full minute, I sighed, disgruntled. "It's not working."

"I can see that," he stated.

I gave him a dirty look and held up the relic. "Do you want to try?"

He took a step back. "Unlike my father, I don't want to be near that thing. Gives me the creeps."

"A lot of help you are." I tapped my nail on the handle of the scepter, wracking my brain for information. As many dead banshees as I'd talked to, one of them must have said something of importance, something to help me. Rose. Mom. Celeste.

A halo of light dinged in my brain. That was it. Celeste had spoken of a blood sacrifice. Power doesn't come without a price, she had said. The relic didn't want my power. It wanted my blood.

Not a fan of needles, I shuddered as I stared at the sharp tip, perfect for piercing the skin and thin enough to be a tube.

This was going to suck.

Palm flattened, I took a deep breath, and before I could think about how much it was going to hurt, I plunged my hand onto the needle.

Crash gasped. "Jesus Christ. A little warning next time you decide to self-mutilate."

Hissing through my teeth, pain lanced down my arm, extending to the rest of my body. I couldn't breathe. I couldn't even cry. The cold seeped through my skin, reaching my inner core. Silly me for thinking saving the world would be painless. I clenched my jaw against the sting, keeping my hand secured over the globe.

The glass began to swirl with my blood, little droplets floating in the chamber like bubbles, but that was all. Nothing amazing or epic happened. I'd assumed I'd feel something. A tremble. A surge. The only thing I felt was my entire being buzzing with thwarted hope and a heavy disappointment settling in my chest.

Shit. Shit. Shit.

I wanted to scream, the kind that would shatter glass, burst eardrums, and cause destruction. "Why didn't that work?" I raged.

Crash had his WTF look on his face. "Uh, I'm still getting over the fact you stabbed yourself with it."

I started to mutter. "Blood. Sacrifice. Power. What else could it need?"

He rubbed the sandy scruff on the side of his cheeks. "My father never mentioned anything about blood, only something about it taking two souls to trigger the veil."

I glanced up. "Why didn't you say something sooner?" My eyes locked with Zane's across the lawn. I could have whispered his name, I wasn't sure, but I had drawn his attention.

Soul symmetry.

My blood alone wasn't going to save us. It needed our blood. Together.

"If you really want to help," I said to Crash. "Keep your father occupied while Zane and I crack ancient history."

"You do realize he is going to kill me."

"We're all going to die if Zane and I don't do this."

"Point taken. You owe me." The air around him stirred, following the network of red veins enveloping his body. I blinked, and he was no longer human. The wolf at my feet winked before bounding off toward his father.

This better work.

The stench of death was everywhere. Zane's head swung in my direction, his eyes a deep blue under the dim light shining like diamonds. Damp bits of hair clung to his forehead and temples. He took one look at my face and then was off, flying toward me. Shadows shimmered around him, heavy in the air, cloaking us from the chaos. Power invaded my system.

He had a way of making me feel invincible, which was crazy, because I didn't know if we'd ever truly be safe.

"Is that your blood?" he asked, eyeballing the glowing artifact in my grasp.

I nodded. "I think I figured out how to activate the scepter, but it is missing one key ingredient."

"Don't tell me."

"Yep, your blood, but we need to merge our souls first."

He held out a hand. "What are we waiting for?"

We hadn't even touched, and I could already feel my soul reaching out to him, drawing him to me. It wanted the connection, urged for it, and I gave it what it begged for. Our powers conjoined, pulsing. Another time, another place, I would have just liked to revel in the sheer awesomeness pouring through us. Someday, I swore, we'd be able to use our soul symmetry for something other than fighting.

Our fingers linked, and the energy flared—lightness and darkness. I closed my eyes, knowing what came next, and let Zane take the lead. My head tipped back as the first icy bite of the needle pierced Zane's hand.

No pain. No gain.

"Piper," he said in a strangled voice, and a tremor went through him, rippling to me.

I gasped, my eyes popping open. It was an odd sensation, filled with both agony and bliss. The merging of our souls was a high, but the extraction of blood was a sensation I never wanted to feel again. Time seemed to slow, dragging out the process and emphasizing the agony. I wanted to cry out, but the sound was caught in my throat.

While Zane and I were tangled up, Declan slashed at a nearby hallow, only to have him spring back. Another leapt in from behind, cornering him. He wasn't the only one with his back to the wall. As I winced, Aspyn, Parker, Zoe, Zach, and many, many others fought desperately to keep the hallows at bay, but it didn't look promising. If something major didn't happen, there was no way we were going to win this war.

Never had I seen such a horrid sight. Ripping my gaze from the destruction, I stumbled, unprepared for the instant relief. Zane had dislodged his hand and released mine. Gulping, I took huge, deep breaths of air, clearing the fog of bewilderment.

I should be used to the surreal, but seeing my blood blend with

Zane's was captivating. A red mist swirled in the glass chamber like a magic potion. It shimmered, fluid and alive, eager to do its purpose: to rid the earth of those who didn't belong in this realm, sending them back to the other side of the veil.

Blood was trickling down my face, dripping a path down my cheek like a giant red tear. My body throbbed, and each movement brought on a new onslaught of pain, but I kept everything in sharp focus, ignoring it all but the relic.

"Here goes nothing," I mumbled and raised the scepter over my head, smashing it down into the ground. The dirt shook under my feet, followed promptly by a burst of blinding light that raced across the garden and spread over the island. My blood and Zane's oozed out of the chamber, seeping into the earth.

Lights exploded behind my eyes, and before my next breath, I was flown back into a corner. My head whacked on something hard, and stars burst as I slumped to the grass. The relic became like a black hole, drawing all the hallows to it and sucking them up.

Oh. My. God. We did it. I couldn't believe it. I must have blinked fifty times, but the fire in my belly was already celebrating. Zane had the same dumbstruck look. I moved to throw my arms around his neck, doing a little victory dance, until a low voice stole my moment.

"Do you know what you've done?" There was no mistaking the intense bitterness.

How could I have forgotten about Heath for even a second? I turned around, and Zane placed his hand on the small of my back. "Yes. I do. I undid everything corrupt you started."

His lips curved. "Not everything."

My stomach twisted, and a lump rose to my throat. A great sense of foreboding took root. "Just admit defeat and maybe I'll spare your life." ... But not my power.

He wasn't having it. "You're going to have to kill me."

I kept my voice light and even. "With pleasure." A murmur went through the ranks of the reapers, all eyes turning to me.

Everything happened at once. I extended my hand, intending to siphon Heath's reaper powers right from his slimy core. At the same time, he grabbed his son, throwing Crash in front of him. "If you're going to kill me, you might as well take out my entire bloodline."

Bastard.

I hesitated, as he knew I would, my hand stopping a centimeter from Crash's heart.

"Cutting it a bit close, luv," Crash said, keeping his voice light, but I caught the slightest tremble.

Zane growled.

Crash observed me with solemn gray eyes, and I knew he was going to do something I wouldn't like. My heart splintered. I had begun to think he wouldn't betray me, that all the things he had said to me had been the truth.

My eyes couldn't believe it. What kind of father did that—sacrificed his son to save himself?

A monster.

A coward.

Heath was nothing more than a spineless douchebag. He didn't deserve to be a reaper. I vowed before this night was over, I would kill him—rid the Earth of such a foul being.

As soon as I got an opening.

"I'm sorry," Crash uttered. "It had to be this way."

The truth hit me in the chest. Crash had never betrayed me. He might have even saved me—saved us all.

He deliberately stared his father in the eyes as he spoke, but he had been apologizing to me. Smart move. It was never wise to take your eyes off a snake like his father. Heath wasn't a fool. He knew his son. Moving so fast, Heath was like lightning, his hands on either side of Crash's head.

A sickening crack echoed in the night, followed by Crash hitting the ground. His body flickered between human and wolf.

I yelled his name, frightened he might die. Zane has his hands on my waist, keeping me at his side. I forced myself to stay calm and stretched out my abilities to see if I could still sense Crash. He was indeed alive, but his breathing faltered. Crash thrashed on the ground, blood pooling at his hands. Anger flared in my chest as I lifted my chin, eyes burning into Heath.

In horror, I opened my mouth to scream. Heath had lifted his weapon for the killing blow. I tore from Zane's hold, and I didn't stop, not even when he called my name.

But I was too late. Crash somehow managed to steady his form and roll to the left, just as Heath swung out with his sword, nicking Crash on the top of the shoulder. He winced as his shirt soaked in blood, but it was the least of his concerns. Heath wasn't going to quit until the job was done. His blade sliced in the air. Heath might be old and wise, but Crash was young and quick. Anticipating his father's move, he knocked into Heath's arm, dislodging the weapon. It clattered to the ground with Heath staggering backwards. Crash took advantage, stepping within Heath's guard and plunging his own dagger through his father's chest.

Time ceased. Heath stood there, a look of shock on his face, staring at the blade in his chest. Crash had used such force the knife had erupted out of Heath's back. "What have you done?" Heath gurgled, eyes blank and confused.

Then Crash yanked the blade free, and Heath's eyes rolled up in his head. He crumbled to the floor like a decrepit old man. Red veins slithered over his entire body, followed by the dark shadow of death, hiding him from view.

"I was never going to be the son you wanted," Crash said, looming over Heath's body.

He had killed his father.

I shuddered, torn between passing out and throwing up. Strange how I was a harbinger of death, yet I still wasn't desensitized to the sight of blood.

Heath might be dead, but I knew better than anyone, he wasn't really gone, not until his soul was destroyed. "Zane," I prompted.

Crash had proven his loyalty, but I couldn't risk the chance of his father coming back as a hallow to be reckoned with. I'd rather avoid that encounter altogether, and there was only one way to ensure I'd never see Heath's ugly mug again. His soul needed to be destroyed.

There would always be hallows who lingered on Earth, and the Crows would destroy them—that was how the cycle worked: balance. It felt epic to level the scale.

Zane crouched over the source of all my problems and put his palm on Heath's chest. As the essence of the overlord pumped into Zane, his veins darkened, spidering over his body. And just like that, the source of all my problems—my mother's death, Rose's death, the ruin between two realms—dissipated at the hands of my husband.

It was finally over.

CHAPTER 29

"Sit down," Zane instructed. "Let me see your face."

My body trembled from the aftermath of shock and adrenaline. I sat down, folding my hands together to keep them from shaking. The cut wasn't deep and already had begun to heal. Although now that he had brought it to the forefront of my mind, it stung like hell. Zane knelt at the side of the couch, studying the gash. He pressed a cold, damp cloth to my cheek. I instinctively flinched and jerked away.

"That hurt," I hissed through my teeth.

Zane shook his head, the corner of his lip lifting. "I haven't even touched you yet."

I grimaced. "It's been a long night."

He lifted the towel, blotting it very carefully to my face. He was as gentle as possible. "It has been, but it's over. And now we can rebuild." He took my hand and pressed a kiss on the center of my palm. "There, all better."

"I can't believe it's really over." The truth of it exploded inside me. It was hard to imagine what my life was going to be like. I'd grown so used to the constant fear, always waiting for the next attack or the next attempt on my life.

Zane squeezed my hip. All we could do was stare at each other.

I wasn't the only one in need of tending. I pulled my gaze from Zane's, searching the parlor for our group of friends. They were really okay. Warming near the fireplace, Zoe was patching Parker up. I caught his eye, and he smiled.

Pure, sweet relief poured through me. He was safe.

Crash, Declan, Aspyn, and Zach were huddled near the window. Declan had his arm secured around Aspyn as she wiped at her eyes. I looked up into Crash's tired face, and he winked. There was so much to be joyous over, but I found myself thinking about all those we'd lost, including Oliver.

I swallowed back a fresh bout of tears.

It was then, as I was quashing the raw emotions, that TJ wandered into the room. He took one look around and blurted out, "What happened? What did I miss?"

"Your sister just saved the world," Parker said proudly, his glasses crooked on his nose. Zoe straightened them, smiling.

TJ busted out laughing. "Yeah right. You guys are hilarious."

"He wasn't joking," Declan jumped to my defense. "She really did just save us all from extinction."

I cleared my throat. "I didn't do it alone."

TJ took a closer look around, seeing the cuts, the blood, and the weary expressions. "I literally miss everything."

It didn't matter that TJ was bummed. What mattered was he was alive, and the world wasn't going to be overtaken by psychotic ghosts. "Trust me, it was better you missed it."

Concern wrinkled his forehead. "Do you think we should call Dad? Make sure he is okay?"

I cringed and stiffened. Damn. How could I have forgotten? I'd told TJ the truth about myself but had failed to tell him the truth about his father. I was so exhausted, and the last thing I wanted to do was tell my little brother I was his only living relative. "Sit down," I said, leveling my voice. "There's something I need to explain."

"Why do you have that look like you're going to tell me he's dead?" he tossed at me.

I winced again. He made it sound so heartless. "Because he is." I laid it straight. The timing sucked, but that's what I got for procrastinating. I had been distracted between Zane and the veil, but it was no excuse. TJ was the only family I had left. We needed each other.

"How are you so sure?" Doubt weaseled its way into his pinched expression.

"I saw him. The night before you came back to the island, he showed up."

"As one of those ghosts," he concluded.

I nodded, my face going still and white. What else could I say? Congratulations, you're now an orphan?

He finally took a seat, robotically sitting on the edge of the mattress. "No." He rejected the notion.

I watched as his eyes worked through what I was telling him, and I felt my gut clench, blinking so hard so I wouldn't start bawling like a baby. "I'm sorry," I whispered. "He won't be coming back."

The color drained from his face, and I knew I had just turned his world inside out, a feeling both of us knew well. I could only hope he would lean on me and the new family we had here in Raven Hollow.

I didn't tell him that he wasn't my biological father. I didn't tell him that James had threatened to kill him. Instead, I let him remember his father as he was.

My hair was a mess, tangled and crusted with blood; my clothes were worse, torn and disgusting. I peeled them off, discarding them into the trash as I walked into the bathroom for a long soak in the tub. I needed warmth to heat me from the inside out.

As I returned to my room, freshly showered and semi-normal, a chill coasted along the floor. I glanced up and gasped. "Zander?"

His smile widened. "I told you we'd see each other again."

I managed to swallow the squeak of surprise before Zane came barreling through the door to check on me. Looking at Zander, even the ghost of him, brought a fresh memory of his death. It still haunted me. I smiled, tears shining in my eyes. "You did."

Gaze twinkling, his eyes moved to my loosely tied robe. "Not the best timing, but timing never seemed to be our thing."

I laughed, tightening the terry cloth around me. "No, it wasn't."

Zander was lounging on the edge of my bed. "You did it, Piper. Always knew you would save us all."

I leaned my hip against the vanity. "You did, huh?"

He nodded. "From the first time I saw you at the bonfire, I knew you were going to change everything. Zane did too. We all did."

"I wish someone would have told me."

He chuckled. "What fun would that have been?"

I snorted. Seeing Zander drudged up raw feelings, and my emotions got the best of me. I couldn't help but think of Zane. "He misses you, ya know," I said, rubbing my arms. "He doesn't need to tell me. I can feel how much it pains him to not have you around anymore."

Zander's pale face fell flat. "It's a good thing he has you. Take care of him. He needs you more than he would ever admit."

I pressed my lips together. "It goes both ways."

"The universe knew what it was doing when it paired you with him."

"I guess," I conceded. "But some days I'd argue that the universe has a cruel sense of humor."

A ghost of a smile curled on his lips. "He might not be the easiest person to love, but he loves you fiercely. The almighty Death Scythe was willing to thwart the council in the name of love. He might have stretched the limits of the council's rules, but never outwardly spurned them. What will you do now?"

"Assign new council members," I joked … sort of.

"I think that's exactly what you should do. Out with the old, in with the new," he encouraged me.

"And how do you think Death would feel about that?"

"Have you met my father?" he replied directly. "I would take him making Zane his heir as a sign. He would welcome the change."

I twirled my wedding band. "Maybe you're right."

A smug smile stretched across his face. "Of course I'm right."

"Things like that remind me you're related to Zane."

"He learned from the best." His smug smile faded a little, and I knew our time was coming to an end. "Take care of him."

I stepped forward. "Do you have to go?" I asked, thinking maybe he would like to see Zane.

He nodded, and I understood. It would be harder for them both to see each other. "No good-byes."

I forced a smile on my lips. "See you later."

He grinned in return—the Hunter killer smile, dimples and all. "I'll be seeing you, Piper."

I watched in a sad, wistful silence as Zander's form began to break up, flickering like a faulty lightbulb. In a matter of seconds, I was staring at the empty spot where he had been.

Dragging my feet across the floor, I collapsed on my bed, and no sooner did my head hit the pillow, when tingles tiptoed down my spine. Zane sauntered into the room looking like everything I ever needed. A warrior, a lover, a friend, a savior. And he looked damn good too. Seeing his face caused a slew of emotions to materialize, including all the ones I'd been suppressing. I had a feeling I wouldn't be able to hold the dam much longer.

He climbed onto the bed, lying down beside me, our faces close. "I love you," he whispered softly.

Oh gosh.

He had no idea how much I needed to hear him say that. I pressed my lips to his, fighting back the messy balloon of emotions rising to the surface. It had been a helluva day, and now that it was over, really over, I had all these feelings I didn't know what to do with. I was going to cry.

Yep, I was definitely going to shed hot, messy tears. Some for those we lost, some for being alive, some for the relief and happiness.

We'd defied the rules, fought back, and won.

Staring into Zane's gleaming eyes, I was feeling pretty good. We had brought an end to the apocalypse, and every ending was also a beginning. Zane and I were just about to start ours.

EPILOGUE

TWO YEARS LATER...

I was being shaken awake. Blinking in the darkness, a tiny cry rang in my ears.

"Piper," Zane murmured, "wake up." He was sitting on the edge of the bed, blue eyes sparkling through the shadows.

Exhaustion pulled at me. Sleep made my eyes heavy, and I was more tired than I'd imagined I would be. Being woken multiple times a night made my thoughts swirl muddily.

He slipped a hand onto my waist. "Your daughter is hungry."

"Why is it she is *my* daughter when she is either wet or hungry, but *your* daughter when she is smiling or cooing?" I asked, my voice still muffled from sleep. Being a mother was hard work, sometimes harder than being the White Raven.

He chuckled lowly. "She's perfect, isn't she?"

I opened an eye and glanced at the clock. "At four in the morning? Adorable, I'll give her that. When she sleeps through the night, that will be perfect."

There wasn't a more heartwarming sight than seeing Zane hold our petite daughter in his arms. She looked so fragile against his chest.

Arabella wrinkled her little nose, her tiny fists flailing in the air, and a sweet smile on her rosy lips. She had hair as dark as midnight and eyes as crystal clear as the ocean, just like her father.

Yeah, the middle of the night feedings were killer, but when she peered up at me as she did now, I would do it all a thousand times over.

She let out a cry that could have woken a small village. Our daughter might have gotten her stunning looks from her father, but she had the lungs of a banshee.

There wasn't a day that went by that I didn't think about the night we closed the veil, preventing an apocalypse in the making.

Life had resumed. The aftermath of what Heath had done was like a bloodstain. It had left its mark on all of us, and no matter how much you scrubbed, it was impossible to rid all of the remnants of that day from your mind.

But we had managed to pick up the pieces, putting order back into the world and among the reapers. We still had work to do, but anything worth fighting for took backbreaking labor.

Aunt Zoe and Uncle Parks had moved into the south wing of the manor shortly after. They still couldn't keep their hands off one another. It was sickening … and really nice to see Parker so happy. It was all I had ever wanted for him.

Parker took to being a reaper like a duck to water. Who would have thought?

Zoe spoiled our daughter rotten, but then again, so did everyone, including Death. He was one proud, big papa.

Zoe and Parker weren't the only ones locking lips nowadays. Aspyn and Declan—after the battle, they had found solace and comfort in each other's arms … or maybe it was more like in bed.

Aspyn needed someone like Declan in her life to balance her wild side.

It was all about finding that perfect symmetry.

I sighed, pressing a soft kiss to the top of our daughter's downy head. She was content to lie upon Zane's chest, sucking on her fingers, at least for the moment. It would be only a matter of time before she exercised those lungs again.

From the moment Arabella was born, the council had had a change of heart. They turned into a bunch of baby babbling softies, except for the divine. He didn't have a heart.

I couldn't blame the council for their acceptance of Arabella. She was charming and could thaw the iciest of hearts.

"She looks so peaceful like this, like a little princess." Zane looked at me, his eyes all melty.

God, I loved them both, more than I loved coffee, and that was hardcore, because my love for vanilla lattes was just short of me attending caffeine anonymous meetings. "I thought I was your princess," I said softly.

"You're my queen," he replied with a smirk.

THE END

Thank you so much for joining me in Piper & Zane's adventure.

If you're looking for your next fix, grab a copy of SAVING ANGEL, book one in the Divisa Series! You can get two of the novellas in the series for FREE by signing up for my VIP Readers email list at www.jlweil.com.

Thank you for reading.

xoxo

Jennifer

ABOUT THE AUTHOR

USA TODAY Bestselling author J.L. Weil lives in Illinois where she writes Teen & New Adult Paranormal Romances about spunky, smart mouth girls who always wind up in dire situations. For every sassy girl, there is an equally mouthwatering, overprotective guy. Of course, there is lots of kissing. And stuff.

An admitted addict to Love Pink clothes, raspberry mochas from Starbucks, and Jensen Ackles. She loves gushing about books and Supernatural with her readers.

She is the author of the International Bestselling Raven & Divisa series.

Stalk Me Online

www.jlweil.com
jenniferlweil@gmail.com

CPSIA information can be obtained
at www.ICGtesting.com
Printed in the USA
LVHW112033131022
730641LV00025B/854/J